RULES ROSES & RIVALS

I0699878

RULES, ROSES, AND RIVALS

UNTOUCHABLE

WHAT IF EDITION
BOOK ONE

HEATHER LONG

Copyright © 2025 by Heather Long

Cover: Smoking Hot Covers

Editing: Leavens Editing

All rights reserved.

This is a work of fiction. Names, characters, places, brands, media, and incidents are either the product of the authors imagination or are used fictitiously. The author acknowledges the trademark status and trademark owners of various products referred to in this work of fiction, which have been used without permission. The publication/ use of these trademarks is not authorized, associated with, or sponsored by the trademark owners.

Rules, Roses, and Rivals/Heather Long

ISBN: 978-1-966724-09-4

*To the road not taken—look at you now, covered in teenage
angst, poor decisions, and questionable romantic timing.
To the characters who wouldn't shut up about this version—
congrats, you got your way.
And to my patrons: you absolute chaos gremlins.
You said, "What if?" and I said, "Fine, but it's going to hurt."
You're welcome.*

FOREWORD

Dear Reader,

Welcome to *Rules, Roses, and Rivals*, the first book in the *What If for the Untouchable* series.

Before we dive into this twisty, emotional, and (hopefully) delightful reimagining, I want to take a moment to thank the people who helped bring it to life—my incredible Patreon members. Your encouragement, chapter after chapter, kept this project moving forward. This story exists because you believed in it from the very beginning.

For those of you who are new here, let me explain. This *What If* is something a little different—think of it as *Author-Written Fan Fiction* for my own series. Same characters. Same world. But a new path.

How? Let me tell you a story...

In August of 2019, I began work on the first book of what would become a thirteen-book series: *Rules and Roses*. When I sat down to write it, I found myself at a crossroads—two very different roads that would shape everything.

In one version, Frankie meets the French exchange student on the first day of school. In the other, she meets him over the summer, during a time when she's estranged from her four best friends. I went back and forth on that decision for a while, weighing what each path could unlock for the characters and their emotional arcs. Ultimately, I chose the version where their worlds collide on the first day of school.

But I never forgot about that other path.

What if I had chosen differently?

That question stayed with me through the entire series. And that's how *Rules, Roses, and Rivals* was born—a chance to walk the road not taken. To explore what might have happened if Frankie and the exchange student met under different stars, in a different summer, with different baggage and stakes.

This isn't a rewrite—it's a reimagining. A parallel story that plays with choice, timing, and chemistry. Some scenes may feel familiar, some entirely new. But all of it is rooted in the same love I have for these characters and their messy, complicated, passionate lives.

So whether you're a longtime fan of the *Untouchable* series or just discovering this world for the first time, I hope this story sweeps you up all the same.

xoxo

Heather

P.S. If you are wondering can you read it without reading the original series? The answer is yes. It will stand on its own.

ONE

FRANKIE

"Frankie," Mom called. "You're going to be late."

"No," I yelled back as I flattened myself to the floor to find my shoes under the bed. "I'm not." I had plenty of time to get out of here, pick up Mathieu, and get to school. There they were. I hauled the shoes out and stuffed my feet into them before lacing them up.

I had a packed academic schedule and work at the Mason's this week. It was the first day of senior year and I was ready to get out there and face my demons, former best friends included.

Slinging my backpack over my shoulder, I hurried out of the bedroom and slid into the bathroom to run a brush through my hair before pulling it up into a ponytail. A little lip gloss and I was ready to go. The gloss wouldn't last and I didn't care, I had lip balm in my bag.

Kissing made that a necessity. I hurried to the kitchen where Mom was drinking her coffee. She glanced up, her head tilted as she swept her gaze over me.

"That's what you're wearing?" Judgment salted the question, but I was used to it so I offered up a one-shouldered shrug as I grabbed the toast out of the toaster and held it with my teeth while pouring coffee into my tumbler.

"Yep," I said, after I swallowed a bite and snagged my keys. "I gotta go."

I didn't offer her up any other explanations. Dating this summer had taught me that Mom was not a fan of me seeing *any* boys and she lost her mind when I mentioned I was hanging out with a guy after work one night.

So, if she didn't ask then I wasn't lying and all I had to do was avoid the question.

"Wait," she said as I got to the door.

Dammit. So close.

"Mom," I said, only half-turning. "I don't want to be late."

"I know, but I wanted to make sure you had this." She peeled off two twenties. "I may be gone the next couple of nights. I'm waiting for word on whether I have to fly out to handle a situation."

"You're going out of town?" I just barely managed to bite off the word "again" before it slipped. She'd been gone more than she'd been at home all summer. Instead of college visits, I'd spent my summer working and getting to know Mathieu.

The one truly good thing to have come out of this summer. That certain knowledge helped to cool the flames of irritation crackling their way through me.

"Can't be helped," she said, and considering her mood, I let it go. She wasn't snapping at me or making snide remarks. If anything, she'd just been happier about a lot of stuff. I'd take it.

"Okay, just pin the money to the board? I can grab some groceries tomorrow. We have plenty right now." The board was on the fridge. "Did you pick up cat litter?"

The thought just dawned on me. Mom was supposed to grab that over the weekend but she'd been pulled out of town. I wasn't even sure what time she got in the night before.

"No, I'll leave another twenty." Then she air-kissed next to each of my cheeks before retreating from the kitchen with her coffee.

Right. Of course, she forgot. No apologies, just throw a little money at it. Not that we had a lot of money. Mom had a good job, but she made every dime stretch. That meant no extras for me. The fact I had a car was because she "sold" me her old one and I paid for it with tips.

I saved money from tips for college. I had a small allowance to cover a sudden growth spurt in the middle of a school year, but thankfully, those seemed to have stopped. So for the past eighteen months, I'd banked that small allowance too.

"Be good," I told Tabby, who was washing her paws in the living room. She spared me a look like "was I serious?" and I laughed.

No, I really wasn't. I ate my toast on the way to the car and brushed off the crumbs just in time to see a familiar figure leaning against the driver's side door. Some of my pleasure in the day fled. I'd managed to avoid them most of the summer.

I'd made one attempt to see them at Bubba's birthday and what a mistake that had been. Thankfully, Mathieu had waited for me in the car and gave me a great reason to escape. He'd also listened…

"Hey," Coop Brennen, my best friend—or so I'd thought —since kindergarten stood there with his backpack slung over one shoulder, his eyes half-closed, and a five o'clock shadow on his cheeks. The sandy blond hair on his face was darker, but from experience I knew it lightened if he grew it out.

"You look like crap," I said by way of greeting. The partying lifestyle was bound to catch up with them. Their antics had been all over social media *all* summer long. It was enough to make me sick.

But I wasn't going to let it get to me.

Not anymore. I had my own life now and they didn't get to control me anymore.

"Look better than you," Coop retaliated, and I snorted.

"Impossible." I seized onto normal with two fists and gave him a light shove away from the driver's side door.

He mock-stumbled before straightening. At six foot, he topped me by six and a half inches.

"Let me guess, you need a ride?"

"Kind of obvious, isn't it?" He smirked and circled around the car. I'd already unlocked the doors, so he all but fell into the passenger seat. "I'll cover half the gas."

"You'll also ride in the back." I set my backpack into the backseat before climbing into the driver's seat. The ten-year-old Toyota wasn't flashy or sexy, but she was reliable and got me where I needed to go. Freedom came in all shapes and sizes.

"Why would I ride in the back?" Coop asked as he pulled on his seatbelt. I snapped myself in before I started the car. It was already hot outside and I wanted to get the air conditioner running.

"Because I'm picking up my boyfriend and if you behave, I'll let you meet him. Either way... you're sitting in his seat."

The shock on his face was worth the pronouncement. I spared him one look before I backed out of my spot. Then ignored him as he sputtered.

"Right, you have a boyfriend. Who are we picking up? Some kid you got stuck tutoring?"

His utter disbelief and scoffing managed to smother the faint joy I'd taken in surprising him. Maybe it was the expression on his face or the snark in his tone, but now I really wanted to stick it to him.

I'd spent years watching them with girls. All the while, they spent years keeping everyone away from me. Not anymore.

"You'll see," I told him and hit the indicator before I turned out of the apartments where we'd lived for the past thirteen years.

"Wait," Coop said, all of his humor fleeing. "You're serious?"

Yes.

I was.

But I bit my tongue and kept every vitriolic comment to myself. It was better to show than to tell.

TWO

All the way to Mathieu's place—well his host family's home—Coop prodded at me. "Who are we picking up?"

"I told you," I said, attempting to stay patient. Irritation raked through me at the doubt in his frown. "We're picking up my boyfriend, so get ready to sit in the backseat." At least the distance gave the air conditioner time to cool the vehicle down. It was already hot as hell outside and the humidity wasn't helping.

"Since when do you have a boyfriend?" Oh, look, Coop's smartass sobered up as he frowned at me. "I haven't seen any guys hanging out at your place."

"I'm not going to comment on the idea of you 'watching' my place for who might be coming or going." Acid burned on my tongue. There was just so much more I wanted to say. Rachel Manning all but slapped sense into me the past spring as our junior year wound down.

The guys all had girlfriends, dates, and sex. Lots of sex. Sex I'd heard about. Sex I'd found myself imagining based on some of their comments. And... more than once I'd had to listen to their complaints about said girlfriends. Girls who were all supposedly *my* friends before they hooked up with them.

On some level, I think that hurt more than finding out the guys had chased off anyone from asking me out. They'd made me "untouchable."

Ass. Holes.

My temper threatened to boil over once more and I swallowed it. Stuffed it down deep. I'd taken off the day school ended to visit a friend in San Antonio. Thankfully, Jennifer didn't mind and her parents were happy to let me crash there for a couple of weeks.

It was far away from everything and everyone. During my time there... I met Mathieu. He'd been playing tourist and his French accent was a dead giveaway that he wasn't local. Even more, he was working on his English and I wasn't bad at French, so I ended up playing tourist with him and his host family.

"Frankie," Coop said, a bit of a snap in his voice. Oh, I'd been thinking about San Antonio and wrestling with my temper.

"What?" I might have snapped back, then sucked in a deep breath and blew it out as I flexed my hands on the steering wheel. The word "sorry" stuck to my tongue. Mitigating moods was something I was good at, I preferred to soothe ruffled feathers and smooth out all the jagged bits.

Before.

I preferred to do that before.

Before I found out that they cut me off from a chance to be happy like they were.

Before I found out they made a rule for me. A rule they clearly didn't follow.

Before I found out just how much that hurt.

So no, I wouldn't apologize.

"I have a lot on my mind, Coop," I told him. "First day of school. I need to walk my schedule…"

"Yeah," he said, and I swore his tone softened. "I'll walk it with you if you want. Then we can head to the caf…"

"I'm fine to walk it with Mathieu. It's his first day too and he doesn't know the layout of the school."

Then we were on the street where the host family lived. A little thrill curved through the aggravation Coop had left scraping through me. I hated being angry with my best friends. Hated it because they were supposed to be my best friends and that betrayal was not one I'd seen coming.

"There really is a guy." All the animation drained out of Coop's voice.

"Yeah," I told him as I pulled up to the curb. "Be nice."

"Be *nice?*"

"Yes," I ordered. "And get in the back."

Protest flooded his expression but Mathieu glanced at him before he reached for the rear door behind me.

"Hey," I told him. "Coop can move."

"It's fine," Mathieu said, the rich smoothness of his accent rolled over me. "I'm Mathieu," he introduced himself and offered Coop a hand. Coop had twisted in the seat. Expressionless, he stared at Mathieu.

My heart fisted in my chest, but then Coop seemed to summon a tight smile. He gripped his hand and shook it. "Coop."

"Ah, the kindergarten friend." Mathieu chuckled. "Frankie has mentioned you."

"Yeah," Coop said slowly, elongating the syllable. "She hasn't said a word about you."

I glared at Coop but Mathieu continued to smile. "That

is because she has been spending her time with me instead of talking about me."

His jaw dropped, but I cut in before Coop could respond. "Yes, this is Coop. That's Mathieu and now, we need to get to school. You got your schedule printed out last night alright?" I'd walked him through it on the phone because it was late and he hadn't realized he needed to print his own.

"I did—though I don't think we'll have as many classes together as I would have liked."

We'd gone over my schedule.

"That happens," Coop said. "Frankie's in a lot of advanced classes." The absolute lack of lightness in his tone was a tell-tale sign he was pissed. Too bad. Maybe he should have believed me.

"We'll figure it out," I told him. "You ready for your first day?"

Real excitement began to invade me again. Mathieu grinned. "I am very ready, *mon chou*." He waited until I'd turned the car around to head toward the school before he continued in French, "Are you well?"

"Oui," I told him, with a glance to the rearview mirror. Hopefully he would take the answer at that. I had confessed some about my so-called friends and the crap they'd pulled. He found it kind of charming but also seemed to understand my dislike.

"Great," Coop mutters. "He speaks French."

"I'm sorry?" Mathieu said from the back and Coop had pulled out his phone.

"Nothing."

I rolled my eyes. Despite having to go an extra few blocks to pick up Mathieu, we made it to school with plenty of time. I'd paid for a parking spot for senior year. It was near the drama and music halls. While I didn't have classes in those halls, my spot was less than 25 feet from the doors, which meant I get inside out of the heat faster.

Win-win in my book.

Coop helped me get the sunscreen up in the windshield and then he was out. Mathieu opened my door for me and he already had my backpack.

"Thank you," I told him.

"You're welcome," he murmured before he dipped his head and brushed his lips to mine. Another thrill went through me that I didn't get to really enjoy before the door slammed on the other side of the car.

Mathieu actually chuckled as he lifted his head and I could feel the burn in my cheeks.

"Shut up," I muttered but I couldn't stop my grin.

"You are beautiful when you blush." Then he wrapped an arm around my shoulders as I locked the car and I turned to find Coop staring at us. Boy did he look pissed.

That killed some of my good mood, but I just lifted my chin. I practically dared him to say something. Finally, he said, "You want to walk your schedule?"

"I was planning on it."

"Well, then," Coop continued giving me a tight-lipped smile. "Let's introduce Frenchy to the school."

"He has a name," I reminded him as Coop led the way.

"I heard," Coop said, then flicked a look at Mathieu. "But I think Frenchy fits."

Mathieu gave me a gentle squeeze and I sighed.

"The guys are waiting for us in the caf, so we can introduce Frenchy after the tour."

My stomach plummeted. At least Coop was *trying* to be nice. I wasn't one hundred percent positive about the rest of the guys.

THREE

"Are you seriously doing this *right now?*" I hissed the demand while Mathieu spoke to his math instructor. Currently, I only had one class with Mathieu, advanced French.

Which was fantastic, because it was highly unlikely any of the guys would be in it. That said, I wished I had more classes with Mathieu but we would make it work.

"What am I doing?" Coop asked, his innocence utterly belied by the little horns holding up his supposed halo. He barely glanced at me though, he had his phone in hand and his gaze fixed on Mathieu.

I pinched the back of Coop's biceps just behind his elbow and he jerked his arm away.

"Ow."

"You know what you're doing. Stop glaring at him."

While Coop was still glaring, he'd at least transferred his attention to me. Over the past couple of years, he'd gained a few inches on me in height. Not that it mattered. We'd known each other for way too long for him to intimidate me.

Not that being my best friend since kindergarten did me any favors with the crap he and the others pulled. Just that reminder was enough to stiffen my spine.

"I don't *know* him," Coop countered, anger threading through his voice. "He's a *stranger* and you're *dating* him." Distaste curled his lip and I snorted.

"What bothers you more? That you don't know him or that I'm dating him?"

"Yes," he countered. "What's wrong with you? You vanished on us all summer—for *him*?" The accusation carried elements of hurt and irritation. Worse, he glared at me like I'd done this to hurt him on purpose.

I stared at him. "You are one to talk," I said. "Do I need to remind you of your girlfriends—plural, not singular, over the years? Not to mention the only person or persons you have to blame for where I was this summer is yourselves."

Mathieu was done and I abandoned the argument with Coop to hold out a hand to my boyfriend. Although Mathieu gave me a searching look before he glanced at Coop, when I squeezed his hand he just said, "One more class?"

"Absolutely." Agitation surged under my skin. I couldn't believe Coop. Then again, of course I could. They were the ones who made all the calls and decisions. But not anymore.

I took *my* dating life out of their hands.

And I was happy about it.

I wanted to stomp my foot at the end of that thought, but instead, I just smiled at Mathieu.

"You two are arguing?" He lowered his voice even if he switched to French.

"It's fine," I lied to him. It wasn't fine. But it would be. "We argue. He's an idiot. I'm stubborn. We'll work it out."

Mathieu wore a skeptical look, but he let it go. Rachel Manning sailed past us in the hall and she shot me a grin. "Looking good there, Curtis. Like the new accessory." Her smile dimmed a notch when she glanced past us. "You really shouldn't keep pulling out last year's colors."

I snorted and shook my head. The humor that flashed in her eyes softened the snark. But Rachel confused me. She could be funny, then biting in her commentary. We had this love-hate relationship, like she seemed to live to irk me, while I wasn't sure if I hated that I adored her or loved to hate on her.

Maybe both?

Then again, I owed her.

"Hey, Manning," I called, twisting to catch her eye. She paused. "What French class did you get?"

"Third."

"Then we're together for that."

"Excellent. You're my study buddy." She waved and I shook my head.

"Good friend?" Mathieu asked and I laughed.

"Honestly? I don't know. But she's got her charms."

Coop followed us as we stopped at Mathieu's last class. I'd located all of mine, but I wanted him to know his way. It was going to be tough since other than third period—where he was the teacher's assistant—we had no classes together and our classes were all over the place.

Then it was time to head to the caf.

"Fucking finally," Coop muttered as he strode ahead. His bad mood descended into worse with each classroom stop. A part of me just wanted to drag my feet.

If *he* was this pissed off about Mathieu, I wasn't sure I wanted Archie, Jake, or Bubba to meet him. Not with Coop in this mood. Would it be worse if they all hated him?

My mood plummeted, then Mathieu took my hand. The ease in his casual affection helped. "Brace yourself," I warned him. "I'm sure Coop's already told them."

Very little doubt existed in me on that subject. Coop's gradually worsening mood wore at me all the way through our tour. My stomach kept bottoming out and nerves prickled over my skin.

I flushed hot and cold. The sound inside the cafeteria swelled out and washed over us as Coop pushed in the doors. Girls laughing. Guys talking. Whistles. Whoops. Music. It was the sound of high school, and I'd known most of these people for years.

All at once, my fear evaporated. I *knew* these people. I knew my so-called best friends every single person they'd ever dated. I also knew the secret they'd been keeping from me.

I didn't need to be afraid. They weren't going to like me dating. If Coop's reaction was an indicator. They were going to hate it.

Well, that was too damn bad.

"Ready?" I asked Mathieu and his smile grew as he glanced down at me. He gave me a subtle wink.

"*Oui, mon chou.* You?"

"*Oui.*" His confidence bolstered mine and I let it filter into my walk as I raised my chin. Coop shifted as he reached the table where the guys were waiting

Jake Benton, Archie Standish, and Bubba—well his real name was Ian—Rhys all stared. Their gazes were on Coop, but I damn near felt the physical force of their attention when they shifted their gazes to me.

The last time I'd seen all four of them had been at Bubba's birthday party. They'd been partying hard, drinking, and hanging out with their girlfriends. It was a good reminder that life went on, whether we liked it or not.

"Here we go…" I said under my breath. "Hey guys…"

FOUR

The sudden crash of their attention hit me like a hammer striking a gong. The vibrations of it rattled through to my bones. Mathieu gave my hand a squeeze. Or maybe that was me digging my fingers into him.

Over the years, plenty of their girlfriends had joined us at the table in the morning. They'd come and they'd gone. In all that time, not once had I brought someone to the table. All the irritation fueling my courage seemed to fall away as Jake's brow tightened and Archie sat forward.

I let my gaze skip from one to the other. Finally, I settled on Bubba, because he didn't seem as intense as the others. Sucking in a deep breath and determined to fake it until I made it, I summoned up a smile and pressed onward.

"Wanted to introduce you guys to my boyfriend, this is Mathieu—"

"Your *what* now?" Jake interrupted.

"Boyfriend," Coop answered. "He's a dude. And her friend. Ergo, boyfriend."

I didn't roll my eyes because that was almost helpful. "Thank you."

"You're welcome." Coop dragged out a chair. "Archie got coffee. Didn't get anything for the boyfriend we didn't know you had."

Okay, so much for being helpful.

Jake stood and circled the table and I had to fight the urge to step right between. Jake and Bubba were both football players, tall, broad-shouldered, and over the past couple of years, they'd both put on a lot of muscle.

"Jake Benton," he said in a tone that didn't remotely offer friendship. "When did you meet Frankie and where?"

"Over the summer," Mathieu answered easily. "And actually, we met in San Antonio briefly then I found out she lived here. We ended up talking and I am very glad for it. She's wonderful."

Mathieu gave my hand another squeeze then he offered his hand to Jake. All the air backed up in my lungs. Hostility rolled off Jake in waves and his ice blue eyes were chilly. He finally took Mathieu's hand, but the greeting was brief.

Bubba rose and shouldered Jake gently. If nothing else, it made Jake let go of Mathieu.

"Ian Rhys," Bubba said. "Friends call me Bubba though."

"Frankie told me," Mathieu said easily as he shook Bubba's hand. "Would you prefer I not? As we do not know each other yet?"

Surprise flickered over Coop's face before he caught me looking and then his whole expression shut down. Jake snagged my backpack and tugged it down my arm.

"You should sit," he said, half pulling me away from Mathieu before I'd even realized what he was doing.

"Nah," Bubba said. "Bubba is fine. Probably wouldn't answer anything else."

I was on the other side of the table and Bubba had Mathieu cut off as Coop pushed out a chair on their side. "Matty can sit with me."

"Guys..."

I didn't get to say more than that because Archie stood up abruptly and hooked his arm through mine. "Frankie needs a minute. In fact, Frankie needs five minutes. You guys entertain Frenchy. We'll be back."

"Hey—"

"Maybe." Then Archie tugged me away from the table even as he offered me one of the coffee cups.

My options were limited considering half the cafeteria was watching us. The hum of conversation had dropped significantly since Mathieu and I walked in. My stomach bottomed out and sweat prickled over my skin.

The last thing I wanted was to be the subject of more gossip at the school. The untouchable badge was humiliating enough.

"I'll be right back," I said over my shoulder as Archie started walking. Mathieu frowned but Bubba cut off his line of sight. The only one not staring at him was Coop, who stared after me and Archie.

Archie, who didn't slow down until we were out of the cafeteria and the door closed behind us, cutting off the noise. Then he pivoted and stared at me.

The glare in his brown eyes gave me pause. More, the hard slash of his mouth and absolute anger that seemed to be floating off him in waves.

I tugged my arm free of him and backed up a step. That just seemed to piss him off more and I lifted my chin. "Problem?"

It was like waving a red flag at a bull. Maybe I should have expected it. A part of me did expect the anger and the irritation—from Jake. Maybe from Coop. They always got bitchy about new people—guys now that I thought about it.

But Archie? He'd always been the most relaxed.

He'd also been the one with the most girlfriends too. They never stuck around for long. He didn't seem to be that interested in them, or if he was, the interest waned fast.

"You're way too smart to ask such a stupid question." He practically ground out the words like they needed to be turned to grit between his teeth. "Who the fuck is Frenchy?"

"I introduced him. I would have given you a last name, but you guys got a bit dramatic."

That was underselling it.

Archie's hands twitched like he was going to reach out to me, then he folded his arms. "Frankie..."

"Don't you Frankie me. I have a boyfriend. Shouldn't be a big deal. If it is, he and I can sit somewhere else."

He blew out an explosive breath. "It *is* a big deal."

"Why?" I raised my brows as I stared at him. "You guys date like you're eating potato chips. Can't just have one. Always going back for more. I finally get a date, and a guy who likes me, and suddenly it's a problem?"

I swore I could hear the clack of his teeth as they snapped together. "Not the point. First day of the school year is about us—"

"It used to be." The words slipped out before I could pull them back. Maybe it was the fact he'd dragged me out here and we were alone. Maybe it was his proprietary tone. Maybe it was the fact that guilt was actually scrabbling around inside of me and I refused to feel guilty.

"It *used* to be?" Archie asked, his voice going deadly quiet and he narrowed the distance between us until he loomed over me. "What the hell does that mean?"

I held his gaze and didn't retreat. "It means that we've done things your way—all of your ways for years. You called the shots. You got to set the tone. You dated. You got laid. You brought your rotating door of girlfriends to hang out and I've been supportive *every single step of the way*."

Anger flooded me, chasing away even the vaguest sense of unease. Anger *and* hurt. I jabbed his chest with my finger once for each of the past six words.

"I listened to your complaints. I helped you pick out presents. I warned you when they were taking things more seriously than you thought. *And* I was there for you. How did you guys repay me?"

"By protecting you and being *your* friend?" The rawness in his tone took me aback. "You want an apology for *that*? You can forget it. You don't get to just spend the whole summer ignoring us, treating us like crap, then waltzing back in here with some stranger—who you can't *possibly* know what he wants from you—then think we're going to be okay with it."

"Sucks when you turn out to be wrong about the person you thought had your back." I needed to defuse the situation. Some rational part of my brain made list after list of why I should.

But the rest of me? The part that cried herself to sleep the night after Rachel told me what they'd done? The part that watched for it in the days that followed and realized how much she'd underplayed it? The me who went to the spring dance by herself when all four of those assholes took a date?

That part of me? Yeah, that part wanted to slap him upside the head.

"Frankie, this isn't you..." Archie said.

"Of course it's me. It's the me you don't get to control anymore. It's the me who dates who she wants when she wants and does with him what she wants."

He jerked back.

"Yeah, not so untouchable now. Not anymore. You four think you're so clever—chasing off anyone who wanted to ask me out. Making me feel like no one could possibly be interested in me, all the while, I'm there thinking you guys are my best friends. When you were anything but—"

"That's bullshit," he snapped. "We've always been your friends. That will never change and I don't know who put that shit in your—"

"Did you guys warn off anyone who wanted to ask me out?"

"That's not the point," he said, waving his hand as if to dismiss it.

"Oh it's very much the point. Matt Tanner. Jason Martin. Barney Jackson."

The recognition in his eyes as I ticked off the list of names. Matt and I had been friends for about fifteen minutes in sophomore year. Then one day, he went out of his way to avoid me and never looked back.

Jason Martin and Barney Jackson had both been guys that seemed interested for a minute. I'd been tutoring Jason, but then he quit that and Barney changed classes to get away from me. I'd always thought *I* had done something wrong.

"Yeah, see—I know what you did. Rachel told me."

That actually made him back up a step.

"She told me why no one would *ever* ask me out. Why

I'd never have a date to a dance or to a party or anything else." I fought the sudden surge of hot tears to my eyes. "You guys were supposed to be my best friends and the whole time—you were sabotaging me. So no more. Mathieu? He's my boyfriend. Get used to it."

Tears threatened to fall and I pivoted on my heel and stalked back inside. I was so angry that I dropped the coffee in the trash. A crime. But my stomach hurt at the thought of drinking it.

It felt like the whole damn cafeteria stared at me as I made my way back to Mathieu. His eyes darkened with worry so I forced a smile to my lips.

"How about we go check out the library," I suggested as I snagged my backpack. I'd really had enough of the guys

"As you wish," Mathieu said, then glanced past me. His expression tightened, but he just wrapped an arm around my shoulders after I grabbed my backpack. We left the cafeteria via a different door. I had no idea if Archie was still in the hall.

I didn't really want to run into him right now, but the weight of three particular stares seemed to burn between my shoulder blades.

Misery made for poor company, but I'd almost found a way to stifle the tears by the time we got to the library.

Almost.

FIVE

FRANKIE

Leaving Mathieu was harder for me than for him. I didn't make a big production out of it. He was excited about his semester here in an American high school. It was one of the things we'd bonded on over the summer. As I watched him walk down the hall, it was a reminder all over again about the clock on our relationship.

When winter break came, he would be flying back to France and to his family. I rubbed a spot on my breast bone where my heart seemed intent on punching its way through. I slipped through the door of my first period class and dropped into a seat near the back.

Archie followed me right through the door and grabbed the desk next to me. I could practically feel him staring at me, but I didn't want to meet his gaze. I made it through most of the class *not* focusing on Archie but when the bell rang, he blocked my path.

"Lunch?"

I stared at him.

"I have to get to class."

"So do I," he countered, then snagged my book bag before I could. "I'll walk you there and you can have all that time to say yes."

I rolled my eyes as he set off *with* my bag.

Dammit.

I hurried after him. "Archie…"

"Hey look," he said, a slow grin on his lips. "You remembered my name."

"Don't be an ass," I grumbled, refusing to laugh at the smart-ass tone. It was so Archie.

"Can't help it, babe," he said, wrapping an arm around my shoulders. "I was born to be an ass."

I snorted, about to protest again when I realized he was heading on a direct route for my next class. "Coop gave you my schedule."

"I'll never reveal my sources." His smirk, however, was one hundred percent Archie. I wanted to punch and hug him in the same moment. "Now," he said when we were at the classroom door. "Lunch?"

"No promises." I took my bag from him. "I want to see how Mathieu is doing and it's his first day."

A muscle twitched in Archie's jaw. "Bring him with."

After this morning? "Are you serious right now?"

"Yes," he said, locking his gaze on mine. "Say yes, Frankie."

"How about I'll think about it?"

"That's yes," he murmured, releasing the bag and when I raised my brows, his grin grew. "It's yes, but you're not letting me off the hook. See you at lunch."

He strode off before I could say anything and I stared after him. What the hell had gotten into him? Into all of them? Had they always been so…

"Hey," Bubba said and I swallowed my irritation to pivot and face him. He really was the only one I'd had any kind of conversation with over the summer. Even if dropping into his birthday party at Archie's place had reminded me *why* I'd been so angry with them and their double-standard.

"Hey."

"I saved you a seat." He motioned for me to go ahead of him and sure enough, he had parked some of his stuff on the desk next to him. "Thanks for being in the class still. Not sure I'll make it through without you."

Right. We'd discussed doing this together last spring. Before...

"Sure," I said with far more cheer than I was feeling. Archie's behavior had always been...over the top but this *felt* different. He was mad. No matter how he tried to cover it.

Math blew past us and I caught Bubba's grimace at the homework. Thankfully, he didn't kidnap my backpack or follow me to my next class. It was French. Madame was one of my favorite teachers, but Mathieu was also in it and to my absolute delight, serving as the TA.

The warmth of his smile boosted my mood and chased away some of the grief from earlier. It even helped when Rachel Manning claimed the desk on my other side. She was so—relaxed.

Considering how abrasive she could be, we had a kind of like-hate relationship. That same bluntness, however, had opened my eyes and... "Hey Rach," I said by way of greeting as I sat down.

"Bonjour," she replied in the most Texan way possible, horrible accent and all. I cracked up and some of the tension choking me all day evaporated.

I got a couple of minutes with Mathieu after class. "Archie has invited us to lunch with the guys. We don't have to join them..."

"Of course not. Madame, however, and a couple of the other French teachers have asked me to join them for lunch. I believe they want to talk about France and more. I can change it..."

Okay, I was a little jealous. I never got invited to lunch with the teachers. Except, it would give me time alone to deal with the boys and maybe that would be better. Fighting with them was hard enough. Fighting with them in front of Mathieu was worse

"Don't. Getting to know them is important too," I told him. "And I have work this week. So, I know we're both going to be busy at times." I'd already given him my schedule. "But I can share you with others."

He chuckled, flicking a glance around before he dropped a kiss on my lips. A sigh went through me. PDAs were not always okay in the halls, but none of the teachers were looking our way.

With a caress of his fingers, he nodded. "If you want to avoid them some more, you can come to lunch with me."

I did want to avoid them, but I also wanted to solve all of this. Somehow.

"Merci," I whispered.

Then we had to part because I had to get AP Lit and there was Coop. Like Archie and Bubba before him—and Rachel for that matter—he claimed the desk next to mine.

Our very first assignment required partners, he smirked at me. We ended up spending the class arguing about the summer reading. It was almost fun. Somewhere between books, movies, and books that became movies, I relaxed.

This was Coop, and we had been friends practically our

whole lives. I could be pissed at him for being a dick and still enjoy him being him.

"Yo," Coop said as he caught my arm when I started to follow the flow of students toward the cafeteria. "Not that way."

I hadn't answered Archie yet, even if I did plan to have lunch with them. Coop, it seemed, had either gotten a different memo or decided to make the decision for me.

"We're not eating lunch?" Yes, I played dumb while I let him drag me through the flow of traffic. The benefit to his height and laconic manner was most people did get out of his way.

"We're eating lunch," he said.

"Cooper!" Laura Zaverman—his *girlfriend*—appeared in front of us. She hooked her arm through Coop's free one. "I've been looking for you."

"Yeah?" He barely glanced at her. "Don't have time right now, Laur. Maybe later."

"But it's lunch..."

"Exactly." He extracted himself from her grasp even as he kept a firm grip on me. What did he think I was going to do? Vanish into the flow of the crowd? Half-turned, but still moving, Coop pivoted to give Laura a once over. The weight of those piercing gray-green eyes was impossible to deny, and Laura straightened, her chin and chest lifting. Definitely *not* a coincidence. "See you later."

He didn't wait for her response, just tugged me to keep walking. Laura's gaze skipped from Coop to me. A part of me wanted to apologize because Coop was an idiot. The rest of me just shrugged. Coop was also Coop. If Laura wanted to swap spit with him, she should get used to it. He did what he did on his schedule and no one else's.

I knew that better than anyone else.

Then we were out in the blistering sunshine and I pulled away so I could get my sunglasses out. It was an oven outside, the heat rising in merciless waves from the pavement. I'd kill for a hat.

"Keep up." Coop produced his own sunglasses and tucked them into place. The hot breeze rifled his hair as he led the way toward the parking lot.

"Let's go," Jake yelled as soon as we rounded the corner. He stood on the running board of the driver's side of his sunshine yellow SUV. The thing was just so bright. He'd gotten it at the end of our junior year when he boot-strapped his class placement to the top ten percent.

"I take it we're going off campus for lunch." Yep, I was testy. Archie had invited Mathieu, told me to bring him, but here was Coop hustling me out of the school without asking and before I even *answered* Archie.

Archie already sat in the front passenger seat and Bubba had the backseat. Coop herded me into the middle between him and Bubba. I hated the middle, and he damn well knew it. The seat cushion there was not comfortable, but I stripped out of my backpack.

Bubba snagged it from me to drop it into the rear with theirs before I settled. Coop's backpack followed. No sooner did Coop close his door than Jake settled in the driver's seat, seatbelt on, and eased the SUV into motion.

Getting out of the parking lot was a pain in the ass, but if we went out by the football stadium, we could slip out a far less used entrance.

Bubba stretched his arm along the back of the seat, and the lack of space left me sandwiched between him and Coop. Leaning forward, I said, "Turn up the A/C?" Even with me in shorts, being sandwiched between the guys was going to roast me back here.

As Jake turned it up, his phone rang. He just hit ignore as Maria's name popped up on the dash.

Jake and Maria. Archie and Patty, Bubba and Sharon, Coop and Laura. "Are you guys playing hooky from the girl-friends?"

That might actually explain the high-handed behavior.

"Broke up," Archie said over his shoulder.

"Not dating," Bubba said, his eyes still closed as he tipped his head back. Why the hell was he so tired today?

"Not my girlfriend," Jake said with a flick of his fingers.

Coop, however, said nothing. When I glanced at him, he made a face.

Yeah. Really, what could he say? We'd run into her in the hall.

Five minutes later, we slid into the parking lot at Blaze's. The pizza place was a longtime favorite of ours. I snagged my backpack on the way out of the car and Coop said, "You can leave it, it'll be fine."

"Yeah, but I brought my lunch."

"We're having pizza." Jake tugged the backpack out of my grasp and slid it back in the car. "My treat. You skipped the pizza party in June, so now we're making up for it."

I hated when they paid for me. But Bubba and Archie had already vanished inside, and Coop gave me his smug, *I-know-something-you-don't* look.

We had so much else to argue about. I let this go. "Thanks, Jake."

"You're welcome, Frankie." He winked then shoulder-checked Coop as we passed him. Inside, the restaurant was darker, so it took a minute for my eyes to adjust. The smell of pizza hit me from everywhere. My stomach let out a growl.

Right behind me in line, Jake loaded his plate. We

grabbed cups when we got to the register. He paid, and I waited a beat for him, then we got our drinks and went in search of the guys. They'd claimed a rear table with Coop following right behind us.

"Congratulations to us for having made it to senior year. Only one-hundred eighty days left until we graduate," Archie said. He toasted us with his soda and I wanted to laugh.

I really did.

It seemed like forever and no time at all.

Instead of saying anything, I dug into my food. The pizza was perfect. The peanut butter and jelly sandwich I'd made would have satisfied the need, but it wouldn't be this tasty.

Across the table, Jake stared at me as he bit into his slice. The weight of his regard was almost crushing. It didn't help that Archie was also staring at me. At least Bubba and Coop were on my side of the table.

Still.

Their presumptuous behavior continued to annoy me even if it was as familiar as the halls of the high school. It was just the way they had always behaved. Pushy, occasionally kind, and always looking after each other.

I used to think that applied to me. Eating the pizza Jake paid for reminded me of that same feeling. But we all knew better. Twice, I'd considered asking them and twice I'd discarded the idea, words unspoken. For all that we'd hung out for years, I was and wasn't a part of their group.

My choice.

Not theirs.

I didn't *run* with any one crowd. I'd avoided pigeon-holing at all costs. I'd read the books and seen the movies. High school was often depicted as a nightmare gauntlet, but I hadn't let it touch me. I had too many other things I needed to do, and I wouldn't make the mistake of thinking high school was the rest of my life.

Today, introducing them to Mathieu reminded me of all the times they made all the calls and I just went along with it.

No more.

A foot collided with mine. "Hey," Bubba said, nudging me. "You're not listening."

Nope. I hadn't been. Instead, I'd been thinking about the fight we needed to have.

The real one.

"You have my attention now," I said, rather than apologize. I'd been apologizing for a long time.

I wasn't going to anymore.

Archie studied me for a long moment and I lifted my chin as I met his gaze.

"Do we?" His murmured question shut everyone else up.

"Yes," I answered easily enough.

"Good. Thanks for ditching Frenchy." He actually sounded genuinely happy about it.

Coop groaned and Bubba sighed, but Jake said nothing. In fact, the muteness from him worried me more than the smugness from Archie.

"He had other plans," I said. "Don't get used to it."

Archie's good mood fled and guilt prickled under my skin even as I enjoyed puncturing his attitude.

"Maybe we save all of this for later?" Bubba suggested.

"Sure," I agreed, reaching for another slice of pizza. "No problem."

I put up with their girlfriends for *years*. They would

learn to be polite to Mathieu or they wouldn't be seeing me at all.

That idea was far more disquieting than it should be, but I refused to look at it too closely. Giving in had never gotten me anywhere and I needed to hold onto this anger.

If I didn't, our history had long since proven they'd all just mow right over me.

SIX

ARCHIE

Matthew. Mathieu. Matty. Disdain curled through every syllable as I repeated them in my head.

Mah-*tew*.

Matt-*pew*.

All the way through our first class of the day and the year, Frankie had *ignored* me. No, not ignored. No, she pretended this was all fine. That her *dating* some stranger was fine.

Since when did she date?

That was the stinger.

She ripped into me about her *right* to date. I never said she didn't have a damn right to date. I'd been asking her out for years. I'd *taken* her on dates.

But for some reason, she never noticed. Whether it was me or Jake or Bubba or even Coop. She hung out with us, cuddled, leaned on, but ultimately, we weren't—fuck it, *I* wasn't her boyfriend.

I should have been.

We should *be* one of those couples that made it from

freshman to senior year as unbeatable. It had taken a long time to admit, that maybe, just maybe, I wasn't her type. None of us were. Maybe she liked girls too? Like us?

That would suck—even if it was kind of hot to imagine—but like, I'd learn to live with it. But nope. Rachel Manning had been hitting on her for two years and it went right over her head. I'd seen other guys try, and she just didn't respond to the flirting.

So maybe she was asexual?

That was a thing. I didn't totally get it, but I'd done some research. Talked to Coop about it. Based on the way my phone was blowing up, I wasn't the only one at a loss.

Jake was stalking the guy. Bubba was trying to talk us all down, but he couldn't fool me. I'd seen him at lunch. For just a little while, we got Frankie to ourselves.

Then she reminded me I had to get used to fucking Frenchy.

Not. Gonna. Happen.

Coop had sweet talked a girl in the counselor's office into giving him Frenchy's schedule. He'd sent us all photos of it.

We had no classes in common. None.

He was in Frankie's French class. Bastard.

Foreign exchange student. There had to be rules, right? Conditions they had to obey? Chasing American tail had to be against the rule? She was under eighteen. At least for a few more months.

The more I thought about it. The more all of it annoyed me. She went to San Antonio and just happened to meet him there? Why the fuck did she go to San Antonio?

Her diatribe from the hall echoed in my ears and the gleam of tears that had sheened over her green eyes waited like an assassin to stab me.

That was what had shut me up before she stalked off. The glimmer of *hurt*.

"Mr. Standish," came the officious voice of Mr. Belden, "are we boring you?"

"Yes," I answered bluntly. "But don't let that stop you."

Snorts of laughter rippled across the room. The class was AP Physics focusing on electricity and magnetism. Jake was supposed to take it with me, but he had an independent study class with Frankie instead.

Lucky bastard. Maybe I should have done that.

Mr. Belden eyed me over the top of his glasses. The man was a mad scientist stereotype down to the wispy whites of his hair, and the plaid of his jacket. I swore he smelled like the peppermints he was always fishing out of his pockets.

Shaking his head, Mr. Belden motioned to the board. "Do try to pay attention, Mr. Standish. Missing a question on the test about any of this material would be particularly embarrassing if you think you know it all."

A snort escaped me at the scolding note in his voice and I saluted him. The man wasn't wrong. Even if I could answer all the formulas on the board as he discussed them.

I liked taking things apart. I liked knowing things. I liked putting them back together again, making them better. If only people were as easy to deconstruct.

No, a snide little voice in the back of my mind corrected me, *if only* Frankie *were as easy to deconstruct. You have been trying to solve her for years and you're no closer now than you were then.*

That thought was going to linger like a bad bruise. As it was, I managed to focus on the class all the way to the end and took notes. Then it was time to go. The original plan had been to meet at the diner, get food, shakes, and talk homework plans. We always divided up the week between the four of us on who got Frankie when.

I left the class on a quest for the parking lot. I wasn't even sure she would show up this week. If Coop had anything to say on it, she would. But how cooperative would she be with the new guy in the mix?

He had to go. There was just no two ways about it. I had to share her with our best friends, I was not sharing her with some French lothario with delusions of romance on his mind.

"Archie," a shrill voice penetrated my focus and I cut a look at Patty who dug her nails into my arm.

"What? And why are you shouting?" God the girl was decent enough at sucking dick, but I really didn't want to listen to her voice.

Color bloomed in her cheeks and her eyes narrowed as she glared at me. "Because I called your name three times and you were ignoring me."

I hadn't heard her, but that could be self-defense. I shrugged off her grip. "Then take a hint."

With that I started walking again, but the click of her heels against the tiles of the hall floor promised she was following me. "Archie."

"No."

"You don't even know what I was going to ask."

"Don't care," I told her without looking back or slowing my step. If she wanted to chase me to the parking lot, that was on her. "The answer isn't changing."

"You are such an asshole."

Yes, I was. I almost chuckled.

"Too bad you already missed out with the new guy in town."

That ground me to a halt and I pivoted to face her. The smirk on her face was positively triumphant.

"What?"

"French guy, very sexy, about this tall…" She mimed that he was a little taller than me. He wasn't, but whatever. "Very hot for a certain blonde that you adore. Apparently, *she's* hot for him."

Students streaming out of their classes and down the hall split as they reached us and went around. I closed the gap between us and Patty's eyes widened. She backed up and then stopped when she hit the lockers.

"*Don't* talk about her like you know her. *Don't* start spreading shit about her either. I don't need to remind you what I can and will do if you go after her." I didn't give a flying fuck about me. Patty could spread all the gossip she wanted.

She didn't get to pick on Frankie.

"You have it for her so bad and you can't even see it. She doesn't want you and that has to sting. Instead, she's putting out for someone else." Her victorious smile vanished at my smirk.

"Green isn't your color. It looks more like puke." Cruelty edged the words and I didn't care. She should know better than to provoke me. "Keep her name out of your mouth. Shut the fuck up about her."

"Or what?" She dared me.

"Or photographs from this summer can get leaked. Accidents do happen."

She paled even as the hostility in her eyes increased. I raised my eyebrows, daring her to say another word. To try me… I knew how to destroy people. You didn't grow up where I had or gone to the schools I had without swiftly learning how to protect yourself by taking out the competition.

Patty was less than nothing to me. There wasn't anything I wouldn't do to protect Frankie.

"We understand each other." It wasn't a question. Despite the fury radiating off of her, she nodded jerkily. A little fear would go a long way.

Done with her, I pivoted and stalked down the hallway. Frenchy had to go. We had to know someone that could get his visa revoked.

He'd need one to study here, right?

If he was back in France, he would be away from Frankie. I also packed away the idea of Frankie "putting out" for anyone. If he'd laid a finger on her, I'd let Jake kill him.

After I got my pound of flesh.

SEVEN

JAKE

Mr. G was always cool, part of the reason I'd signed up for the AP European History with Frankie was that Mr. G would be the teacher overseeing it. But that was only part of the reason. The rest was the blonde sitting two feet to my left and doing her level best to *ignore* me.

I could let it get on my nerves. I could let it piss me off. I could—I was more than capable of picking a damn fight. Thing was, I didn't *want* to fight with her. So, I divided my time between the reading and watching her.

Her distance over the summer had stung. Even when Archie had his surgery, she hadn't shown up, which was my first clue something had to be really wrong. I thought it was her bitch of a mother. Apparently, that wasn't it at all.

Coop hadn't mentioned her being out of town. Had he not known? I only found out later that she came to Bubba's party. If I'd seen her there, I might have ditched to take off with her. But she didn't return messages or calls. The only time I'd seen her had been when she was at work.

The fact she'd given me such a cold shoulder had pissed

me off, so I brought Maria with me the next time. When the fuck had this French guy really entered the picture? Before the party? After?

When did she suddenly develop an interest in dating? Goddammit, I had a thousand questions and her ignoring me wasn't working for me.

"All right, you have your reading for the week," Mr. G was saying. "I need to go down and prep for tomorrow. I'll trust you two to behave for the last fifteen minutes of the day, yeah?"

"You got it, Mr. G." I almost fist pumped that he was leaving. Fifteen minutes with me and Frankie.

"See you tomorrow," Frankie said, though she sounded a little less enthused. Her sigh as he closed the door confirmed it and that gave me more than a little pause.

"You really hate the idea of being alone with me that much?" The blunt question probably wasn't what she wanted to hear, but I needed some guidance on what the fuck was going on.

Surprise flickered in those gorgeous green eyes as she finally looked at me. Surprise, not fear. That part was at least good. If she were afraid of me... Yeah, just no.

Lips pursed, Frankie glanced down at the book in front of her before flipping it closed. She put it and the notebook she'd been using into her backpack. I did the same, we still had thirteen minutes to go. Still, she was right, we weren't going to do any more work.

Packed up, she twisted to meet my gaze again. "Are you going to yell at me too?"

Brows raised, I fisted my temper and gripped the edge of the desk. "Someone is yelling at you?"

"Well, expressing their irritation, I suppose." The little

shrug offered no comfort. "Not that any of you have the right to be irritated."

"I think I'll reserve the right to feel however the fuck I want," I told her. "And I'll defend your right to do the same." The air around her crackled or maybe that was just me. "Who yelled at you?"

Since she hadn't answered me earlier. I wanted a name. They wouldn't be yelling again.

"It doesn't matter," she said, then picked at something on the desk.

"It matters to me," I reminded her. "You used to be able to tell me anything. If someone is picking on you, you know I'll take care of it."

"I'm a big girl, Jake. I can take care of myself."

"Didn't say you couldn't." Then I hooked my foot against her desk and turned it, with her in it, to face me. She gave a little start, and there—for just an instant—the flash of a smile curved her lips. I'd missed that damn smile. "I've seen your right hook. Your left might need some work, but your right is vicious."

Another smile appeared, this one lasting longer. "Thank you, I appreciate the compliment."

"Are you not going to tell me who yelled at you?" I cocked my head to the side. "Not Coop. He's usually the last one to start yelling."

"Jake," she said on a huff of a sigh. "Don't try—"

"Probably not Bubba. He can yell, but he was pissed earlier that he didn't really get to talk to you much at lunch." Not that Bubba said that, but I knew the guy. Played sports with him. I could read the body language. "That leaves our pal Archie..."

Her lips compressed and there was my answer. So,

Archie got in her face. While I understood it, even *he* didn't get to yell at her.

"I'll take care of it," I promised and then reached over to put my hand on hers. Her gaze darted up to mine again. Her skin was ice and the air conditioning in here wasn't that efficient. "You're freezing."

"I'm not," she said, shaking her head. For a moment, I thought she'd pull her hand away but she didn't. Small win, but I'd take it. "Jake—look, you guys..."

I flicked a look toward the clock then back to her. It was marching toward the bell. She showed every indication of bolting the moment it rang. We needed more time.

"Us guys?" I prompted her.

"Never mind," she said, shaking her head. The slide of her blonde hair dropping over her shoulder had me wanting to sink my fingers into it. Fist it, tilt her head back, and then kiss her until she gave up every one of those secrets she housed behind her eyes.

"Talk to me," I said, going for coaxing rather than ordering. "You're *upset* and I don't like it. I need to fix this. Whatever happened that made you cut town and walk away from all of us. Tell me... Let me help."

Her lashes dipped downwards, hiding her eyes from me. "I don't know if you can. Archie's mad at me cause I'm dating. Coop's acting weird cause I'm dating and..." She snapped her eyes open and pinned me with a look. "You..."

I guess Bubba wasn't making the cut here. Probably in watch and wait mode. He could be patient as hell. Then again, she actually *spoke* to him at his birthday party.

Yes, I was jealous as hell over that.

"What about me?"

"You're just like them. Annoyed that I have a boyfriend all of a sudden. You've been dating since freshman year and

Archie is pretty much the same. So why is it okay for all of you to date and not me?"

"I never told you that you couldn't date." I never would have either. "Hell, I've asked you out on dates."

The disbelief in her eyes wasn't humbling in the slightest. Or insulting. "We've never dated…"

Fisting my temper with both hands, I fought to keep my smile from turning into a grimace. "Frankie, we've been hanging out for years. We ate lunch together every day for the past seven years—or however long. When it comes to the parties, you are the first person I ask."

Confusion filled her eyes and I finally clenched on fist to hold onto that temper. "Jake—you and Maria were the item."

"*Were* an item as in the past tense. We broke up a few weeks ago." It was two weeks when we made it official, but the summer had been one long experiment in how unhappy I was without Frankie even around to hang out with. "Never should have dated her in the first place."

"Then why did you?" There it was, that directness I adored. She didn't flinch away from my gaze.

"Because she was pretty and she was nice and…" I didn't stand a chance with you.

"You wanted to get laid," Frankie summed it up and now I grimaced.

"I'm not *that* much of an asshole."

"No," she said, actually agreeing with me. "You're kind of worse."

"Excuse me?" The temper I'd been holding back slipped free. "How am I *worse*?"

She gripped her backpack and blew out a breath. "You, Archie, Coop, and Bubba. My *best* friends. People I thought I could trust with anything and everything."

"You can. What the hell are you talking about?"

"Last spring, you know the dance was coming up and I kept waiting to see if someone would ask me. You guys were all making plans with the various girlfriends…"

"We included you," I snapped. There was no way in hell we wouldn't have included her. "Coop and I both told you we'd take care of your ticket. Archie would make sure the car picked you up too. Bubba said his mom wanted to help you find a dress…"

It would let us pay for it since she never had money for a lot of extras. The girls weren't a huge fan of Frankie running with all of us, but I'd rather have dumped Maria and gone with Frankie to the dance more than anything else.

We could have skipped the damn dance.

"Included me," she said, then touched her tongue to her teeth. "*Included* me? So telling every guy in school that I'm untouchable and no one should ever ask me out, was 'including' me? You kicking the ass of any guy who looked at me twice—*that* was including me? You four parading your girlfriends around while making sure I was always *alone*—was including me?"

I don't think she could have hit me harder if she'd actually opened her hand and slapped me.

"You broke my heart," she admitted and my anger sank like a rock. "All of you. My best friends and you made sure I was miserable and you had no intentions of doing anything else. So yeah, I pulled back and went away. The minute I get away from you four—what happens? I got a date. I found a guy who likes me for me, who made time for me. Someone I could explore all the things with that I wanted—"

She broke off and I couldn't move. Explore all the things? Was she talking about sex? Had Frenchy put his goddamn hands on her? I was going to break them off and beat him to death with them.

The earlier words registered. That choked off my fury for the pain reflected in her voice. "Frankie—"

It was already too late, she had her backpack in hand even as the bell rang. She practically dove for the door. By the time I made it to the hall, she was gone in a sea of students.

I knew where she parked, I could go there.

Or I could go find out who the fuck she'd been talking to that filled her head with all of that. Because the pain in her eyes? That had been real.

She blamed me for that. Me and the rest of the guys. I dug my phone out of my pocket and sent a message to them. We needed to meet and we needed to meet now.

EIGHT

COOP

I was leaning against Frankie's car when she charged out of the door at the same time as Jake's text hit my phone.

We need to talk. All four of us. Now.

The combination of that terse message and the taut, wounded expression Frankie wore knocked the breath right out of me. The moment her troubled gaze locked with mine, however, her face blanked.

Fuck.

It hit me with the force of a truck. My phone vibrated from Bubba and Archie answering Jake. Or maybe they were arguing. Right now, I didn't care.

"Hey—" I started, but she raised a hand, cutting me off.

"Don't," she said and when I would have opened my mouth again, she sliced that hand through the air. "I said, don't." The first word had come out harsh, but the last three were husky with elements of pain.

The last thing I should do was let any of it go, especially if she was hurting. Not even the sheen of tears could extinguish the fire blazing within those green eyes. The desire to push the issue was an almost violent urge, because I wanted to fix whatever it was.

Needed to fix it.

The fact she was taking a minute to get her breathing and mood under control wasn't lost on me. Biting my tongue hurt like a bitch. For Frankie, I could and would do a lot worse. Shoving my vibrating phone into my pocket, I focused, waiting her out in the blazing sun.

After sliding her sunglasses on, she unlocked her car and opened the driver's side door. I could practically see the balloon of hot air that it released. She leaned in to start the car, then rolled all the windows down before she straightened again.

"Do you need a ride home?" The husky alto of her voice rippled straight through me.

A dozen different answers danced through my head, but none made it to my tongue. Not while I considered her mood and her posture. What did she want to hear? The fact I had absolutely no idea gutted me more than I wanted to admit.

"Are you heading that way? Or do you have plans?" It was a safer response, I hoped. "I don't want to just assume."

Cause that was exactly what I'd done that morning, and hadn't that gone so fucking well?

She frowned fiercely, and I clamped my jaw shut on giving her shit. Not yet. The tectonic level shift in our rela-tionship wasn't *just* on her. No way in hell it could be. While her sunglasses still hid those beautiful eyes from me, the tension in her shoulders seemed to ease.

"I was going to take Mathieu home, but he has a meeting with Madame, his exchange advisor, and his host parents." The little note of loss in her voice stabbed me. "So, yeah, I guess I am going that way."

She wasn't looking at me anymore, she'd shifted at the familiar sound of a sports car's engine. Archie pulled in right behind, his orange classic Ferrari all but purring. Jake's SUV was right behind Archie.

Fuck. I wanted to wave them off, this was a bad idea. We did not need to be cornering her. The looseness in Frankie's back vanished as she stiffened. Her chin came up, and I could guarantee the fire in her eyes was back.

The rumble of a motorcycle announced its prowl up past both Jake and Archie. The rider paused on the far side of Frankie's car and braced his feet to the ground, before he flipped his helmet up.

"Bubba?" Shock shifted Frankie's tone again as she took a half-step back and bumped into her driver's side door.

"Surprise," he said, a real smile on his face. "I wanted to show you earlier, but we didn't have time."

"You got a motorcycle?" The bombshell rocked her, clearly.

"Yep, birthday present from my parents." Another smile, he seemed a hell of a lot more relaxed than the rest of us.

"Is that safe?" Worry drenched her question. That eased the first of tension that had been twisting my guts since she basically disappeared on us for the summer.

"Took a class so I could get my license." Yeah, I really did envy Bubba for his ease. "Maybe I can persuade you to take a ride?"

Jake's jaw dropped and Archie whipped off his sunglasses. Good, I wasn't the only jealous one. That fucking helped.

"I've... never ridden on a motorcycle." Far from sounding put off, she actually seemed intrigued.

"Any time you want," he said. "I've got a second helmet just for you."

For real dude? I raised my eyebrows, staring past Frankie and meeting Bubba's brief glance. His grin wasn't quite smug, but it might as well have been.

Jerk.

"She doesn't need to ride the motorcycle until you have a little more experience," Jake announced. He'd turned off his SUV and slid out to stand.

"She is standing right here and can answer for herself," Frankie retaliated.

"Oh, *now* you can say something?" There was no mistaking the bite in Jake's tone.

"Hey," I said, taking a couple of steps forward. "Ease up."

"Or what?" Jake flicked a look past her to me. "I got news for you, saying fuck all hasn't been working."

"Jake," Archie snapped as he slammed out of his car and faced off with Jake. "You don't get to talk to her that way."

That was gonna end well.

"Talk to her like what?" Jake snarled right back and he went toe to toe with Archie. His temper was already burning and none of this was helping. "Like she's important? Or like maybe I give a damn what happens to her?"

Fuck me.

Bubba swung his leg off the bike and it too stopped rumbling. He pulled off his helmet and cut behind Frankie's car to get between the guys and Frankie.

"Guys," he said, pitching his voice down and even. If she said anything after that, I didn't hear it. But both Jake and Archie pivoted to glare at him. Physically, Jake and Bubba were pretty much evenly matched. Archie wasn't a slouch, but he didn't have their muscle mass.

That said, I wouldn't put money on any of them *except* Jake. Archie could eviscerate someone without breaking a sweat when it came to words. Jake, however, was mean and brutal in a straight fight. He also didn't wait for anyone else to start it. The fact his right hand was curling into a fist made up my mind for me.

"I got this," I said to Frankie as I passed her. The heat sweltered around us, rising from the parking lot in waves. Sweat had already soaked the back of my neck and left my hair damp.

Bubba nudged Archie aside even as I collided with Jake to push him back. Good, I wasn't the only one who'd seen the imminent explosion.

"What the fuck?" Jake hissed, transferring his glare to me.

"You want to punch Archie? Do it later," I advised, not raising my voice either. "Not here. Not *now*."

His glower promised me his temper was definitely on a razor thin wire. Probably the only reason he listened was because it hadn't snapped yet.

I flicked my gaze to the side, as though I was going to look over my shoulder. That snared Jake's attention and he followed the gesture to where Frankie stood. With my focus on Jake, I couldn't read her expression. If she was well and truly furious with all of us, well...

Right now, we probably deserved it.

"We should move your cars so Frankie can back out." Her vehicle was the only one still on and probably to let the a/c kick in, which it had plenty of time to do by now and we were just wasting her gas.

Archie blew out a breath. With the rigid line of Jake's

shoulders relaxing, I spared a look to where Bubba had backed Archie up to his car. Hopefully, the crisis had been averted.

"Why don't you just follow us over to the diner?" Archie focused on Frankie and I managed to not slap a hand to my face. "Start of school tradition, we can work out our schedules."

A muscle ticked in Jake's jaw and that surprised me. He didn't want her going to the diner? Really? When I raised my brows at him, he shot me a bland look right back. The demand of his earlier text message resurfaced.

Right. He wanted to talk *about* Frankie. That meant her being there was a bad idea.

Honestly, I didn't think excluding her was a good idea either.

He shrugged, because what else were we supposed to do right now?

It was a whole conversation in a few glances. One Frankie could probably interpret. We'd all known each other so long.

"Maybe she has plans," Bubba suggested, then added, "But you're more than welcome to come with. Archie is right, it's tradition. We usually talk about homework and how we're handling stuff."

"And who I'm tutoring and when?" The snark in her tone was undeniable.

Yeah, still a bad idea.

"If you don't want to tutor anyone," Bubba said, picking up the sarcasm she'd lobbed at him without missing a beat. "You don't have to. Senior year is gonna be tough on all of us—but if you need a hand with *anything*, I hope you'll give us a shot at being able to return the favor."

"Smooth," Jake muttered and he wasn't wrong. Though, now Archie was giving Bubba a sour look.

"You know what," I said, jumping in. "If Frankie has plans, then we can do a call tonight." Twisting, I faced her. "You know, we can do it on video chat, if you want, or voice call. Then you don't have to feel pressured to make any decisions right now, and we can get out of this heat."

It would give *everyone* time to chill. She licked her lips, and I swore I could feel her studying me. Come on, Frankie, give us an opening. "Do you still need a ride home?"

The guys were really going to owe me for this one, but I jerked a thumb at Jake's car. "I'll make him take me home, that way you can do what you need." It was a concession. "Then just text when you want us to call."

It was handing her all the control and I caught Bubba elbowing Archie when he opened his mouth. The air whooshed out of him, but he didn't say anything.

"Okay," Frankie said, then she raked a hand through her hair before she pulled it back and up into a ponytail. "I do have some stuff to do. But I'll text—probably after six, but hopefully before seven."

"Works for me," Bubba said. "Just let us know."

"I will."

It was like winning the goddamn lottery, I could breathe again because she'd agreed.

"Okay, move your car," Bubba said to Archie and I caught Jake glancing from us to her and then back.

"You too," I said, then moved around to get in the passenger side of Jake's SUV.

I half-expected both guys to argue but after a seriously dramatic pause where they glared at each other, they nodded and retreated to their cars.

Bubba just shook his head before he turned to Frankie.

Whatever he said earned a flicker of a smile from her then he was on his bike.

"I fucking hate this," Jake said as he started the engine and the air conditioning started blasting.

"Yeah," I said. "I know." Archie pulled away first, then Jake followed. I glanced over my shoulder as Frankie climbed into her car and slammed the door.

Leaving her there felt plain *wrong*.

"But," I told him as I faced forward again. "She agreed to talk to us later and that's something."

"We need a plan," Jake said and he cut out of the lot and across traffic with a little more recklessness than I cared for, but I got it.

He was pissed.

And scared.

I got the last really hard.

We skipped the diner entirely and headed back to Archie's place. Probably better to sort this out in private. I was grateful for the extra time on the bike, alone with just the music playing inside my helmet. We made an odd little caravan, Archie's deep orange Ferrari followed by Jake's bright yellow Jeep Compass with me and my rather ordinary bike bringing up the rear.

Archie slid his car into the garage while Jake pulled into the circular drive and rounded the fountain in front of the main doors. I parked off to the side in the shade of the trees. My hair stuck to my head when I peeled off the helmet. At least when I was moving, the air flow helped to cool me off.

After setting the helmet aside, I stripped off my backpack, then my jacket. Jake and Coop were arguing inside the still running SUV. I studied them for a beat, debating whether I wanted to interrupt or not.

Jake slammed the palm of his hand against the steering wheel three times, his face a tight mask of anger. Unsurprisingly, Coop didn't flinch nor did he back down. Of all of us, he tended to be the most even. The front door opened and Archie stuck his head out.

"Did you guys get lost?"

"No," I said, carrying my jacket and backpack as I headed inside to the blessed air conditioning. "They're wrapping up some aggressive negotiations in the car."

Archie slanted a look past me toward the car, rolled his eyes, then closed the door. "Come on, they know where the game room is."

Not waiting for me, he snagged his own backpack and took the stairs two at a time. I caught sight of Jeremy, the Standish's butler, house manager, or whatever his actual title was, standing in the archway separating the kitchen from the open formal dining room.

After lifting my chin in a brief greeting, I followed Archie up. Jeremy would let the guys in once they got done with whatever debate they were fighting out in the car. Probably better to let them sort it out there before we added more kindling to the fire between all of us.

Archie was in the game room, already pacing, by the time I got there. Three of the televisions were on, one paused mid-game, another played music videos, and a third mirrored Archie's laptop screen. It had a webpage open to Instagram, featuring Frenchy's page. Most of the recent pictures all featured Frankie.

"When did this shit happen?" Archie demanded as soon as I walked in.

I dropped my backpack on one of the sofas and left my motorcycle jacket on top of it. "This summer, apparently."

The dry response was the only one I had. Even as I tried to study the guy in the photos, it was the smile on Frankie's face and in her eyes that arrested me. She looked so goddamn happy. Hand on the trackpad, I scrolled down the screen.

How had I forgotten how truly blinding that smile of hers could be? How long had it been gone for me to forget the breathtaking force? A part of me wanted to punch the guy in the face for having an arm around her, even more when I saw one of him kissing her.

"Do you see the problem?" Incensed, Archie continued to pace the room. There was a barely restrained violence wreathing him. I glanced at him just as Jake and Coop hit the opening to the game room.

The temperature spiked as Jake zeroed in on the big screen.

"Son of a bitch," he swore, stalking forward.

Coop let out a long sigh as he slid his hands into the pockets of his shorts. "Guys..."

Straightening, I caught Coop's eye and shook my head. Based on Jake's reaction, he wasn't ready to listen to reason. Not yet. Archie was just a seething black hole of tightly wound fury. The two of them in the same room was probably an epically bad idea.

Yet, here we were.

"How the fuck did she meet him in San Antonio?" Jake demanded as he scrolled. "And when..."

"First post is from June." The flat answer from Archie held everything from recrimination—*why the hell hadn't we known*—to pure fury—*what the fuck were we going to do about it?*

"Dammit," Coop muttered and scrubbed a hand over his face.

"How did you miss this?" Jake whirled to glare at Coop. "You said you were still keeping an eye out for her?"

"I was and am." Instead of irritated, Coop sounded a

hell of a lot more patient than I felt. "She didn't bring him back to the apartment. She also has a car and wasn't really interested in talking to me any more than she was with the rest of you."

That stung.

"Whose fault is that?" Archie pounced.

Without missing a beat, Coop just shot him a bland look. "Didn't you ask her?"

Coop didn't respond to either of the twin glares he received from Jake and Archie.

"You know what, we can figure out the rest of that *after* we get rid of the asshole." Folding his arms, Jake fixed a look on Archie. "What else do we know about him?"

"Exchange student from France. He's staying with the Butlers. Standard exchange terms are one semester at best. We can look at making it too uncomfortable for him or we can check into getting his student visa revoked..."

"Are you serious?" I asked, and ignored the stink-eye Jake gave me at the interruption.

"Yes," Archie replied. "I have some calls in to get more information on him. I'll have a full background check by tomorrow at the latest."

"Do you care how we get rid of him?" Jake challenged me and I got it. He was pissed and he wanted somewhere to pour all of that anger.

"Yes," I told him and didn't shake my head at the shock rippling over his face and Archie's. "I care because whether we like it or not, she's clearly into him." I waved a hand to the screen. "If we just get rid of him, that's going to hurt her."

"Not to mention what she'll do if she finds out." The quiet observation from Coop landed like a grenade between all of us. Jake swore and stalked away where he punched the wall.

Archie just sighed. "I also called my attorney about what options we have if just getting him kicked out didn't work, maybe we can make him an offer for a different school or location in another state."

I rubbed both of my hands over my face. That was not any better than just getting him kicked. "I didn't really get to talk to her about him or any of this today." Math had been too busy and lunch had been tense. I'd wanted to show her the bike, which was why I'd headed toward her parking spot after school, but that hadn't worked out well either.

"Yeah," Coop said slowly. "I talked to her some this morning, but she was in a mood to fight. Probably didn't help that I teased her about the boyfriend before I realized he was real."

"She is pissed," Archie muttered. "At us."

"Why?" Jake demanded, facing us again.

"Because of that bitch Rachel." Archie paced over to the drink fridge in the corner bar. He pulled out a soda and unscrewed the cap. "She told her we'd blocked everyone who ever wanted to date her."

"She *didn't* want to *date.*" If Jake spit the words out any harder, I was pretty sure they would catch fire.

"I'm aware." Archie took a long drink. "That was why she stopped talking to us. She believed Rachel. She believed her and then she went to San Antonio and this guy makes moves on her."

"To be fair," I said, already aware that I was going to get some shitty looks. "We did make sure some guys didn't ask her out."

"No," Jake countered. "We made sure the dickweeds left

her alone. If she doesn't want to date, she doesn't need to deal with assholes chasing her. Besides, most of them just wanted to nail some ass, it had nothing to do with her."

While he wasn't wrong, I couldn't escape the fact that we had made sure that the guys at school left her alone. Jake handled most of it. Archie had some. If anyone got really persistent, well... We all dealt with it and that was that.

"She's pissed about us dating too," Coop volunteered.

"Since when?" Jake scowled.

"She mentioned that," Archie admitted and I studied him. He was staring at his drink, as if he could decipher the answers from the bottle's ingredients. "But she never cared before. Just reminded me that she'd always been supportive of us dating."

He chewed the words like they left a rotten taste in his mouth and he had to talk around them. Arms folded, I leaned against the side of the sofa. "What else did she say?"

Archie shook his head. "She's just mad. We can fix this, we just need to get rid of him. If she wants to date, we can do that too."

"Has it occurred to you that maybe she didn't want to date *us*?" I hated the idea. I hated even bringing it up. But here we were. "It's not like we haven't all asked."

Archie might have been the last to roll into our friend group in freshman year, but he'd been interested in her from day one. We all told him she didn't date, but it hadn't deterred him.

If anything, he seemed to relish the challenge. Admittedly, I'd watched his attempts in both amusement and fascination. One, he didn't give up, and two, she just didn't respond like the other girls did. Even when he invited her directly, she always made sure to include all of us.

The fact she didn't respond any differently whether it was Coop whom she'd known the longest or Archie just after we'd all met him, said a lot. She wasn't into guys. If one of the girls tagged along, she always seemed fine with it.

The first time I asked out Sharon, I swore Frankie had her fingers crossed for me. I wasn't even sure how she'd known I asked in the first place, but she'd been enthusiastic.

"No," Archie said bluntly. "That didn't occur to me. We're her best friends. We've always looked out for her. You guys did before I got here and I've been invested since the day I met her."

That was one description for it.

"I'm not giving up now." Like he needed to declare that? Still, Archie lifted his chin. "The only question I have is, are you all in or out?"

"In," Jake said without hesitation. Coop answered half a beat later, but with more skepticism to salt his enthusiasm. When they looked at me, I had a hard time doing more than shrugging.

"I'm not out, but I'm not going to sign off on hurting the guy to get rid of him, especially if it hurts Frankie." I had a hard line and that was it. I also wanted to *talk* to her. Needed to find out what we missed or if we're all just off base.

"We all care," Jake reminded me. "Let's not forget that."

"No one has forgotten, Jake," Coop said with a sigh.

"Except Frankie," Archie admitted. "She doesn't seem to think we do."

That... Yeah, on that, I didn't disagree, we needed to fix that.

TEN

The whole drive home, I fought the urge to sob. The fact they could piss me off so badly and I could practically vibrate with anger, yet I still wanted to cry was unfair. It was also so damn frustrating.

I was still sniffling when I pulled into my parking slot at the apartments. The sun beat down with a vengeance, the heat slapping me as soon as I opened the car door. It followed me all the way into the apartment with my backpack.

Once I was inside, I leaned against the closed door and let the air conditioning wrap around me. The sweat on my skin was already drying. The icy coolness helped not only with my temper but also my tears.

A questioning meow had me opening my eyes to see Tiddles eyeing me from the kitchen doorway. A black cat with the biggest eyes and attitude, he seemed to be waiting for me to get my shit together.

"Hey, baby boy," I murmured, pushing away from the door. I checked the water dish and nodded. They still had plenty. I'd check the litter box later. "Despite your protests,"

I continued on my way to the bedroom with him trotting alongside me. "Your dinner isn't due for another thirty minutes."

That meant I could shower and maybe rinse off the day. Tiddles argued, but when headed for the bathroom and the shower, he hopped up on my bed. It didn't take me long to strip. I started with a cooler shower, and gradually warmed the water up.

By the time I finished, I felt a great deal more human. I'd gone ahead and washed my hair since it would have plenty of time to dry before I went to bed. I changed into a tank top and thinner shorts after. The cats were thrilled that I opened a tin for them before I checked what we had for my dinner.

The shopping list was still on the fridge. There were three twenties also attached to as promised. I made a face. At least I had stuff for sandwiches, so I made myself a grilled cheese, grabbed a soda and retreated to my room.

The apartment was small, two bedrooms, two bathrooms, though Mom's was in her room and an ensuite. The door to her room was also closed to keep the cats out. My bathroom was in the hall. There was a combo living room and dining room for the main room and the galley kitchen.

The compact place made keeping it neat pretty easy. The trash wasn't full, and the litter box wasn't bad so I could take both out in the morning. It was almost too quiet in the apartment, so I put on some music.

Torched's latest album had been released over the summer and I had damn near every song memorized. It resonated with me. It was kind of weird to be tackling my homework and reviewing my syllabi for each class without the guys.

Disappointment clawed its way up through me. I'd

known the moment they learned about Mathieu, they'd be pissed. I'd known it, and it still made my stomach hurt that I was right.

What made it even worse, was even after everything, I'd *really* missed them over the summer. As aggravating as they were being and high-handed, it was actually kind of nice to argue with them.

Tiddles raced in and bounced from the floor up onto the desk where I was getting my notebook organized. At his expectant look, I stroked a hand over his head and down his back.

"Yes, I'm aware that I make no sense. They piss me off, block me from dating, and treat me like I'm some kind of child who doesn't know what she wants and I have the audacity to *miss* them, when I was the one who cut them off in the first place." I sighed even as Tiddles began to purr. When I would have stopped petting him, he bumped my hand again.

Tory and Tabby made their way back into my room with Tory leaping up onto the bed. The sleek white cat sprawled over my pillows like she owned them. Tabby prowled over to leap onto the desk and then over to the window sill where she could keep watch on the neighborhood.

The faint scent of fish lingered, but one by one, they began to fastidiously clean themselves. Even Tiddles.

"So, that's the only opinion I get?" I asked but they didn't pause in their hygiene checks so I went back to checking how much reading I had, what projects were due when and what kind of schedule I'd need.

Normally, we did this together and we divided up tutoring time if the guys needed it or if we shared a class and a project. This was the first time I hadn't already committed every minute of every day for the rest of the semester.

I'd just finished getting my notebooks organized when my phone vibrated.

Mathieu: *I did not consider how many people want to ask me the same questions over and over.*

I laughed.

Me: *You're French. They want to know what you think about everything.*

Mathieu: *Maybe. I am amused by how many wish to discuss the heat.*

Me: *It's not that they want to discuss it, but it's an imperative. Cause damn it's hot in August.*

The laughing faces he sent in response only made my smile grow.

Mathieu: *Noted. I shall not complain until September then.*

Another laugh escaped me.

Me: *Are you home now? Or have they hijacked you longer and taken you out to dinner?*

His answer didn't come immediately, so I set the phone down while I went over the discussion questions for our first lit reading assignment. Reading was never a hardship and at least I didn't actively despise any of the books on the list.

I would have to grab one either from the library or Amazon, if the library didn't have it. I was scrolling through my Kindle to find the first book on the list when my phone vibrated again.

Mathieu: *How did you know?*

He didn't wait for a response before he sent another.

Mathieu: *I had hoped to have dinner with you, but I don't think we will be done for another two hours. I also have some work to do after. Are you free tomorrow?*

Me: *I'll make time. The first week is always the hardest. Call me before you go to sleep?*

Mathieu: *I will make sure you are still awake before I call.*

I sighed.

Me: *If I don't talk to you later tonight, I'll pick you up in the morning...*

Mathieu: *I would like that very much. If anything changes, I'll tell you.*

I sent him a kissy-face emoji and sighed. Yes, the first week would be the worst. We just had to adapt to the new schedule. As much as I would love to be hanging out with him right now, it was probably better for me to get my schedule under control.

Then we could have fun when I wasn't working and my homework would still get done. I found the book I was looking for, then checked the length before I studied the questions again.

Right, I could read this tonight pretty quick, then get the answers started. She hadn't indicated what our first "paper" would look like, but that was part of the fun. We had to prep for the discussion questions period, because it could be anything from a persuasive paper to an essay test to an actual debate in class.

It was one of the things I really loved about Mrs. Fajardo. She challenged us and proved that reading wasn't just about devouring the words, but about processing them. With most of it done, that just left math. We didn't have any homework in there due until Friday.

Bubba had asked me to help him with the class, it was AP Calculus. I took my plate and empty soda can to the kitchen. There was no ice cream in the freezer, but I checked the pantry and reached into the back—score.

I'd hidden peanut butter cups back there and Mom

hadn't found them. So I took the package of Reese's and some water back to my room. My phone buzzed.

Coop: *Ready to video chat?*

I stared at the message. It wasn't that late. It was just after seven. I had most of my homework done, I could curl up and watch videos or a movie or...

Coop: *I know we pissed you off. I'm sorry.*

That made me sigh.

Me: *Are we just going to talk about assignments and stuff?*

He offered that apology and that *helped*. But I wasn't sure if he was apologizing because I *was* angry or for *why* I was angry. Did I dare ask that question? Or would it just start another fight?

Coop: ...

The three little dots flickered as he seemed to be taking a long time to compose his response. I set the phone down, closed out of the documents I was in on my laptop and then flipped open my notebook to my class schedule and the homework schedule I'd worked out already.

Finally, my phone vibrated.

Coop: *I want to hang out. I think they do too. But—Bubba needs help with math and we always kind of figure out the schedule for the week. So—-all of the above?*

I studied the response and chewed the inside of my lip. The earlier desire to sob had evaporated. Most of the tension binding me up in chicken wire had also eased. While I wouldn't have said I'd relaxed, I was a lot closer to it than I'd been at school.

Coop: *I can tell them to fuck off and just come over if you want.*

My pulse increased, almost uncomfortably. The hard thud was probably bruising.

Coop: *C'mon, Frankie... talk to me.*

Me: *Ok.*

Just two letters and I huffed out a long breath. It didn't do much for my stress levels.

Coop: *Ok to the call? Ok to me? Ok to run away to Mexico for a vacation?*

Coop: *Cause we'll have to take your car if it's the 3rd one, but I'm game*

A laugh escaped me.

Me: *Ok to the first 1. Maybe to you. Too much homework for 3.*

I'd barely hit send when my computer began to ring. The video chat invite was right there in the corner. I accepted before I tied myself up in too many knots. The three dots were flashing again in my message with Coop.

The screen opened and there was Coop, a faint, if crooked grin in place. He was in the big square and I was in the little one above. I frowned as I waited for the sound to connect.

Coop's grin widened, and became almost a smirk. "Can you hear me now?"

"Yes," I said. "Where are the guys?"

"Waiting for me to send them the link for the chat." He focused on me, the intensity in his gray-green eyes riveted me. I recognized his bedroom behind him, but even the computer between us couldn't diminish the demand in his gaze. "I wanted to talk to you first."

"Did you?" I went for light, particularly because Coop was damn near unblinking in his stare. "So, you wanted two more than you admitted."

"I didn't admit any of it, but I did want to talk to you whether we chatted with the guys or not."

I could hear the vibrating of his phone as it went off in texts. I'd bet anything the guys were demanding to know what was taking so long. It probably *shouldn't* amuse me but it kind of did.

For his part, Coop just ignored the phone. "Frankie..."

My heart did another slam against my ribs. It damn near hurt because his voice dropped.

"I missed you this summer." The scolding note was there, not loud or even particularly stressed, but still present. "I did come by your apartment a few times."

When I opened my mouth to respond, he raised a hand.

"Let me finish. I'm not asking for an explanation and I'm really not trying to make you feel bad."

I sucked my lower lip in against my teeth.

"But..."

There it was. So much weight tangled around that single word.

"You and me? We're cradle to grave. You have been in my life for as long as I can remember and I'm not willing to let you leave it."

I swallowed.

"French dude. No French dude. The guys? Jake? Archie? Bubba? With them or not—I'm here. Me. You and me, we don't do this to each other. So, if you want to get rid of me, good luck. It won't work."

I forgot how to breathe. I curled my fingers into my palms, digging my nails in.

"You don't have to say anything. I meant it. But that's what I needed you to know," he said, his voice a whisper. Then he nodded, and his expression relaxed and a smile tipped his lips. "Now I'll get the others on so they can bitch, moan, and whine about homework."

His attention flicked off me and I huffed out a breath as one by one the others popped up on the screen. Even with the electronic distance, it was all suffocating.

ELEVEN

If Monday has seemed almost *endless*, Tuesday blew past too swiftly for me to track. French was a lot more interesting with Mathieu shooting me quick smiles during the assignments. Probably because he mentioned that his favorite dessert was tuxedo cake when Coop and I picked him up that morning, and I picked tuxedo cake for my project.

It also helped that the guys weren't giving me as much grief today. I don't know what changed between yesterday and today, but they seem to be doing better with the idea that I was dating Mathieu. When lit ended, Matthew actually met Coop and me on our way downstairs and toward the cafeteria. Coop eyed him but he didn't complain. We barely made it another half dozen steps when Laura intercepted calling Coop's name.

Though he hesitated, Coop glanced from me to Laura, and then back again. I gave him a little shrug, if he wanted to go talk to her I wasn't going to stop him. With a sigh, he lifted his chin and said, "I'll catch up." Then he diverted towards Laura.

"Do you want to wait?" Mathieu asked his gaze tracking after Coop briefly before glancing at me again.

"Nope," I said. "He'll catch up."

With a nod Mathieu gestured towards the room, and I nodded towards the doors that headed outside. "Planning to eat outside today. We've got some great picnic benches. I brought my lunch. Did you bring yours?"

"No," he said slowly with a slight grimace. "I'll go get mine and meet you out there?"

"Of course," I said. "I could go with you, if you want." Not that I wanted to go because if we didn't get out there soon, we were not gonna get one of the picnic tables. Mathieu only smiled, then dropped the kiss on the tip of my nose.

"Go get the table," he said. "I will find you soon."

With that, he headed towards the line and I let out a little sigh. I really did like him so very much. Still smiling, I turned and headed for the doors. I made it to the only open picnic table just three steps ahead of some freshmen. When they hesitated, I just stared at them.

Seniors got perks.

So, disappointed or not, the freshman just shrugged and turned away. And I took my seat with a happy little grin. Despite the suffocating heat of August, the trees and the building created shade back here.

The breeze, as warm as it was, helped to stir the air. It was just kind of nice to be outside where the noise level was definitely at a lower decibel.

I just started unpacking my lunch when Bubba slid a heavily laden tray onto the table across from me. He sat, a familiar smile warming his face.

"Hey, Frankie."

"Hey, Bubba." As irritating as they could all be, Bubba

had the temperament of a golden retriever. Like the day before, he looked tired, despite his smile. He dropped his backpack on the ground and reached for the container of chocolate milk on his tray of—a hamburger, a slice of pizza, and a small stack of fries and what...?

"What is that?" I pointed to the plastic packed item that was upside down.

"Pop tarts," Bubba said with an unabashed grin. "Brought them with me this morning but forgot to eat them, so I figured I'd have them for dessert."

God, that was a lot of food. I bit into my sandwich and shook my head.

"It's frosted strawberry," he said, holding it up like he was trying to tempt me. "I'll share."

"I'm good." I motioned to my carrots. "Got my dessert right there."

"Rabbit food with a—" He canted his head to the side to eye my food. "A PB and J, you're just rocking the top-of-the-line menu choices."

"If it works..."

"...don't change it," Archie finished as he dropped onto the seat next to me. "Why are we eating at school?" Though Bubba was right there, Archie focused his attention on me.

"I don't know, Arch. I'm eating here because I brought my lunch. Bubba appears to have staged a raid on the lunch line."

Bubba laughed.

"Ugh," Archie said, making a face. "I'd rather leave campus."

"No one is keeping you here," I reminded him and took another bite of my sandwich. When he reached for one of my carrots, I pulled them away.

"I don't want to stand in the line," Archie said by way of explanation. "And I don't want to eat by myself."

"You're not by yourself," Jake set his tray on the table on my free side. His was piled higher than Bubba's had been—in that he had two of everything.

"Do they not feed you at home?" It was a rude question, but damn.

"Eh, couldn't make up my mind and didn't know if you had actual food or—" He motioned to the carrots. "Rabbit food." He set a burger and a container of fries in front of me.

"Great," Archie said, shoving his backpack under the table and reaching over me to snag some fries.

Rather than deal with the lean and reach, I transferred the fries to Archie's side along with the burger.

"Hey," Jake growled, and reached past me to put them back. "Those are for Frankie. Go get your own."

"You're all determined to starve me, aren't you?" Archie looked so morose, I couldn't help laughing.

"Poor baby, nobody loves you." He was not remotely chastised by my comment.

"Here," Bubba said. "I'll share." He slid the Pop Tart over to Archie. I had to bite my lip to keep from guffawing. Archie *hated* Pop Tarts. He acted like they'd committed a crime against breakfast food.

"Thanks," Archie said with a scowl. He turned to me. "I'll trade you this for the other half of your sandwich, since you have a burger now."

I didn't want a burger, but it was kind of pathetic...

"What the hell is he doing?" Bubba murmured, scowling. Bubba didn't glare at anyone. A frisson of worry scooted up my spine. Was he glaring at Mathieu?

I twisted along with Archie and Jake to see what, or in this case *who*, had snagged his attention. Coop was strolling toward the parking lot with Laura and a couple of her friends. They were all talking in animated fashion, and he had an arm looped over her shoulders. Sunglasses hid his eyes.

"Being a dumbass," Jake commented, returning his attention to the table.

"He likes her," I reminded them. "And it's not like you all haven't had girlfriends."

Archie snorted. "I've never dumped all of you for a girl."

"You and Patty ate lunch together for two months last year," I reminded him.

"We had a project and it was literally the only time we could work on it," he retaliated. Then he stuffed a fry in his mouth.

"Whatever," Jake said, nudging the burger. "Eat. I don't care where Coop eats lunch. His loss."

But Jake didn't argue with me. They'd all had their girl-friends and there'd been plenty of times they'd individually or en masse disappeared down the dating rabbit hole.

"I'm not sure I'm burger hungry." I held up the other half of my sandwich, only Archie snagged it then took a big bite.

Ass.

I punched him in the shoulder, and he winced, coughing hard a minute later. Served him right if he choked on it.

Bubba snickered. "Don't take her sandwich next time, idiot."

"I was trying to help," Archie said with a wince, rubbing his shoulder. "Did you take up boxing this summer or something?"

"Or something," I said, keeping it vague. The burger was not what I wanted, but I was still hungry.

"What did you do this summer, Frankie? We saw you at my party and at work," Bubba nudged my foot with his. "But Coop said you were really busy and that stuff with your mom wasn't great."

Jake focused on the food in front of him, but Archie and Bubba looked at me expectantly. Apparently, Jake hadn't shared his theories with them.

Before I could answer, Mathieu circled the picnic table and took a seat on Bubba's side. A pleasant smile warmed his mouth as he glanced from Jake to Archie to Bubba, before finally meeting my gaze. "I'm sorry I took so long."

I grinned at him. "I probably should have warned you. You have to haul ass now that they've given all of us the same lunch hour."

"I'll remember that for next time." He flicked a look at Jake and I didn't have to check to see if Jake was staring at him. "Did something come up...?"

"Nope, grab a seat. We have plenty of room." I'd make Jake or Archie move if I thought it wouldn't lead to another argument. As it was, I could live with Mathieu sitting across from me because so far Bubba had been the least antagonistic about all of it.

I'd take my wins where I could.

"You've met these guys briefly yesterday." We'd talked about all of them the week before school started. I didn't want him ambushed. "But as a refresher, that's Bubba," I said, motioning across the table, then patted Jake. "This is Jake and this is Archie. Guys, this is Mathieu Domienier."

"It's good to meet you," Mathieu said, wiping off his hands with a napkin before offering it to Bubba first. I held my breath, because I could practically feel the tension vibrating off of Jake and Archie. Bubba finished chewing his bite of food, and wiped a hand off on his shorts before he took Mathieu's in a brief shake.

"Nice to meet you too." Bubba almost sounded like he meant it. When Mathieu half-rose to reach across the table, Jake stood. Bubba shot Jake a warning look but Jake ignored everyone except Mathieu.

I would have reached up for Jake's arm but Archie dropped his hand onto my thigh and just above my knee and squeezed. It yanked my attention to him. "Wait," he mouthed the word more than said it aloud.

"Jake Benton," Jake said finally, and he took Mathieu's hand. Jake's knuckles went white, but Mathieu's expression never changed. "How long have you known Frankie?"

There was nothing friendly in that question.

"Almost three months," Mathieu said. "Ten weeks?" He sent me a smile before meeting Jake's stare. At six feet, he was roughly Archie's height, so a little shorter than Jake. But if Jake's broader build bothered him, Mathieu didn't act like it.

He had a leaner, more slender build. But he also moved with such confidence. His features were sharper than any of the guys. His cheekbones were high, his jawline was strong and defined but his hazel eyes were so damn expressive.

"She's known you since primary school," Mathieu continued even as Jake kept his grip on Mathieu's hand. "You are important to her and clearly she is important to you."

"Let him go," Bubba said quietly. But neither Jake nor Mathieu moved. "Jake."

At the sharpness in Bubba's tone, Jake switched his attention to Bubba then he huffed out a sigh and released Mathieu's hand. There was no missing the red marks Jake's grip had left.

Still, Mathieu glanced at Archie as though debating whether to offer him his hand or not. Rather than rise, Archie waved him off after he took his hand off my thigh. Without saying a word, Archie stuffed the rest of my sandwich into his mouth.

Nodding once, Mathieu sat once more and gave me a smile. The air around us crackled with all the things the guys weren't saying and that just made the sweat trickle down my spine. A foot bumped mine and I tried to smile at Mathieu.

The discomfort thickened and I sighed. "Bubba..."

He turned those blue eyes on me and gave me an encouraging look. "Frankie?"

"Did you get those calculus questions done?" It was a stretch to come up with something to fill in the quiet, but we needed something.

"Most of them," he admitted. "I think the last one had an error in it."

I frowned. "A typo?"

"Maybe," he said. "I don't know. Maybe we can go over it later?"

"You still want tutoring?"

"Yes," he said firmly. "I can come to you. Or we can meet somewhere. Whatever works for you." He slid a look at Mathieu then me. "I was hoping for today, but I don't want to assume."

Mathieu and I didn't have plans for any day after school this week, mostly because he was trying to get a feel for his schedule and balancing everything. He also didn't offer that information, letting me decide.

Another reason I adored him.

"I'll check to see what I've got during study hall and text you, okay?" It was me avoiding making a decision now, but I didn't want to do it here with Jake half-seething next to me and Archie's icy silence.

"Whenever," Bubba told me. "Really."

He meant it.

That helped.

When the first bell sounded warning us lunch was almost over, I'd never been so glad for a chance to escape.

TWELVE

FRANKIE

I wrestled with myself about heading over to Bubba's after school or having him come back to my place. Tutoring would have to be today or it would have to wait until Friday. I had work on Wednesday and Thursday. But he usually had games on Friday, so that would be tricky.

Mathieu: *I look forward to having all of these meetings dealt with this week. The program liaisons have arranged a meal this evening for all of us in the area. It's almost ninety minutes away.*

I wanted to pout with him, but there were more exchange students in the greater metroplex area. It made more sense for Mathieu and his host family to go to them than the other way around.

Me: *Try to get some sleep tonight. I work tomorrow and Thursday after school.*

Mathieu: *You said. Your friends? Are things still uncomfortable?*

Uncomfortable. That was a word. I shrugged, not that Mathieu could see me. I headed out to my car as I turned my answer over in my head. Hitting the crossbar to open the door with my hip, I typed in a quick response.

Me: *Working on it. Sorry about lunch.*

Jake hadn't said a word about it during AP Euro, which was probably because Mr. G had been present for the whole hour. The fact Jake had been trying to intimidate Mathieu hadn't been lost on me. Nor had Mathieu's refusal to back down.

The whole thing made my stomach jitter. Being angry with them for how they treated me was one thing. But I refused to let them treat Mathieu that way. I *liked* him and they needed to deal with it. I was prepared to face off with them on this subject if necessary.

What I wasn't prepared for was the rose sitting on top of my car or Coop and Bubba standing side-by-side and staring at it.

Mathieu: *They care, ma poupée. I suspect they care more than they have told you. Do not be so hard on them.*

The message had me blinking almost as much as the presence of the flowers. The door opened behind me and Jake came to a hard halt next to me. I hadn't even realized he was following me.

Coop spotted us and held up his hands. "I didn't do it."

"Neither did I," Bubba said slowly. "Wish I had."

I clicked the screen off on my phone as I closed the distance to where the purple rose sat. It was definitely purple and beautiful. It also smelled fantastic. Despite the steamy temperature and the fact, it was parked on the hot roof of my car, the vase was still cool.

There was a note on the side of it and Jake took hold of the vase, balancing it. We might need to discuss the hovering, but I pushed that aside for now. Though, admittedly, the idea I was avoiding dealing with it made me pause. Why was I letting them still get away with stuff?

"Is it from Frenchy?" Jake asked, yanking my attention back to the present.

"Mathieu," I corrected him.

"Whatever. Is it from him?"

"I don't know, I haven't opened it yet." Still, the butterflies in my stomach were thrilled at the idea. Someone had left me a rose. Mathieu hadn't said anything about it, but maybe that was the point. It was supposed to be a surprise.

The note inside was typed.

Lavender roses signify mystery, *enchantment, and attraction at first sight. You enchanted me from the beginning. I hope you enjoy a little mystery. You deserve far more.*

That was it.

"No one signed it," Jake said before he glanced at me. Maybe it was from Mathieu. I'd send him a thank you later.

I reached for the rose and Jake's frown turned fierce. For a split-second, I worried he wouldn't surrender the vase but he handed it over.

"It doesn't say who it's from?" Coop asked. Jake had scanned the card, no way had he missed it from where he stood.

With that in mind, I shook my head and handed the card over. "No, but it's really sweet."

Coop and Bubba wore twin frowns as they scanned the note.

"I don't like it," Jake admitted and I elbowed him to get him to back up a step.

"You like very little," I reminded him and ignored his oof.

"I like *you*," he countered as I opened the door to the car and let the hot air balloon out. Coop snorted, but circled around to open the passenger door. I set the vase back on the roof before I shrugged out of my backpack.

Jake caught it before I could, then he bypassed me to set the backpack into the backseat. I bent in to slide the key into the ignition and get the car started so I could get the a/c on.

Straightening, I glanced at where Bubba stood as I put my sunglasses on. "I'm going to take Coop home, feed the cats and do some chores. Then I can come over if you want." I'd thought about inviting him, but I had no idea what Mom's schedule was. She said she had to go out of town. As sudden as the trip came up, they could also suddenly end. The last thing I wanted to deal with was her irritation if we were in her space and working on calculus.

"I'll order pizza," Bubba offered. "Want to grab your suit and bring it? We can take breaks in the pool. Probably keep me from wanting to drown myself over numbers."

He made a face and I laughed. "I'll think about it. But you don't have to feed me."

"Feeding me too," Bubba said with a wink.

"Why don't we all—" Jake began, but Bubba shifted his gaze to look past me. Whatever Jake had been about to add, he let go with a long sigh. "Never mind. I have to grab Blake and Becca for dance classes."

Despite what the growl in his voice might suggest, the frustration wasn't directed at his sisters. He just didn't want to have to go. He raked a hand through his hair, then gave Coop a hard look followed by a second directed at Bubba.

"I'll call you later," Jake said with another half-growl turned sigh. He wrapped a hand around my biceps, tugging me around. "Frankie...I'm definitely calling *you* later. I want to be perfectly clear on that."

While his grip was firm, it wasn't painful nor did his fingers dig in. This close, I couldn't miss a single bit of the way his pale blue eyes lasered onto me.

"I don't like you dating, Frenchy." Flat. Imperious.

"No shit," I muttered, even as his nostrils flared. "You made that clear earlier."

"No, earlier was me not liking *Frenchy*," Jake countered. "This is me *telling* you, I don't like you dating Frenchy. I don't *want* you dating him. And we're not done with this conversation."

"Jake..." Bubba said, locking a hand over Jake's wrist even as Coop came around the other side.

"Let her go, Jake." Coop's expression was a lot easier than Jake's or Bubba's, but his mouth firmed into a line. "We're not doing this here."

"Correction," I said, yanking my arm free. "We're not doing this at all. You're not the boss of me, Jake. *None* of you are. You're my friends, not my keepers. I don't tell you who to date and you don't get to say the same to me."

A muscle ticked in his jaw as we glared at each other. It was seriously the angriest I'd ever seen him and all of it directed right at me. Pissed or not, Jake didn't scare me. He might be a dick to the people around us, but he would *never* hurt me.

Bubba shoved between us and pushed Jake backwards. Head snapping up, Jake transferred that fury to Bubba and I caught the curl of his fist.

"Don't," I said, wading between them once more and wrapping my hand over Jake's fist.

We weren't alone out here and there were kids still streaming out to their cars. More than one seemed to be lingering and watching us.

"Don't," I repeated in a lower voice. "You two start fighting out here and you're going to get suspended from the team." It was the first thing that came to mind.

The hostility upped the temperature of the muggy air to boiling.

"C'mon," Coop said, his voice dipping as mine had. "Ease back, Jake. We're all hot and a little bitchy at the moment."

"I am not bitchy," I said with an exaggerated sniff, even as I kept one hand over Jake's fist and the other one his chest. Bubba was right against my back. There was no way I could keep them apart if they really decided to rip into each other. "I'm *fussy*, remember?"

I made a face at Coop, then stuck my tongue at him as he rolled his eyes. "Fussy. Right. I forgot."

Whether it was my tongue sticking out or Coop's deadpan response, Jake let out a snort of laughter. His hot glare eased and he dropped his gaze down to me. The fist under my palm relaxed and he blew out a breath.

"You're not fussy," Jake argued. "Coop's just a lazy ass."

"Hey," Coop complained. "When did this become 'pick on Coop' day?"

"It's pick on Coop Day, every day," I said in damn near the same breath as Jake.

All at once the last of the ballooning tension burst around us and I could breathe. Jake took a step back, but not before he turned his hand over underneath mine and squeezed my fingers gently.

Coop just snorted, but he didn't dispute us.

"Right," Jake said with another squeeze to my hand.

"I'll call you later." Then he pivoted and strode away. Coop watched him go and I could read the worry etched into his expression. Or maybe I was projecting.

Warm hands settled on my hips. Bubba lifted me and pivoted so I was next to the car and he was on the other side of me. "Get in the car," he said. "Cool off and go feed your cats before they starve to death."

It was almost playful, but his smile didn't quite touch his eyes.

"If you want to skip after this," he offered but I shook my head.

"No, I won't have time before the weekend if we don't do it today." I glanced to where Jake disappeared then summoned another smile for Bubba. "I said I would help." Then because I didn't want him to think it was just an obligation, I added, "I want to help... and I want pizza."

That pulled a real laugh out of him. "Go on then, I'll see you soon. Text when you're on the way okay?" He dropped a kiss on my forehead, damn near muting any other words from escaping me.

Like Jake before him, he strode away. I glanced at Coop who just raised his brows. "You okay?"

"I have no idea," I admitted. "But we should go." Because I wasn't sure I could take anymore upheaval at the moment. Pivoting, I retrieved my lavender rose and slid into the car. Thank fuck the air conditioning had kicked in and the cooler air washed over me.

Coop dropped into the passenger seat and dragged on his seatbelt. He was silent until I pulled out of the parking lot.

"Frankie?"

I didn't hold my breath. "Yeah?"

"I don't like you dating Mathieu either." At least he

didn't call him Frenchy. "And I don't want you dating him either."

I cut a look at him. "How was your lunch date with Laura?"

He frowned, then glanced at me. I could see his mouth open then close without saying anything. Finally, he leaned back and stared out the passenger window

"Yeah," I said with a sigh. "That's what I thought."

THIRTEEN

BUBBA

I pulled my helmet on and got the engine started on the bike.

"Bubba!" Sharon called my name and I spared a look in her direction, but just shook my head. She was the last person I wanted to see at the moment. More than once, she'd dropped hints about grabbing a ride on the bike,

So not happening.

Ever.

Today I'd planned to invite Frankie to take a ride with me. From the first time I'd gotten the keys to this bike, I'd thought about taking Frankie for a long ride. Her showing up at my birthday party had been a good sign, or so I hoped. She'd never been this mad at us—hell at me—for this long before.

Finding out she was dating the French foreign exchange student was a punch to the nuts. The fact I wasn't alone in floundering over what the hell happened, didn't help as much as one might have thought.

Jake and Archie were all in on just getting rid of the guy. Since at least one of their plans had bordered on straight up violence, Coop and I were taking turns trying to talk them down. Wanting the guy gone and wanting him *dead* were two entirely different things.

And Frankie likes him.

The thought was enough to make me sick. Why *him*? What had he done that none of us managed? How had he convinced her to go on a date? I had a dozen questions, none of which I could answer. Not yet.

Now someone put flowers on her car. Yeah, a second someone putting moves on her wasn't any more appealing than the first guy. It did, however, give me an idea. Specifically, that Frankie deserved to be treated like gold.

It never occurred to me to get flowers for her before or any of the stuff other girls seemed to like. Those had just never seemed to be something she was interested in. As I cruised toward my neighborhood, I balled up a lot of what I'd "known" about Frankie over the last few years and threw it out.

She was one of my best friends. She and the guys kept me sane and I'd do anything for any of them. I wanted more with her, I'd *always* wanted more. As I slowed near my driveway, I blew out a breath.

I may have to accept that she really wasn't interested in *us* that way. That would *suck*. But I needed to know for sure. Frenchy opened the door, fine. I'd live with it.

Didn't mean we couldn't kick his ass out while wedging the door open so I could ask her out or Archie could or Jake...

Though honestly, the idea of them asking her out too made me grimace. We'd all been on equal footing for so long that if one of them succeeded in getting her to date them—would it change everything between all of us? What if I did? What if I could convince her to be my girlfriend?

I pulled into the garage and set the kickstand down just in time to see Mom and Dad coming out through the garage door.

"Hey, Ian," Mom said with a smile as she led Dad out to their car. When she paused next to the bike, I removed my helmet and climbed off. Then I dropped an obedient kiss on her cheek. "There's leftovers in the fridge."

When she paused a beat and glanced behind me, I parked the helmet on the bike. "Frankie's still coming over. She went home to feed her cats first and drop Coop off."

"Oh, well, I was hoping to get to see her. You tell her to stop being a stranger." She glanced out again as if she could will Frankie to arrive faster if she kept watching.

"C'mon, sweetheart. We're already running a little late and we still have a drive to get to the restaurant." Dad nudged Mom along and gave me a firm look. "Don't keep Frankie here too late."

Not something I was going to worry about right now. "You guys have fun. I'll see you later." In fact, the sooner they left, the sooner I could go upstairs and change into my suit and grab my guitar.

We had more than math homework tonight. I had some samples I wanted Frankie to hear. I had—a lot to share with her. Three months' worth of stories, music, events—*stuff*. Honestly, I just wanted time with her.

It didn't take me long to change into swim shorts, grab my guitar, and head back downstairs. We had big towels for swimmers in the linen closet downstairs. A glance at my watch said it hadn't been that long, but I still unlocked the front door and glanced out for her.

My phone buzzed a couple of times on the table while I grabbed some Cokes out of the fridge. Untwisting the bottle top, I let out a sigh when it released a fizzy sound. Yeah, I was definitely ready for a drink.

The first message was from Archie. He wanted to know if Frankie was here. The second message was Jake in my group chat with the guys asking if she was here. A third message had come in while I was upstairs. Frankie was on her way.

It was only a ten-minute drive from her apartment to my house, slightly longer if she got caught at the light. Excellent, she'd be here soon. My phone vibrated with another message from Archie.

Archie: *WTF? Is she there or not?*

Me: *She's on her way. What's eating you?*

Archie: *Some asshole sent her flowers?*

Well, I couldn't exactly argue with that, but I wasn't going to take that out on Frankie or one of them.

Me: *Someone sending her flowers has nothing to do with her coming over.*

I headed over to the door and leaned against the wall where I could see the driveway from the side window. Archie was still typing something based on the three little dots flashing on the screen.

Me: *She's here. I'll catch up with you guys later.*

I sent that to the group chat rather than just Archie. I exited the app as a message from Sharon came in. Rolling my eyes, I swiped away the notification and muted her chat. She could stay unread. I didn't need or want to talk to her.

Shoving the phone into the pocket of my swim shorts, I opened the door. The heat was a sucker punch after cooling down inside. But that was Texas.

Frankie was wearing a one-piece green bathing suit that I'd never seen before with a pair of shorts over it. She'd ditched her Chucks and had on sandals. She grabbed her backpack out and closed the door with her hip before I could get there.

"Hey," she said, an actual grin on her face even if she was flushed and sweating a little. It was hot, I didn't blame her for turning red. The sunglasses hid the deep green of her eyes. She'd pulled all that blonde hair up into a high ponytail, and it really emphasized how slender her throat was.

"You wore your suit," I said, catching her backpack. The fact pleased me way more than it probably should have. It was hardly the first time we'd have gone swimming together. For that matter, we had guest suits upstairs if she needed one.

"You did mention swimming, right?" The teasing snark in her voice just made me grin wider. Especially when she motioned to me. "Or did you just lose your shirt somewhere?"

Laughing, I jerked my head to the house. "C'mon in, I grabbed what I needed from upstairs. I got cold Cokes out. We have the house to ourselves, it's date night for Mom and Dad."

"Oh," she murmured, closing the door behind us once we were in. I didn't have to glance back to know she locked it. Locking the door after she was inside was a habit. "Oh, it's so nice and cold right here."

I glanced back to find her standing just under the vent, head tilted back as the air conditioning pushed all the cooler air out. I'd bet her eyes were closed under her sunglasses.

"Cold drinks this way," I reminded her with a verbal nudge and she made a playful groaning sound before she trudged after me.

Once in the kitchen, she pushed her sunglasses up and made a face. "I'm here. Give me cold libation and tell me what we're doing." The additional drama to the statement just made me snort.

I tugged out my phone, muted the messages app entirely so it wouldn't keep sending notifications, then pulled up one of the songs I recorded. "Have your drink, and listen to this." I hit play and put the phone and soda in front of her.

Music had been my passion project for the past couple of summers. The guys knew I played but I didn't really talk about the songs I wrote or the music I recorded. The only one I shared that with was the gorgeous angel now sitting at my kitchen table.

Her intent expression told me she was listening to the music. I had to make myself look away so I didn't try to read anything into every move she made. Frankie was the best critic for my songs. She told me when she didn't like something or if it sounded off. When she made suggestions, they were almost always solid.

I'd get her to sing with me, but someone had convinced her she couldn't sing so she lip sync'd along and just hung out when I played. Someday, I'd find the person who sold her that bullshit and I'd kick their ass. For now, I tried not to fidget.

This past summer I'd written and discarded easily a dozen songs. A couple of really morose ones about missing her. While I had absolutely missed her, the melancholy was a little too dark. This one held memories of who we had been and what we had done. Still balladic, but not so depressing.

"Bubba," she said on a long exhale and I locked my gaze on hers. "This is amazing."

"Yeah?" My palms were sweating so I wiped them off on my shorts before I dragged a chair out to sit near her. "You really like it?"

"Like it? I *love* it." It was impossible to not believe her when she used that tone. "It's a head and shoulders, hell, it's a whole body above your old stuff. When did you write this? And what is it called?"

"Doesn't really have a title yet, it's just one of a few I wrote this summer. The melody was in my head and it wouldn't go away." Mostly because I couldn't stop thinking about you, but I kept that part to myself.

"So I go away for a few months and you make magic." She widened her eyes at me. "Maybe I should go away more often."

"Bite your tongue," I said, catching her hand in mine. "Seriously. I'd rather have you around than write a song ever again."

"Bubba…"

"No," I said, giving her hand a firm squeeze, but not looking away from her eyes. "I mean it. I *missed* you this summer. Missed you like I'd miss my damn arm. Worse, because I had no idea why you were so determined to stay away from us. To stay away from me."

If I were one hundred percent honest, I was hurt too. That was more about me than us.

"I'm serious, Frankie. You're important to me. You've always been important to me. Not having you around, sucked. Not having you to talk to sucked more. If all we do today is hang out, swim, maybe order a pizza—then I'll be happy." Especially because we'd be doing it together.

"What about calculus?" She raised her eyebrows even as she squirmed a little in her seat. But she didn't pull her hand away from mine. I'd take all the progress I could get.

"Okay, I might have to cave on that because I would like to graduate with a decent grade this year." Though I had time to drop if I really needed to get rid of it.

Not that I wanted to drop. The stupid math class was the only one I had with her. This year sucked for how different all our schedules were.

"I think we can make that work," she told me, and when she would have pulled her hand back, I wanted to tighten my grip and hold on.

That was why I made myself let go. As much as I wanted to push everything, I needed her to be on board with it. "Thank you."

"Do you have more songs recorded?"

"Yeah, but not sure I want to play those for you." They were all so dark the more I thought about it. "What do you say we throw ourselves in the pool? Take an hour where we just play. Then we can do homework and stuff."

"And stuff," she murmured, glancing to the side as if she needed to think about this. I held my breath when it seemed like this was an idea that she really seemed to struggle with. Her phone buzzed and she shot me an apologetic look before she tugged it out.

Her scowl was epic. Whoever just messaged her had pissed her off.

"What's wrong?"

"Just more double standards," she muttered, clicking her screen off and turning it face down. "You know what, I do want to swim. I didn't get to spend as much time in the pool this summer."

The words "well you should have come around more" burned on the tip of my tongue, but I swallowed them unsaid. "Then we should make up for lost time."

Outside, I got to enjoy watching her tug off her shorts

and lay them over a chair under the table's umbrella. After I put our sodas on the table, I went ahead and dived in. The water was "cold" compared to the heat, but it felt damn good. I swam the length of the pool and emerged in the shallows.

It gave me a perfect view of her diving in. She really was gorgeous. For the next few minutes, we alternated between floating and swimming. When she drifted closer, I snaked an arm around her and pulled her back against my chest.

"Bubba?" There was just a note of warning in her voice. Warning and inquiry.

"Just let me say this," I said against her ear. Maybe it was cheating to do it with her looking away from me. It was definitely shitty to make a move on someone else's girl. But she wasn't someone else's girl. I didn't care who she was dating.

Frenchy was the interloper. Not me.

"I've wanted to date you since I understood that guys could like girls and it wasn't weird. You might be one of my best friends, but you have a body that I enjoy looking at and a brain I love learning from. You're also funny and adorable."

She'd gone completely still.

"For way too long, I didn't think you were interested in dating anyone. Not guys. Not girls. Nothing I did seemed to shift your opinion. But now you are dating…" Fuck, I hated saying that. "Dating someone we don't know and that bugs me because I want you to be happy, *and* safe. More, I want you to date *me*."

Her little jerk didn't bruise my ego at all.

"This is a lot to dump on you right here and right now, but if I didn't rip the Band-Aid off and just say it, I have a feeling I never would. So, this is me, Ian Rhys, telling you, Frankie Curtis, that I like you and I want to date you."

"You have a girlfriend…" It came out almost a strangled whisper.

"No. I don't. Sharon and I broke up. I don't have a girlfriend."

"But Mathieu and I…" She put her hand over mine on her stomach. I kept my hips back from hers even if her back was to my chest, cause my dick was all about broadcasting how happy we were to be holding her.

"Keep dating him," I said, and almost couldn't believe I was saying it. "If you want to, just—don't be exclusive. Let me have a chance." Then because that was enough pressure, I pressed a kiss to the nape of her neck. One brush of my lips to the damp skin there. "You don't have to say anything now or decide anything. Think about it. Please."

I waited, then let her go and pushed backward to swim to the far side of the pool again. I needed to burn off some of the desire that had me harder than a stone at the moment. Each time I passed her, I wanted to touch her, but I kept my hands to myself.

After a half-dozen laps, I headed over to where she sat on the steps. Time to face the music, literally and figuratively. She tilted her head as I approached and I straightened.

"Few more minutes," she said finally. "Then we can order pizza, do math homework, and talk essays."

I blew out a breath.

"If…" she continued, holding up a finger. "You play me another new song after."

Relief crashed into me and I made a face. "You drive a hard bargain."

"Those are my terms," she quipped. "Take it or leave it."

"Oh, I'll definitely take it." Take you. I was in.

FOURTEEN

FRANKIE

My phone vibrated in my pocket more than once during my shift, but it was nonstop here. Kids poured in after practices had started letting out. Football players, cheerleaders, members of the band—though the band typically drilled in the morning.

If I wasn't taking an order or delivering food to a table, I was making milkshakes. The grind and growl of the machine had become a constant chorus. My hand and wrist were both getting sore from fighting to scoop the ice cream. The freezer was broken, in that it had one temperature setting—subarctic.

Still, I supposed that was better than if it were more like the equator. If it wasn't possible to keep the ice cream cold, we'd have to stop serving shakes. While my hand and wrist would appreciate it, the rest of me wouldn't.

The bitching from the customers would be epic, particularly while Texas continued to play host to the seventh circle of hell. So, as much as my hand was cramping, I'd take the subzero freezer thank you very much.

"Hey, Curtis..." A familiar voice cut through the din and

I lifted a hand, then turned to shoot a smile over my shoulder. Never ignore the customer, no matter how busy you were.

My gaze collided with Rachel Manning's, who leaned with both hands on the countertop. "Be right with you. One minute." The sixty seconds was a promise I might struggle to keep but I finished scooping the ice cream, added the syrup and the milk then got this one hooked onto the shake machine.

The other two I had running weren't quite done yet. There was food in the window, so I snagged that and sailed over to deliver it to the table with some of Bubba and Jake's football buddies.

"Hey, Frankie," Rip said. "Settle a bet for us."

I raised my brows.

"If it's a quick one."

Both guys popped their biceps up to show off their arm muscles.

"Who's bigger? Me or Kent here?" I glanced from Rip to Kent. They were practically the same size.

"Kent," I said, his was a fraction higher. "Can I get you guys anything else?"

Rip's whole expression fell as the guys hooted and hollered, but they shook their heads. Leaving them to their great muscle debate I did a sweep of the packed tables.

I just needed to get those shakes out then wait for new orders to be ready, but I thought I had everyone covered.

Scooting back around the counter, I headed for Rachel. I put out a napkin and a glass of water for her. "Sorry about that." It had definitely been longer than a minute.

"Yeah, making me wait a whole extra thirty seconds," Rachel deadpanned. "How dare you?"

Amusement tickled through me at the open mocking in

Rachel's expression as she rolled her hazel eyes dramatically.

"I could make it longer," I offered in a dry tone with a glance at my watchless wrist.

She snorted, sliding onto one of the counter seats. "I appreciate the thought, but I'd rather go ahead and order."

Grinning, I pulled out a damp cloth from the clean stack and wiped down the counter. I was pretty sure I had already cleaned it up, but better to be sure. "Well, if you insist. What can I get you?"

"Big and thick," she said, lips twitching. "Innuendo implied but not necessary."

It was my turn to roll my eyes.

"And a strawberry shake." But she glanced over at the case. "If you can chip it out of the frozen tundra."

"I can," I told her. "It'll be a minute or three."

"Sounds good." She pulled out a notebook and flipped it open. There was reading material in there and she had a pen and paper. When she caught my look, she said, "Homework. I think better when I take notes."

"God," I said on an exhale. "I feel that." Taking notes was definitely how I could commit info to memory faster. The shake machine cut off. "Be right back."

"Take your time," she drawled but I was already turning away. Two of the three shakes were done blending and I got them poured, whip cream added, and slid in tall spoons and grabbed straws before whipping out to deliver them.

On the way back, I checked on my other tables, pre-bussing dishes where they were finished, and getting fresh drink orders for those who wanted refills. Back behind the counter, I sorted the dirty dishes into the bus tubs, then wiped my hands and cleaned out the shake cups and poured the third shake to get it delivered along with food, then got more shakes going.

Heating up the scoop in hot water seemed to help but I was going to end up pulling a muscle at this rate. I caught Rachel's snorting laugh and glanced over to see her shaking her head.

"Sorry, it's not funny."

"No, it's funny," I corrected and made a face at her. Then I amped up the drama of trying to free the ice cream and that earned me a real laugh. Once those shakes were started, there were people at the register to pay and more people coming in the door.

I still had two more hours of this. Packing away the exhaustion, I kept moving. Rachel waited patiently for her shake, though her burger and fries were ready at almost the same time.

Despite the temperatures outside she wore her long, dark brown hair in loose waves around her face. Her cosmetics, almost minimal, seemed natural and on point today. Whatever she'd done made her hazel eyes pop and also gave the more angular parts of her cheeks and chin a softer look.

I swore, she could look so severe when she wanted, and yet utterly relaxed in others. Most of the time, she wore layered outfits—dark jeans, graphic tees, hoodies, and leather or army-style jackets—in a vibe that seemed far more 90s than now, but maybe that was just the nonconformist in her. She did wear shorts and make allowances for the heat, but not today.

While her look was understated, I admired the confidence she wore like a crown over all of it. If only I were half that brave. The thought was as much envy as it was irritation. Rachel and I had such a love-hate relationship. This week, we seemed to be in "love" mode. Next week, we'd probably be back to armed enemies again.

Whatever we were, though, I had to admit, I owed her. If she hadn't told me the truth about the guys, I might never have seen it. In some of my darker moments, I wished I didn't know. Living in delusion hadn't been as lonely as this, but the truth was better.

The truth also led to me meeting Mathieu, so I would take what I could get. We stayed almost furiously busy through the dinner rush. Rachel lingered at the counter, working on her homework and swapping her shake for a soda.

She was still there near the end of my shift when Jake came through the door. The pressure in the room seemed to increase and turn the air almost electric, like a thunder boomer was rolling in. I had a big tub of dirty dishes in hand when my gaze locked with his for what could have been an endless eternity or a scant few seconds.

Looking away took genuine effort. Since I was almost done, I wasn't taking new tables. Marsha, the manager was already on the floor, along with Zabra, the other waitress. The kitchen would be closed in the next hour. I just needed to finish my side work—most of which was done, and clean off any tables of mine that emptied before I left.

When I made it back out front, Jake had taken a seat at the counter right next to Rachel and they were glaring at each other.

"Hey, Jake," I said as I stopped in front of them. "You okay, Rach?"

"I'm fine," she said, a smirk curving her lips. "Jake's just reminding me why I nominated him for jackass of the year in ninth grade."

"Leave her alone, Jake," I told him. It was as much an

order as anything else and it snagged his dour look off of her and onto me.

"You're off shift, right?"

"In a few, yes. I still have some stuff to do. If you want to order anything—"

"I don't want to order anything," he told me. "I want to talk to you after you're done."

Groaning, I stared up at the ceiling for a minute. "I'm tired, Jake..."

"I can wait," he said. "I'll make sure you get home too."

"I have a car," I reminded him but he just met me stare for stare. Nothing about him said he was backing down on this issue.

"If it's really an issue," Rachel interjected. "I have a car and a taser."

Jake cut a look at her. "Could you possibly just fuck off and leave us alone?"

"Jake!" I punched his shoulder across the counter, not that it fazed him. Hell, it barely moved him—big galumph. "Leave Rachel alone."

A muscle ticked in his jaw, but it was Rachel who waved me off. "I'm not worried about him, Frankie. He's just got a bug up his ass because you called them out on their bullshit after years of putting up with it."

Another sigh tore out of me.

"You know what, Manning..." Jake's voice had dipped into threatening territory.

"If you want to talk to me after my shift," I said, cutting in. "Then you're going to need to wait for me and stop bugging the customers, particularly the ones who are my friends."

"Let him say—" Rachel started but cut off when I sliced my hand through the air.

They both glared at each other, then looked away wearing expressions that seemed more akin to someone sucking on a jalapeño-flavored lemon.

"Fine," she muttered and Jake grunted. It was better than nothing, so I left them to finish my work.

Marsha caught me in the back as I slung a bag over my shoulder. "Everything alright, out there?"

"It's fine. Jake just wants to talk and he and Rachel rub each other the wrong way." That was the politest way I could put it.

"If you want me to walk you out to your car, we can shake them both off." She would do it too. Marsha didn't take shit from anyone. One of the best parts of working here was having Marsha for a boss.

"Really, it's fine," I repeated. "I'm just tired. Jake probably wants me to answer some message that I've ignored while I was on shift."

That reminded me, I needed to check my messages when I got home. Marsha's frown didn't lessen. If anything, she seemed more skeptical.

"I'll keep an eye on you through the window. Just hit the car alarm if you want me out there." That seemed a bit extreme, but also sweet.

"Thanks, Marsha. I'll see you tomorrow."

"Night, hon." She followed me out front. Rachel wasn't at the counter anymore and Jake waited by the door. He pushed it open at my approach, and the jingle seemed to signify that my ebbing energy could just falter completely now. I really was tired.

It had gotten dark, but the sun setting didn't do much for the temperatures. If anything, it seemed even stickier out here now than it had earlier.

I made a face because not only was it unpleasant out

here, I smelled like hamburgers and fries. Jake walked with me to where he'd parked his yellow SUV right next to my car. Once there, I opened the car up and got it started to get the a/c going then looked at him.

"Did you chase Rachel off?" I kept my tone even, but I did want to know. She'd hung out all evening.

"No," he answered with a grimace. "Wish I could say I had, but she mentioned something about needing to finish homework or something."

I nodded slowly. I could always message her later and figure it out. "Okay." I folded my arms. "What's up?"

He didn't answer immediately. Instead, he just *stared* at me.

"Jake?"

"I hate this," he said abruptly. "I hate that you're pretending we're not friends. I hate that you're pushing us —pushing *me* away. I hate that you're seeing some guy I don't know and I definitely don't like. I hate more than anything the way you're looking at me right now."

Every sentence landed like a bomb released in a strafing run. I swore, I could almost hear the whistle of air displacing as they plunged downwards to crash against me.

"How am I looking at you right now?" I couldn't really address the rest. Not yet.

"Like I'm an asshole."

Something moved in his pale blue eyes as the light seemed to catch them. It wasn't anger or defiance. If it had been either of those, I'd have been able to handle it.

But what I saw there took me out at the knees.

What I saw was hurt.

Shit.

FIFTEEN

JAKE

The last place I thought I would be was so far on the outs with Frankie that I didn't even know what to say to her. Talking to Frankie was *easy*. She'd always been easy. Ever since Rachel filled her head with that bullshit about us...

Fuck.

I raked a hand through my hair. "You look tired," I said finally, staring at her. She did look tired. Even her hair which she'd pulled up in a high ponytail looked like it was sagging.

"I am tired," she said with a shrug. "It's been a long day. Tomorrow is going to be a long day. I still have some reading to do."

A part of me reasoned I should let her go home, let her get some sleep. The rest of me dug in my heels. I wanted to see her, I wanted to spend time with her.

"Have you had dinner?" Because we had to start somewhere dammit. If she was looking at me like I was the bad guy then I needed to fix it. That started *right* now.

"The idea of eating a burger is..." She made a gagging face.

"I bet." The faint sway to how she stood there kicked me squarely in the ass. She was tired, so... "How about I go grab us pizza, you go and grab a shower?" I paused a beat. "Your mom gonna flip if i come by this late?"

"Probably, if she were home," Frankie said, smothering a half-yawn. "She left a message this morning that she had to go out of town for something for work. I don't know. She won't be back until this weekend."

What a bitch. Mrs. Curtis was just a shit mother. Yay that she wasn't there which meant one obstacle out of the way, but Frankie deserved a hell of a lot better.

"Okay, well, then we don't have to worry if she won't like it." I opened the driver's side door of Frankie's car for her. "Pizza?"

"Um—is *your* mom going to be okay with you staying out this late?'

"Mom knows I was planning to hang out with you. She's cool with it." I held up my phone. "And she knows how to reach me." Since I said I might crash on Frankie's sofa if we went too late, she'd given me a long look but finally nodded. So, yeah, Mom and I knew what was what.

"Then, yeah...though if I pass out on you, I'm sorry in advance." She smothered another yawn and guilt took a bite out of me. If she was this damn tired, I should let her sleep.

I would, but I was selfish too and I wanted this time.

"No sweat," I promised. "Go home. I'll go grab the pizza." I swiped over to the app where I already had the order ready to go. Before she could get in though, I caught her arm. "Frankie?"

"Yeah?"

"We're going to figure this out, you and me." It was as much an oath as anything. "But three things you need to know as facts."

Her green eyes were troubled as she studied me. "Those are?"

"I'm *not* dating Maria. I haven't in a while. It was over a long time ago and I coasted. Should have cut her loose before and that shit is on me."

Her nose wrinkled and that was fair. Maria wasn't bad, but she was never going to be Frankie. Just dating her because she was there was pretty damn shitty.

"The other two things?"

"I hate you dating Frenchy." I raised my free hand at the instant mutinous expression on her face. "I don't like it, Frankie. Never going to like it. He's not good enough for you."

"You don't even *know* him."

"I don't have to know him." This time, I narrowed the distance and cupped her chin. "*No one* is good enough for you." Then I dropped a kiss on her lips before I could over-think it. The simple brush was definitely not enough. It would never be *enough*. Didn't matter. "Not even me."

The stunned look on her face seemed to echo the shock inside me. Nothing about that kiss screamed passion, but the contact branded me. I wanted more.

"The third thing," I said as she blinked up at me. "I want you. I've *always* wanted you. I thought you didn't want me the same way. Maybe you don't... but Frenchy isn't just getting you by default. There's competition here and I plan to win."

She ran her tongue over her lower lip. "Jake..."

"What? You forget that I like a good fight?" I tried to

inject some humor into my voice, but I was too damn serious for that.

Rolling her eyes, she tilted her head back. "You guys are determined to drive me crazy."

"Not at all," I promised. "Now. In the car. You need to go home and shower. I'll be there in a few."

That earned me a sour look. "You're bossy."

"Yes," I agreed with her. "I am. In you go, baby girl."

The endearment slipped out, but I didn't regret its escape. It suited her. She flushed, pink staining her cheeks and it was adorable. But I pocketed that particular description for now.

"Straight home. I'll be right behind you. Ten minutes?"

She blinked up at me as she snapped the seatbelt into place. "Ten minutes."

After I closed her door, I retreated to the Jeep and waited for her to back out and leave before I got in the car. The drive to the pizza place didn't take two minutes. Fortunately, they weren't busy and our pizzas were being cut, so it didn't take long for me to carry the boxes out and head for Frankie's.

Tracking the time, I actually pulled into the slot next to Frankie's on the far side of the lot closest to her apartment in under ten. Then waited another minute before I headed up. I'd promised her ten minutes.

She was yawning as she opened the door. Her hair was combed straight, and it was still damp. It always took her thick hair time to dry. She was in pajama bottoms and a tank top. She also wasn't wearing any kind of bra and her nipples peaked at the front of the tank. Everything about her was sleepy and deliciously rumpled. As good as the pizza smelled, I'd rather eat her.

I locked the door behind me as she retreated through

the galley kitchen to the living room and I followed. "You really do look tired."

"Keep telling me how bad I look. It's really doing it for me," she actually made a face at me and it was the most normal she'd sounded in months. *That's it, baby girl, give me shit.* God I'd missed that. "Crap..."

"What?" I asked as I joined her on the sofa, she was half sprawled backwards and looked like she'd just been dumped there.

"I need to text Coop and tell him I'm home."

Since her phone wasn't in evidence, I pulled mine out of my pocket. "I got it."

Me: *Frankie's home, safe and sound. Leave her alone, she's exhausted and needs to sleep.*

Coop: *<middle finger emoji> Thanks for the update.*

Smirking, I clicked off the screen and shoved the phone back in my pocket. "Done. I also told him not to come over cause you're tired. That cool?"

"You know, it's presumptuous but I am tired and I really don't want to argue so—cool."

"Accepted." I shoved off my shoes and dragged one of the pizza boxes onto my lap. Then I patted the sofa next to me. I don't bite."

She snorted. "Yes, you do."

"What?" I scowled at her.

"You bit me in the third grade." The words threw me back in time.

"*You* bit me first." I gave her a smug look. "Can't blame a guy for biting you back."

Her narrow-eyed look jazzed me up. That expression promised me that she was going to retaliate. "You pulled my hair."

"Oh." Shit. "Yeah," I sighed. "I did do that." I'd kind of

forgotten that I had pulled her hair. "Don't even remember why I did it." Certainly wouldn't be for why I'd like to pull her hair now. That thought went straight to my groin and I was glad that the pizza box covered that up. "Point to you."

The soft huff of her laughter was pure music, especially when she scooted over to sit right next to me. Her knees brushed my thigh and a little bubble of contentment spread out through me. "Remotes are there," she said, pointing to the side table.

I turned the television on and scrolled to YouTube. Good, she was already logged in. I tabbed over to her Watch Later and then handed her back the remote. "You pick."

Pizza in one hand and remote in the other, she studied the list. Finally, she picked out a video, it was a funny as fuck history one where the historian debunked a film's accuracy with regard to the actual facts. Yeah, I was nerdy enough to appreciate it.

Much to my delight, however, Frankie mowed through four pieces of pizza without slowing down. I loved that she could eat. She didn't pick at her food or pretend she wasn't hungry when she was starving. It did mean I had to account for her appetite and mine, but that was easy enough.

We pretty much slaughtered the first box and started on the second before she settled back with a little sigh. After setting aside the second box, I wrapped an arm around her shoulders.

"This okay?"

"It's nice," she admitted, but her eyes were drooping some. She started to put her head against my shoulder but then stopped.

"It's fine," I nudged her head back toward my shoulder. I wanted her to lean on me. Her wet hair was hardly going to make me melt.

"You sure?"

"I'm sure," I promised her with a smile. She gave a little shiver. Her nipples were still two hard little pebbles in that tank top. I had to drag my gaze off of them. Goosebumps spread over her arm and I curled my own around her a little more tightly so I could warm her up.

"Jake?" she murmured, and her eyes were practically shut.

"Hmm?"

"This isn't a great evening for you." The sleepy words just added to her.

"I get to spend time with you." I pressed a kiss to the top of her head. "I like it."

"Hmm," she released another jaw popping yawn and her eyes closed all the way. "Funny video next." The words were slurred with sleep. I listened to the video, but I drank in the sight of her all snuggled up to me.

Closing my own eyes, I took a deep breath, filling myself with her nearness. When I twisted a little and lifted her up to settle in my lap, she didn't stir. Yeah, having her warm and pliable against my lap was a torture of its own, but I could wrap her up better and she just seemed to melt against me.

Yeah, no more being cold for her. I watched three more videos as her breathing deepened and grew more regular. Holding her was nice.

Real nice. I'd have to move her to her bed—eventually.

Yes, I'd tuck her in, but first, I just wanted to hold her.

SIXTEEN

FRANKIE

Warmth clung to me like a second skin, thick and suffocating, and for one indulgent moment, I didn't care. I burrowed deeper into it, refusing to open my eyes, refusing to move. My fingers curled around the edge of the blanket as I stretched, slow and content. My nose brushed against what I thought was my pillow, and I inhaled deeply.

Jake. The scent was unmistakable—clean, warm, and unreasonably familiar.

A distant purr buzzed from the direction of my desk, and I thought I felt the faint bounce of a cat leaping off the bed. A yawn tugged at my jaw. I cracked one eye open.

Still dark. Perfect. More sleep.

I shifted to settle deeper, and that's when I felt it—the hand. Heavy. Warm. Sprawled across my stomach... and sliding upward.

My breath caught.

Wait.

What?

My eyes snapped open, and a jolt of adrenaline surged

through me. I was in my bed. Definitely. But there was also someone else in it. Curled tightly against my back, solid and breathing and *real*. The thundering in my chest drowned out everything else.

I twisted, heart slamming against my ribs, and stared into the dim shadows.

"Jake?" My voice cracked.

He grunted, low and lazy, like I hadn't just had a mild cardiac episode.

Then he moved—his hand tightening at my waist, anchoring me. He curled me into him with terrifying ease, pressing his face into my hair, his breath a warm gust against my scalp. His stubble rasped against my skin, sending a ripple of sensation straight down my spine. My stomach twisted as I tried to turn, limbs tangled and awkward.

"It's the middle of the night," he mumbled, barely conscious. Still, he managed to roll to his back and drag me with him, like I was some oversized teddy bear. Dim yellow light leaked in through the edges of the blinds, just enough to catch the shape of him beside me.

His arm remained slung across my shoulders, though his hand had slid away. My own hand, traitorous and confused, settled on his chest—because I didn't know where else to put it.

"Jake." Sharper this time, but quieter. My pulse was racing, sleep a distant memory. "What time is it?"

He groaned, dragging me closer. One of my legs hooked over his without permission. *Why did this feel so normal?* So easy?

"Two-ish," he slurred, breath warm against my temple. "You fell asleep. I carried you in. I was gonna go, but..." He yawned, wide and unbothered. "Didn't want to."

My mouth was dry. "You're sleeping in my bed." The words came out flat, pointless. Obvious.

I blinked rapidly. My eyes burned. My hand was still on his chest, where the steady thud of his heart knocked against my palm, loud and strong. We'd done sleepovers before. Years ago. Back when co-sleeping didn't mean anything.

This wasn't that.

This wasn't innocent.

This was *Jake*. In my bed. Shirtless. Boxers. Pressed against me like he'd always belonged there.

And it wasn't just confusing. It was terrifying.

He shifted to kiss the top of my head, then lazily traced his fingers down my bare arm. The lightness of the touch made me shiver.

"If you want me to leave," he said, voice softer now, more awake. "I will."

He sounded like he meant it.

He also sounded like it would kill him.

I swallowed hard. "No." My voice cracked. "Mom's out of town."

As if that excused *any* of this.

"Cool," he murmured, his hand easing me down like he owned me. I didn't resist. I couldn't. My cheek found his shoulder, and the scent of him hit me all over again, deep in my chest.

Every breath he took was a reminder that he was right there. That I wasn't dreaming. That this could go wrong so easily.

He stroked my arm again, slow, thoughtless. Intimate.

Sleep was impossible now.

Every nerve was singing, jittery with awareness. I could feel every inch of him, warm and firm, and terrifyingly familiar. The way his leg pressed against mine. The beat of his heart, steady and solid beneath my hand. The shape of his body—one I knew, but suddenly felt like I'd never *really* seen.

"Frankie?" he asked, voice threaded with concern. "You okay?"

I closed my eyes. No. I was not okay. My thoughts were racing, colliding. My heart was lodged in my throat, and every breath felt like a gamble.

"I don't think I can sleep like this," I whispered, barely able to admit it.

Because I didn't want to fall asleep.

I didn't want to miss *this.*

"Mmm...I'll fix it..." he murmured. The mattress dipped with a soft bounce as he shifted, and then I was being gathered—rolled gently onto my back, then my side, into heat and solidity. A body. His body. An arm locked snug around my middle, and suddenly I was spooned tight, back pressed to his chest, one of his legs tangled with mine like we were puzzle pieces finally fitting.

One arm curved over my waist, the other slid higher—fingers spreading over my sternum. My tank top had ridden up. His hand was on my skin. His *fingers* were on my skin. The contact was warm and grounding and terrifyingly intimate.

It was... better.

And also so, so much worse.

Then his lips brushed behind my ear, soft, unhurried. A kiss. A *real* kiss. "Go to sleep," he whispered, voice thick with sleep and something else I couldn't name. "I'm not going anywhere. I promise."

I didn't know what to do with that. So, I didn't do anything.

At some point, I drifted off. Somehow.

The next time I opened my eyes, the world was dim but clearer—the black of night shifting to the cold gray blur of dawn. The alarm hadn't gone off yet. Shadows clung to the corners of the room, but light rimmed the blinds. I was still on my side. Jake was still there.

His arm draped across me, loose now, but heavy. Familiar.

Comforting.

Too comforting.

Jake is in my bed.

The thought struck sharper now. Not dreamy. Not hazy. *Clear.*

Jake. Not my boyfriend.

Not Mathieu.

My heart stuttered.

The sudden spike of guilt was a punch to the gut, and yet... I didn't move. Couldn't. My hand hovered over his, then brushed it lightly, fingertips tracing the lines I knew too well. He stirred behind me, catching my hand in his, and then—

A kiss.

Pressed to the back of my shoulder, unhurried. Intimate.

My skin lit up where his lips touched it.

"Morning," he mumbled, voice gravel-edged, the rasp of his stubble grazing against me with every syllable. "Not time to get up yet."

I should've pulled away.

I didn't.

"I don't know what time it is," I said instead, voice low, almost ashamed. I pulled his hand to my chest, anchoring myself there, even as my pulse roared in my ears. His bicep curved across my chest in a way that made my breath catch. I should have shifted his hand. Should have said *something*.

But I didn't want to.

He groaned, stretching, then let go and rolled onto his back. I turned to my stomach, lifting onto my elbows, watching as he blindly fumbled for his phone on the side table. The glow from the screen cut through the shadows and hit his face.

Jake. Rumpled. Stubbled. Hair a mess. No perfect styling. No cocky smile.

Just him. Raw. Real.

And *devastating*.

My throat tightened. My stomach clenched.

I'd seen this version of him before—but never like this. Not in my bed. Not after a night tangled together like... like *that* meant something.

"It's just barely six," he said, dropping the phone beside him. He turned toward me, his voice gentler now. "Hey..."

"Hi," I whispered, suddenly self-conscious, retreating behind the dark again now that the phone screen had gone black. Safer not to be seen. Safer not to look too long.

Jake rolled back toward me, closing the distance like it cost him nothing. His breath brushed my cheek, warm and steady. My heart was doing anything but steady. *Thundering.* Crashing against my ribs like it wanted out.

He didn't smell like sleep or sweat or morning breath.

He just smelled like *Jake*.

And I knew—without question—that my sheets would smell like him long after he was gone.

The thought hit me with a strange, twisted sort of panic.

When his fingers grazed my cheek, tucking my hair

back behind my ear, I flinched—but only a little. Then I sighed. His touch was too soft. Too careful.

"Sleep well?" he asked.

Weird question. Loaded, actually.

Did I sleep well, tangled in the arms of someone who wasn't mine?

Did I sleep well while *forgetting* Mathieu existed?

"Pretty good," I answered, even though my voice shook. "A little weird when I realized you were still here."

He chuckled softly. "Weird good? Or weird bad?"

His fingers traced the curve of my ear, sending shivers that made it hard to think.

I hesitated. And in that silence, I saw it—the flicker in his expression. Hope, maybe. Vulnerability. Something that made my chest ache.

Did this mean something?

Maybe it did.

How the hell...

And the worst part?

I wasn't sure I wanted to correct him.

"Weird undecided," I said, not quite able to keep from smiling. "This is kind of—nice."

His gaze searched mine, hungry but soft. Like this moment had been waiting for both of us to catch up to it.

"Yeah?" he murmured, his hand sliding into my hair, fingers gentle as they coasted down to the back of my neck. "Frankie?"

"Hmm?"

"I'm going to kiss you."

A slow flutter of panic and desire surged through me—sweet, sharp, and terrifying.

There was no teasing in his voice, no smirk. Just sincerity. Intention.

I nodded.

Then he kissed me.

It started soft. Barely-there brushes of his lips against mine, like he was memorizing the shape of my mouth. Then again. And again. Light, teasing, feather-soft. I gasped softly and he caught it, deepened the kiss, and when I opened to him, his tongue swept in—hot, slow, possessive.

The world dropped away.

He shifted, rolling us gently so I was curled into his side, his body lined along mine. One hand slid around my waist, tugging me flush. The other cupped the back of my neck, holding me steady as the kiss turned from searching to *needy*. Every stroke of his mouth, every wet drag of his tongue sent sparks flying across my skin.

My legs tangled with his. His thigh slipped between mine, firm and unrelenting. I rocked against him before I even realized it, chasing that pressure, that burn.

Jake groaned against my mouth, one hand sliding under the hem of my tank top to touch skin. His fingers were warm and a little rough, grazing over my ribs like I was something breakable. He kissed like he was starving. Like he'd been waiting years to do this and couldn't take it slow anymore.

And I—

God, I wanted it. I wanted *him*.

I shouldn't. I couldn't. Then I remembered *why*.

The *why* hit me, hard, cold, and too real.

This was so new. Impossible.

Why *now*?

He kissed me like I was his first—no matter how much I knew that wasn't true. It didn't matter, he made me feel it all. This was *our* first kiss.

And I—

I'd already done this with someone else.

Not just kissed. Not just touched.

I'd gone further.

Much further.

With *Mathieu*.

"Jake—wait," I breathed, heart slamming against my ribs. "Stop."

He froze, his forehead pressed to mine, his breath hot against my cheek.

"What is it?" he whispered, stilling his hands, but not pulling away. Not yet.

I squeezed my eyes shut. "I can't. We have to stop."

Confusion flared in his expression. Hurt started creeping in behind it.

"Too fast?" he asked, voice quiet. "Are you okay?"

I pushed gently against his chest, needing space to breathe. "Jake... We can't—we..."

He pulled back just enough to look at me, lips parted, chest still heaving.

I couldn't meet his eyes. Not yet.

"Frankie?"

"I'm dating someone," I whispered. "Remember?"

Silence.

His hands dropped from me like I'd burned him. I looked up. I had to. The anger in his face made my stomach lurch.

"Frenchy." His voice was cold now. Sharp. Not like Jake at all.

"Mathieu," I said quietly more to remind myself than him. Mathieu didn't deserve this. God, Jake didn't either. What the hell had I done?

He nodded once. No emotion on his face. None I could name. Then: "Did you kiss him?"

I opened my mouth. Closed it.

He laughed. "Never mind. Stupid question. Of course you did. Probably a lot more than that, huh?"

The air turned brittle.

I said nothing.

His smile was tight, humorless. "Frankie. Did you sleep with him?"

My silence gave him the answer he didn't want.

He staggered back like I'd hit him. "Jesus Christ."

His face—God, I'd never seen him look like that. Not even when his dad left. This wasn't heartbreak.

This was betrayal.

And I had done it.

"Jake—" I started, reaching for him, but he flinched like my touch would set him on fire.

"No." His voice cracked, harsh and final. "Don't."

He turned away, grabbing his shirt from the floor in a single, jerky movement. He didn't even put it on—just balled it in his fist and stalked out of the bedroom.

"Please just let me explain—"

"There's nothing to explain," he bit out, jamming his feet into his shoes. "You already did."

He grabbed some things from the coffee table, then slammed open the kitchen door so loud the cats scattered.

I stood there, frozen, heart pounding. What the hell could I say?

He didn't look back.

Didn't slam the door again, but shut it hard enough to shake the glass in its frame.

And then there was nothing but silence.

Silence and the sick, yawning weight of everything I couldn't undo.

SEVENTEEN

FRANKIE

"Morning, Coop," I said, my voice too bright, too brittle. It cracked at the edges, and I hated how fake it sounded. My head was still back at Jake—his rejection sharp as a slap, the flash of fury in his eyes, the way he stormed out without waiting for me to explain. Like I didn't deserve the chance. It burned— his silence, his judgment, the finality of it. I didn't owe him anything. Not really. Not after *everything*. But dammit, it still gutted me to have him look at me like I was nothing. Like I'd betrayed him.

I fumbled with my keys, fingers stiff and clumsy, and all I could think was: *Don't cry. Not here. Not in front of Coop.* I clenched my jaw. *You will not cry.*

Coop didn't look at me.

"Morning," he said, but his gaze slid right past me, like I wasn't even there. The word was clipped, cold—not awkward, not shy. Just distant.

I swallowed hard and opened the car door, forcing my hands to stay steady. My backpack hit the backseat with a dull thud, too loud in the glacial silence. When I shut the door and turned, Coop was finally looking at me—and I almost wished he wasn't.

There was something hollow in his expression, tight around the eyes and mouth. Not quite anger. Not yet. But the kind of disappointment that sank straight into my chest like a stone. Not betrayal. *Hurt.* Quiet, restrained, and sharp enough to leave a bruise.

"You ready?" he asked. It sounded neutral. But it wasn't. Nothing about the way he looked at me was impartial. If anything, it felt like he knew everything, judged me, and found me wanting. That *hurt.*

It didn't help that guilt clawed at my throat.

"Yeah," I managed, and he slid into the passenger seat.

He didn't speak again. Not once as I drove. The silence scraped at me. My heart pounded, like it knew what was coming and wanted to run from it. My fingers clenched the wheel tighter with every street we passed. This was worse than yelling.

Finally, I couldn't take it anymore. "What's wrong?"

His phone buzzed in his pocket. Again. It had been buzzing almost since we got in the car. He didn't even reach for it. Just leaned against the window, fist against his mouth.

"Jake spent the night?"

There it was. Quiet. But sharp.

"We fell asleep watching videos," I said. Flat. Careful. I stared at the road ahead because if I looked at him, the guilt would be unbearable.

"Jake said he wasn't going to stay long. Said you were tired."

"He probably did." My voice cracked. "I was. It was late." *We didn't plan it. It just happened.* None of that made it okay. "It's not the first time he's spent the night."

Coop turned toward me, his tone low. "We were twelve the last time he stayed over there, Frankie."

"Okay." It wasn't okay. I hated that he'd figured it out. That there was *anything* to find out.

"And your mom wasn't home—again."

"Yeah, thanks for the reminder," I snapped. The light turned green. I needed motion. Escape.

"You have a hickey."

My breath caught. I had a hickey? How the hell had I not seen it? Heat flared under my skin, shame crawling up my neck.

"Are you mad I have one—or that I didn't report back to you about every second of my night?" It came out harsher than I meant. But I couldn't take it back.

Coop's jaw clenched. "I don't know," he said after a beat. "I don't know what I feel right now."

That cut deeper than if he'd just yelled. I deflated. "Coop..."

He shook his head. "It's fine, Frankie. I just—seeing Jake's car there earlier. Knowing he was there. It just hit me." His knuckles thudded against the door. "Sorry. I'm not mad at *you*."

I glanced at him. "You sure about that?"

He didn't answer. Not right away. I spotted a motorcycle behind us in the mirror—*Bubba*. Of course. And of course, *now*.

We pulled into the school lot. I couldn't breathe.

"I want to ask you out." Coop didn't look at me as he said that.

"Okay." My voice was a whisper. Okay was only one small step above just "oh." But here we were. For the first time, I had absolutely no idea what to say to Coop right now. About anything.

"Are you—are you and Jake...?" Coop trailed off, but I heard the question. Felt it, razor-sharp in the space between us.

"We haven't gone on a date," I said quickly. Too quickly. Coward. *He asked. Sorta. Then we just fell into bed.*

"And Bubba?"

"He asked." I parked. My hands trembled on the wheel. "Just... we haven't really had time to talk since Tuesday. Not really." Keep dating Frenchy if I had to, but date him too. Yeah, those words were permanently etched into my brain.

"Then there's Frenchy..."

"It's *Mathieu*," I snapped, defensive, exhausted.

"Yeah, I don't care what his name is," Coop said. Then, gentler, he reached for my hand. "I'm not trying to be an ass. I promise."

"I know." I tried to smile. "You're just drawn that way."

He smiled back, just barely. The first real one all morning.

"I meant it, Frankie. I want to take you out."

I looked at him, and for a second, the weight in my chest was unbearable. "Even if...?"

"Even if you're dating *others*."

Bubba knocked on my window. Coop didn't let go of my hand.

I held up one finger—*wait*—then turned back to Coop.

"Are you sure?"

His gaze flicked away. "Do you not want to go out with me? If that's it—"

"Stop," I said. "It's not that. It's just—" *Now I'm lying to my best friend, sleeping with a guy they apparently all hate, and breaking every rule I thought I'd made for myself.* They were all coming at me with offers like this was some kind of game. Like my heart wasn't involved at all.

"You've figured out we all like you," Coop said softly. "A lot."

That was definitely part of it. A part I hadn't been ready for.

"But we've been friends forever. If I mess this up—" We hadn't even repaired the damage from their choices and mine as yet. They all wanted to change it again.

"We'll make it work. Just… make time for me, too? Maybe Monday, after planning and applications?"

I squeezed his hand. "Okay."

But guilt gnawed at the back of my throat.

Because I already had no idea how to fix what I'd broken.

I pulled my hand away gently and grabbed my backpack. Coop got out with me, rounding the front of the car. Bubba stood a few feet away, watching us, hands in his jacket pockets. His brows pulled together as his gaze flicked between us, then stopped—just for a second—on my neck.

I resisted the urge to touch it.

The air seemed to shift between us, thick with things unsaid. Bubba didn't smile. He didn't tease. He didn't even speak. Just looked at me like he wanted to, then looked away instead.

They were both close—Coop on my right, Bubba on my left—but neither of them touched me. Not a brush of the hand. Not a hug. Just space, tight and uncomfortable. Like I was radioactive. Like they didn't know where to step.

We started toward the school building in silence. Each step made my skin itch. I hated how self-conscious I suddenly was—how *visible* the hickey must be. How much they noticed. How much they *didn't* say.

Inside, the halls were still mostly quiet. Early.

Archie was waiting at our usual table in the cafeteria

with coffee for everyone. He had his in one hand, phone in the other. He looked up when he saw us, smile twitching onto his face—but it faltered the second he saw me.

Then I saw *Jake*.

He was sitting at the end of the table, two boxes of donuts next to him. His jaw was tight. His expression unreadable.

My stomach dropped.

Because all of them were here.

And the way they looked at me—every one of them—made my chest squeeze tight. Like they were waiting for something. Like they were *bracing*.

Archie's gaze flicked to my neck, then away. Bubba didn't look at me at all. Coop's hand was back in his pocket.

Jake didn't say a word.

And I stood there, halfway between all of them, like a pulled thread in a sweater. One wrong move, and the whole thing would unravel.

EIGHTEEN

ARCHIE

They came in like they were already halfway broken.

Frankie walked between Bubba and Coop, and none of them spoke. She looked like she was trying not to shrink under the weight of all their silence, which was almost funny considering she was the center of everything right now. Usually, Frankie moved with this confidence—head up, smart mouth ready. But today, she looked... wrong. Off. Like she knew the wolves were circling and didn't quite know where to run.

I caught the mark on her neck the second she stepped near the table. So did Bubba, though he didn't say a word. His eyes just hardened and slid away.

Coop tried to play normal, but his shoulders were stiff. How his hand twitched like he wanted to reach for her and didn't.

And then there was Jake.

He sat on the edge of the table with the boxes of donuts at his side, but there was nothing warm in him. No smile, no smug little nod. Just flat, controlled nothingness. Which, for Jake? Might as well be rage.

Frankie saw him and stopped cold. Her expression wavered—just for a second—but enough that I felt it in my gut.

He didn't say a word to her.

Didn't offer a donut. Didn't crack open the box with the fritters. Didn't even look up.

She said his name, soft and unsure. He still didn't speak.

Then she did something I didn't expect.

She just... walked away. She didn't ask anyone to follow her. She didn't even look back.

I watched her go, and something about it made me furious.

She hadn't done this alone. Whatever mess she was in, *they* were in it too. And yet they all stood there, acting like she'd blown up the house while they just watched from the sidewalk.

Coop sighed and dropped into a chair. Bubba grabbed a donut without asking. Jake stared straight ahead like he was alone in the damn room.

"So," I said, not bothering to hide the edge in my voice. "We gonna pretend this is normal?"

No one answered.

Jake took a long drink from the coffee I knew wasn't his usual order. He was off, too. Everyone was.

"What happened?" I asked, leveling it at Jake.

He didn't look at me.

"Jake."

He blinked once. "Go to hell."

The silence that followed that? Thick enough to chew.

"Excuse me?" I rose before I even decided to.

Jake finally met my eyes. His jaw ticked. "You heard me."

It would've taken one more word. One more push. We were that close. Fists clenched, blood up, tension radiating off both of us. Coop moved like he might intervene, but I didn't need him. I could handle Jake just fine. Hell, I *wanted* to.

But Bubba stepped in first, throwing himself between us. "Okay, no one's fighting in front of the donuts," he said without looking at either of us.

"You're really not gonna tell me what happened?" I asked, still staring Jake down.

Jake turned his head. "It doesn't matter."

The hell it didn't.

I stood there for a second longer, willing someone to give me a reason not to shove Jake into a locker and demand answers. But Coop said nothing. Bubba just ate his donut like it was all above his pay grade.

Fine.

They didn't want to fix this? I would.

Because something had shifted. Frankie was out there alone, and whether they were mad, jealous, confused, or just plain stupid, they were letting her drown. And that made *me* mad.

She'd let her guard down. Told us she was finally open to something—dating, maybe more—and now they were treating her like she'd cheated on all of them at once.

I looked around the commons, where we used to sit and laugh and argue about nothing. Now it felt like a war room. And if that wasn't bad enough, I already knew where the next bomb was coming from.

Frenchy.

Mathieu, whatever.

He was a problem. Too slick, too polished, too charming —and none of us knew a damn thing about him. I'd seen the way he watched Frankie when he thought no one else was paying attention. And I didn't like it.

He was the only one who *hadn't* grown up with us. He hadn't been there for the late-night group chats or the trashy convenience store runs or helping Frankie fix her busted faucet because her mom forgot again. He didn't know her. Not really.

But he wanted something. I could see it all over him.

And now, with the rest of the guys too wrapped up in their own hurt feelings, no one was paying attention to the fact that *he* was making moves in all the cracks she didn't know she had.

So if no one else was going to look out for her?

I'd do it myself.

I'd figure out what Frenchy wanted.

And then I'd make sure he didn't get it.

IT STARTED with me catching sight of her in the hallway, walking next to Coop. Frankie was nodding at something he's saying, but she's not really there. Her smile was on her face, sure—but her eyes? They were somewhere else. Distant. Quiet. Like someone turned the volume down on her.

I hated that look on her.

I didn't mean to be the villain here. Not today anyway. But she walked next to Coop, looking all dimmed down and agreeable, and I couldn't take it.

So I slid in beside them like the chaos I was, smirking just enough to irritate him and amuse her.

"Hey, Frankie," I said casually. Then I turned to Coop without missing a beat. "Mind if I borrow your lunch date?"

Coop opened his mouth, ready to assert his moral territory or whatever, but I cut him off, all sunshine.

"Perfect. That's a yes. Thanks, Coop."

Just like that, I gently looped my arm around Frankie's shoulder, steering her away from him and into the current of the hallway crowd. She half-laughed, resisting slightly but not pulling away.

"Archie—what are you doing?" she asked, but the smallest ghost of a smile twitched at her lips.

"I'm abducting you." I grinned. "Classic lunch heist. You looked far too agreeable back there. It was disturbing."

"You can't just—" She glanced back at Coop, that reflexive politeness kicking in. "We had plans."

"Cancel them. Or reschedule. Or send him a postcard." I shrugged. "Frankie, come on—when's the last time you blew something off?"

She hesitated. "...I don't know. Never?"

"Exactly," I said, walking backward toward the front doors like I had a spotlight on me and a theme song playing in my head. "I dare you to remember how to have fun. Just for one lunch break. What's the worst that happens? You laugh? You smile like you mean it?"

That got her. I saw it in the flicker of her expression—something warm trying to push past the fog.

"Live dangerously," I added, shooting her a wink. "Have fries."

Outside, the sun was obnoxiously bright, which was exactly how I liked it. The Ferrari—orange and completely over-the-top—was parked in my usual spot, practically humming with ego. I walked over and popped the passenger door open with a theatrical bow.

"Madam," I said. "Your carriage awaits."

She stood there on the curb, arms crossed. "You know we still have class."

"Sure. But we also have freedom, gasoline, and my impeccable playlist." I shot her a look, lowering my voice slightly. "Let's ditch. Just this once. Let's go be stupid for an hour. Or two."

She was quiet, and when I looked at her—really looked—I saw it again. That sadness. Big green eyes, too heavy with something I couldn't name. Something old. Something she's been carrying alone.

And I hated it. Hated that I couldn't fix it. So I did what I do best.

I distracted.

Then she said, "Okay."

It hit me like a left hook I didn't see coming. "Wait—really?"

"Yeah." She stepped toward the car. "Let's go be stupid."

I blinked, stunned for a beat. I wasn't ready for that yes.

But I wasn't wasting it. I waited for her to climb in then closed the door after her. After, I rushed around to the driver's side, heart beating a little too fast. I slid in, fired up the engine, and the Ferrari growled like it was just as hungry to escape as we were.

We peeled out of the parking lot like two kids running from something we couldn't name.

The hum of the engine settled into a low purr as we hit the open road. I snuck a glance at her. She leaned her head back against the seat, while she wound a bit of her hair absently around one finger. I couldn't help but wonder how long it'd been since she let herself do nothing. Just breathe.

The silence stretched. Comfortable for a second. Then it turned weird.

I drummed my fingers on the steering wheel, trying to work out how the hell to talk to her. She wasn't like other people. You couldn't always poke and get a reaction. You had to wait, gently, like coaxing a stray animal to eat from your palm.

I cleared my throat. "Hey," I said, eyes still on the road. "What do you want to do?"

She turned her head slightly, brow creasing.

"I mean," I continued, a little faster, "what do *you* want to talk about? Where do *you* want to go? This is your detour, Frankie. You call it."

She stared out the window for a second longer, but there was the faintest twitch at the corner of her mouth— like I've cracked something, just a little. Not a smile yet. But maybe. Just maybe.

My phone buzzed in the center console.

Edward.

I glanced at it. My gut clenched. I don't answer. Not now. Not today. Answering would mean dealing with *him*, and worse, dealing with the thing he's doing—the thing with *her*. With Frankie's mom.

I shoved that thought down hard and kept my eyes on the road.

"There's a little place out past the lake," she said suddenly. "Kind of ridiculous. Bright chairs, milkshakes bigger than your head."

I grinned. "Say less."

She gave me a look. "It's sort of dumb."

"Perfect," I said. "We're being dumb today. That's the whole point."

She hesitated. "I was supposed to review history notes before work."

I shot her a quick side-eye. "Uh uh. Nope. From now until I drop you off to get ready, we're on *our* time."

"Our time?"

"No worries, no school, no guys, no Frenchy, no problems, nothing. Just us."

She shifted slowly to look at me. One eyebrow arched.

"Just us," she tested the words, skeptical. "And no problems?"

"Exactly," I said, tapping the steering wheel like I'm sealing a deal. "Just us and no problems."

For a beat, she studied me. And then—*then*—it happened. The smallest smile, barely there. But it was real. Not polite. Not painted on. Real.

In that second, I swore, I'd drive us straight into the sun if it meant she'd keep smiling like that.

CHAPTER

NINETEEN

FRANKIE

The booth seat was sticky from the heat, the kind that clung to your skin and made your thighs stick to the vinyl like it was trying to claim you. The place looked the same as it always had—plastic flamingos out front, checkered floors inside, faded posters of Elvis and old hot rods on the walls. But somehow, it felt like everything was vibrating. Off. Like the air itself knew something was about to happen.

I stirred my milkshake with a straw, watching the swirl of chocolate and vanilla like it held answers. It didn't.

Archie sat across from me, arms stretched along the back of the booth, sunglasses pushed up into that mess of dark hair like he didn't have a care in the world. But he did. I could feel it. His eyes kept flicking to me like he was working up to something. And I didn't know whether to be curious or terrified.

"So," I said finally, just to fill the space. "Nice kidnapping. Five stars. Would get abducted again."

He grinned, but it didn't quite reach his eyes. "Only the best for you."

145

My stomach twisted. I didn't know why. Maybe because this was the first time we'd been alone in weeks where it didn't feel like we were running from something. Or maybe it was because, deep down, I knew what he was about to say and I didn't know how to feel about it.

He leaned forward, elbows on the table. "Frankie."

Uh-oh.

"Yeah?"

"I need to say something, and I need you to actually listen. Not joke. Not deflect. Just... hear me, okay?"

I sat straighter, nerves crackling in my fingertips. "Okay."

His eyes searched mine. "I like you."

I blinked. "You *what*?"

Archie chuckled, but there was a tightness in his jaw. "Don't look at me like I've grown a second head."

"I—no, it's just..." I set my milkshake down. My heart was racing. "Archie, we've been friends forever."

"Yeah. Then I started driving you home after I got my car, and bringing you snacks when your mom forgot dinner, and dragging you to movie nights even when you said you had to study. How many times have I taken you to play mini-golf?"

"A lot," I said slowly.

He gave me a look. "Frankie. It was a *date*. You wore my hoodie. You let me win."

"I didn't let you win," I muttered. "You cheated."

"Still counts." His smirk appeared briefly, but it didn't last.

I stared at him. "But why didn't you ever say anything?"

He shrugged, fidgeting with his straw wrapper. "Because you weren't ready. You never seemed to respond to it. Because I wasn't ready to be rejected. I thought maybe if I waited long enough, you'd figure it out on your own."

I looked down at the table. "Archie..."

"I know it's not good timing," he said. "I know you're fighting with Jake, that Coop is in this, probably Bubba too, and whatever the hell is happening with Frenchy. I get that I might be one too many."

"It's not that," I said quickly. Too quickly. "I'm just—shocked. That's all. You've always been... *you*. Funny. Safe."

His expression didn't change, but something about his posture pulled inward. "Right. 'Safe.' Every guy wants to hear that."

"No," I said, reaching across the table before I could stop myself. My fingers brushed his wrist. "That's not what I meant. I just—Archie, we've always been easy. But now... nothing feels easy."

He studied me for a long moment. "So let's make this easy. Just one question, Frankie. Just answer it honestly."

"Okay."

He tilted his head. "Does it *really* surprise you that I have a thing for you? Or did you just not want to deal with what it meant if I did?"

The truth hit me like a gut punch.

"You know, you have dated, right?" Was I a being a bitch to point it out? "Like, a lot."

"Yes, I'm aware I've dated other girls—like Patty," he said quietly, eyes flicking away. "None of them meant anything. A distraction. But if I'm honest... I thought you really weren't interested. I didn't want to make you uncomfortable. So I kept my distance, tried to keep things casual. Maybe dating others would take the edge off."

A sigh escaped me. He had gone through a lot of girls, always keeping it casual, light. Patty had lasted the longest, but was it because he liked her or because she didn't irritate him enough to shake off?

Raking a hand through his hair, he looked at me with a kind of raw honesty I only ever saw from him when it was just us. Vulnerability hidden behind a sharp tongue and eyes that saw too much. "Now... I'm worried. Worried I might've lost you before I even had a chance."

Had I known? I tried to turn it all over in my head. The guys were—the guys. My best friends. We did everything together until we didn't. My throat was dry. First Coop. Bubba. Jake. Now Archie. I couldn't even decide if this was a *good* thing.

Dating would change everything. The last thing I wanted was to lose him. Lose any of them. Walking away this summer had been the hardest damn thing I'd ever done. Now, not even a few days into senior year and...

What?

What did all of this mean?

"I don't know what to do with this." *With you.* I didn't say the last part aloud as I dropped my gaze, feeling the burn behind my eyes.

He didn't move. Didn't speak. Just let the silence hang between us like a sheer curtain.

"I don't know how to be what everyone wants," I admitted. "I keep screwing it up. Jake hates me. Coop's upset. Bubba asked me to not just choose one guy. And now you..."

"I don't want you to be what I *want*," Archie said softly. "I want you to be *you*. Even if it's messy. Even if it's not with me."

I looked up, throat tight. "Liar."

He raised his brows.

A watery laugh escaped me. "You hate to lose."

"True. As long as I'm in your life, there's always a chance."

"That's not fair." I scowled.

"Nothing about this is fair," he said. "But it's real. And I had to say it before someone else did."

I opened my mouth, but I didn't know what to say.

So I reached for my milkshake instead. Took a sip. Then pushed it toward him with a forced smile.

"Want the rest?"

Archie didn't push. Didn't prod. Just leaned forward and took the straw, smiling that cocky, broken smile of his.

"Sure," he said. "But only if we split fries next."

And just like that, it was easy again. For a second.

But I knew the hard part was still waiting. Waiting for me to make a choice I wasn't ready to make.

Because this wasn't a game anymore.

This was real.

And someone was going to get hurt.

Maybe all of us.

Maybe me most of all.

By the time we left the diner, the air shimmered and sunlight made the chrome on every car just shine. Or maybe it was the brutal heat sending waves up from everything. Archie's sunglasses were back on, but I could still see the corner of his mouth twitching every time I caught him looking at me.

"I'm full of fries and feelings," I muttered as we stepped outside. "That's dangerous."

He snorted. "You didn't even *finish* the fries."

"I panicked. Too much emotional honesty. Salted carbs couldn't compete."

"Fair. But you owe me now. I know how you're gonna pay me back."

"Oh god," I said, mock-weary. "Please don't say karaoke."

He waggled his eyebrows. "Worse. Mini golf."

I stopped mid-step, blinking at him. "You're kidding."

Archie just smirked and unlocked the car. "Dead serious. You and me. Glorified putting. Loser buys Coke slushies."

"But we haven't done that since—"

"I know." He didn't let me finish, just slid into the driver's seat like it was nothing, like this wasn't déjà vu crashing into me like a freight train.

He used to do this. Take me out for milkshakes and then mini golf. Back when the world felt lighter and we didn't have to talk about feelings or heartbreak or whatever weird, soft thing was growing between us.

I climbed in, my heartbeat loud in my ears.

The drive to Lakeside Putt & Go was short. Familiar. It was the same chipped green turf, the same dusty animatronic gator on hole seven that always blinked out of sync. The neon sign buzzed like a tired bee. And still—my chest squeezed as we stepped out of the car. Like some part of me *knew* this wasn't the same as it had been.

Because it wasn't.

This wasn't *just* a game.

"Okay," I said slowly as I grabbed a putter, trying not to look at him. "Is this a date now?"

Archie handed me a pink golf ball like it was a peace offering. "Yeah. It's a date."

I looked up sharply.

"But—" he held up a hand, "there's no pressure. You don't owe me anything. You don't even have to win. You *will*, because you always cheat on the gator hole, but still."

I narrowed my eyes. "That's slander."

"That's fact."

I took the ball and stepped onto the first green. "You don't even *like* mini golf."

He hesitated. "Yeah, I know."

I'd meant it as a joke, but his response made me turn. "Wait, seriously?"

"I *hate* it," he said, dragging a hand through his hair, sheepish. "Always have. It's sticky and loud, and the clubs are too short and the balls don't roll straight. I swear the turf on hole five is cursed."

"So why—" I started, then stopped, blinking.

Archie shrugged. "Because *you* love it. You light up every time we come here. You get competitive and trash talk the windmill and yell at the rubber duck mascot. It's worth it."

I just stared at him, golf club limp in my hand.

He smiled again—but this time, it was soft. Gentle. "You get this look when you play. Like nothing else matters. Not school, not your mom, not... any of the guys. Just you and this ridiculous pink ball and victory."

My throat felt too small. "Archie..."

"You don't have to say anything," he added quickly. "I told you, no pressure. But let me have this. Let me make you laugh today. Let me watch you beat the hell out of that gator again. That's all I want."

God help me, I felt the laugh bubble up. Because this? This was *so* Archie.

All bravado and bad plans and casually dropping confessions like grenades.

So I tapped the ball into place and looked him dead in the eye.

"I'm going to destroy you."

His grin was full of teeth. "There she is."

When I took the first swing—way too hard, sending the ball ricocheting off the side wall and into a plastic flamingo—I *did* laugh. Loud and unfiltered. The kind that came from somewhere I hadn't touched in weeks.

And Archie? He laughed, too.

Even if he *did* groan when I sank a hole-in-one on number three and did a smug little dance in celebration.

And maybe—just maybe—this date wasn't about golf.

Maybe it was about giving *me* something I hadn't known I needed. Something *he* needed.

Something real.

We played three full rounds, after I won the first game and he won the second. Third was the tie-breaker. I kicked his ass.

The sun was down by the time Archie pulled into the school parking lot, his headlights cutting across the empty rows like searchlights. The place looked strange in the dark—quiet, abandoned, like a memory already fading.

He parked near my car without saying anything, and for a second, neither of us moved. The silence between us was thick, but not uncomfortable. More like a pause we both didn't want to break.

Then I saw it.

Another rose.

Balanced delicately on my windshield, petals a little wilted, edges curled from the heat of the day and the faint suggestion of cooling off as night crept in. But it was there. Still waiting. Still chosen.

A soft breath left my chest, as Archie glanced over.

He didn't ask.

His eyes lingered on the small, folded card nestled beneath the bloom—edges lifting in the breeze—but he didn't speak. Just stared at it for a second longer than casual, then looked away, jaw tightening almost imperceptibly.

I still didn't know who the secret admirer was. The roses were nice, but I was already walking a tightrope between too much and not enough.

"Thanks for today," I said instead, turning to him.

Archie smiled, soft and crooked. "Anytime."

He meant it. That was the hardest part.

His hand flexed on the steering wheel like he wasn't ready to let go of the moment yet. Like maybe, if he stalled long enough, I'd lean across the console and kiss him. Or confess something. Or say I'd chosen him.

But I didn't.

Because I hadn't.

Not yet.

What would it be like to kiss him?

"You wanna come over?" he asked, casual, like it was just another offer, like there wasn't a world of meaning tucked behind the question. Or like I wasn't imagining what his lips would feel like on mine.

I gave a little half-laugh, more exhale than sound. "I can't. I have to feed the cats."

His lips twitched. "You're already late. They're gonna be mad."

I shrugged, chuckling "You don't *know* the half of it."

He chuckled. "Oh, I've heard Tiddles bitch you out. He is not subtle."

"Exactly."

There was a beat of silence between us. The good kind. The safe kind. The kind we used to live in before everything got complicated. Today had been the strangest combination of wonderful and weird. I called out of work, something I never did, and Marsha hadn't batted an eyelash. She just told me to rest.

He nodded slowly, then leaned back in his seat. "Call me when you get home?"

I looked at him. "Archie—"

"Don't make it a thing," he said gently. "Just... call. That way I know you got in safe. That's all."

I hesitated, then nodded. "Okay. I will."

He waited as I got out, watched me walk to my car. He didn't drive off. Not until I was inside, door shut, engine turned over.

Only when my headlights flicked on did he finally pull away.

I sat there a moment longer, my fingers loose on the steering wheel, the scent of the rose already filling the car—faint and fading, but still there.

Still *him*.

Whoever he was.

I picked up the flower and stared at it, but didn't touch the card.

Couldn't.

Instead, I leaned back against the seat, blew out a breath so deep it felt like I was trying to exhale all the confusion out of my lungs.

Then I whispered to myself, barely audible, the question I didn't want to answer:

"What the hell am I going to do?"

And I had no idea.

Not yet.

CHAPTER

TWENTY

COOP

Coop

The house always looked so expensive. The green grass was a testament to regular watering despite soaring temperatures and city water restrictions. The cut of it precise, not inching over onto the drive by even a millimeter. The flowers always looked in bloom. Nothing wilted. Nothing out of place. No debris dared to clutter the drive.

The damn fountain was on, the trickle of water almost soothing despite the waves of heat rising up around it. It was an oasis that suggested tranquility and refinement. I used to feel out of place here. The first time Archie invited us over, I didn't want to touch *anything*. Mom would kill me if I broke something. Archie had more money than all of our families put together. Hell, more than most of our class.

I had no idea when that stopped mattering. When Archie just became Archie and his house a house. Today, however, it served as a huge reminder of the difference between all of us. Of what he could do for her. What he had and I hadn't felt this *alien* in a long time.

155

I *hated* it.

The front door opened before we even reached it. I'd ridden over with Jake while Bubba followed us. I wasn't even sure whose idea it was to come. I thought maybe Bubba said it first, in the locker room after practice, towel slung over his shoulder, chin streaked with sweat. "We should talk to him. Tonight."

We all knew who *him* was.

Jake didn't say anything at first. Just kept stuffing gear into his bag with that short, jerky aggression that usually meant someone was going to bleed soon. Preferably Archie. Preferably not himself. The only reason I'd been there was Frankie hadn't come back to school so I'd hung out at football practice to get a ride after.

Jeremy opened the door. Jeremy, who was butler, chef, driver, and house manager for the Standishes. Jeremy, who was always there even when Archie's parents weren't. I liked Jeremy. More than I could say for Archie's standoffish mother. His dad was... Well, maybe I was biased against dads at the moment so I just left it alone.

"Good evening Mr. Bubba, Mr. Coop, Mr. Jake—we've been expecting you. Mr. Archie is upstairs in the game room and the pizzas have arrived." The last he delivered with a kind of wry amusement. Jeremy might work for the Standishes, but I swore he took more of a decisive hand with what Archie did and didn't get to do, despite how much freedom Archie had.

Bubba gave him a quick nod as he strode in. "Thanks, Jeremy." Bad mood still firmly in place, Jake stalked after Bubba and I sighed.

"Is Frankie here?" I didn't even know I was going to ask the question before it came out. Bubba and Jake stopped on the stairs so abruptly no way they didn't hear me.

"No, Mr. Coop, she is not here." The level of kindness in his voice removed any judgment he might have offered.

"Thanks," I repeated and headed up after the guys who'd moved as soon as Jeremy said she wasn't here. As much as I should hurry to follow them, I wasn't looking forward to this fight. But they were waiting for me, impatience swirling in the air around them like we were bracing for war. Ah, united front.

United for what? Well, I guessed we were about to find out.

One knock and Bubba pushed open the door. Archie sat on the couch, TV on but muted, one leg draped lazily over the other like he'd been expecting us. His face was the picture of calm.

"What's up, gentlemen?" he said, voice too casual, too cool. Like we were just stopping by for sodas and Madden.

Jake moved first, stalking past Bubba like a storm and didn't even pretend he wasn't pissed. "You ditched school with her?"

Archie's smirk didn't falter. "Define 'ditch.' We left. Took a drive. Had lunch. I didn't hide it."

Jake's eyes narrowed. "No, you just didn't mention it. Again."

Archie raised his brows. "Frankie needed a break. I offered one."

Jake's voice sharpened. "You offered yourself."

My gut twisted. It had been doing that a lot lately. Ever since she started pulling away. Summer had sucked. I thought we'd begun to make some progress, but Archie swept her away before we could have lunch. She went with him and I hadn't stopped her.

Maybe we were all pushing her.

Bubba shut the door behind us. Locked it.

Archie clocked that. "What, am I about to be jumped?"

"No," Bubba said evenly. "But we're gonna say what needs to be said, and nobody's walking out until it's done."

Jake snorted, the anger crackling around him too much like heat lightning. It would only take one spark. "Oh, how noble of you. Now suddenly you want peace?"

"No," Bubba snapped back. His patience with Jake's temper *also* seemed to be on the verge of breaking. "I want clarity. For Frankie. For us. For this mess."

I hadn't spoken yet. Didn't trust myself to. My stomach had been in knots since the second I saw her and Archie sail out of school for wherever-the-hell.

Archie leaned forward, fingers steepled like he was in some mafia movie. "So? Ask your questions. Let's all lay our cards out, shall we?"

"You've been playing dirty," Jake said flatly. "Undercutting everyone while pretending to be harmless."

Archie stared at him a beat then shrugged. "You make it sound like I'm some Bond villain. I've been honest about her from the first day I met her. I like her. I want to spend time with her."

"Behind everyone's backs."

"One," Archie said coolly raising a single finger. "I asked her out right in front of Coop, that's hardly behind anyone's backs. Two, she didn't ask for a chaperone. Three, we don't owe you a calendar invite."

"She owed me honesty," Jake snapped.

Excuse me? She owed honesty. To who?

"Funny," Archie said, tone flipping to cold before I could interject my own response, "I don't remember you asking permission when you spent the night."

Silence.

I closed my eyes. That one landed hard.

Jake's fists clenched. "That wasn't the same."

"Oh no?" Archie's voice was silk and knives. "You think your brand of secret is more acceptable? That if you're quiet and brooding enough, no one will notice you're breaking the same rules as the rest of us?"

"Enough," Bubba said. Low. Firm. "You two are just slinging mud at each other and pretending it's for her benefit."

"She's not okay," I said. My voice cut through everything. Even surprised me.

They both looked at me.

"She's not okay," I repeated, quieter now. "This—this isn't helping."

Archie's smirk faded. Jake's jaw twitched.

As much as we needed to have this out, I wanted to be at home. No, fuck that, I wanted to be at Frankie's. I wanted to finish the conversation we should have had at lunch. For now, though, I looked at the floor, then up at Bubba. "Say what you were going to say."

Bubba nodded once. "We keep listening to her words, trying to decode what she's telling each of us. But we're missing the bigger picture."

Not quite rolling his eyes, Jake crossed his arms. "That would be?"

"It's not about what she's saying. It's about what she *isn't*."

That hit me square in the chest. Not because I hadn't *heard* those silences. I'd damn near drowned in the one over the summer.

"She's smiling when she's tired. She's laughing when she's scared. She's saying she's fine, but she's *not*. She ran from us all summer. That might be on us."

Bubba raised a hand to stop any protests.

"She has a new boyfriend." He chewed over those words like they left a bitter taste behind. "She has a boyfriend that she met and started dating while none of us were around. She's made it clear she plans to keep him."

I wasn't alone in grimacing.

"Has her mother been home at all this week?" He turned to me now and I sighed.

"No." Not that I'd seen. We'd all made excuses for Maddy over the years. But she had been gone more than she was around. Especially since Frankie started driving.

"That's what I thought." Bubba folded his arms. It gave him an air of restrained violence. "We fucked up somewhere. Whatever else she thinks or believes, we are the reason for it."

"Rachel Manning didn't help," Jake spit out.

"She wouldn't have said anything if it wasn't true." I couldn't believe *I* was defending her. I didn't owe Manning a damn thing, except what had she done *but* told Frankie the truth?

"Why was it her business to tell her anything?" Jake demanded.

"Because she saw something we didn't," I answered. She'd seen Frankie was unhappy.

How the fuck had I missed it?

Archie's voice was quieter now. "You think we're making it worse?"

"I think we're not helping," Bubba said. "I think every time one of us corners her, challenges her, confesses something—she shuts down more."

"She's unraveling," I murmured. "And we're tugging the threads."

No one spoke for a long time.

Jake finally dropped onto the armrest, face buried in his hands. "I thought—if I just told her how I felt..."

"I thought I'd get there first," Archie muttered.

"I thought it wouldn't matter," I admitted. "Because we've always been there. Always been together. That... we always would be."

Accepted that she didn't want to date anyone so I was content to just be her friend. But now?

"She's not a prize," Bubba said. "And we're not opponents."

"Maybe." Archie leaned back, scrubbing his hands down his face.

"Maybe?" I snorted. "No maybes about it. Jake makes moves and stays the night. Archie usurps her away from a lunch date with me and just takes off." Yeah, that still stung. "It feels pretty damn competitive."

Jake glared at Archie, but it lacked the earlier heat. Maybe because Archie wasn't even looking at him.

"Guys..." Bubba said with a sigh. "If we really start fighting over her..."

"We already have." Call me, Mr. Sunshine, but we were fighting over her. That was what brought us here with Jake on a tear and Bubba ready to throw down. Hell, even Archie had been ready for the invasion. "All of you know it."

The last thing I wanted to be was the reasonable one. I almost wouldn't mind punching Archie in his smug face. Almost.

Except as irritated as I was, Archie wasn't who I was mad at.

"We've known each other for years." For a brief moment, I studied Jake. "Elementary school." Then I flicked a glance at Bubba. "Junior High." Finally, I shifted to look at Archie. "High school."

Guilt. Anger. Worry. The room reeked of it.

"We've been friends for most of that time. Frankie was never a sore spot because we were all so sure none of us would be the one."

"Speak for yourself," Archie muttered, but I ignored him.

"We didn't have to fight over her cause we could have our cake and still hang out with her. We all knew where we stood—or at least where we *thought* we stood. We all agreed she needed to be protected from everyone else if she didn't want to date, no one got to pressure her. No one got to talk about her either. Her mother's a bitch, so we did our best to make sure school wasn't."

Bubba leaned his head back and sighed. The weight of it punched through the room.

"Now," I continued. "Everything changes because we *know* she wants to date. I'm not stepping out." I spared each of them a long look. "Don't even think that I'm backing off."

"I already asked her to not just date one guy," Bubba admitted and I almost laughed as Jake *stared* at him.

"I told her today *was* a date," Archie said, spreading his hands in a *hey, it's me* gesture. "Just to make sure she didn't miss it."

That was three of us. We all looked at Jake. He'd been pissed at her. Really pissed. I still had no idea what the hell that was about, but it was something. That bothered me way more than I cared to admit.

"You're all assuming she's gonna drop Frenchy."

I shrugged. "Not assuming a damn thing. He's here until Christmas. Then he leaves."

"Oh, yeah," Archie said and you could hear the smile. "Still too long, but definitely a brighter side."

"Like I said before, I asked her to not limit herself to one guy. Since she is dating Frenchy and she went out with Arch today, maybe she is taking the advice."

"Excellent." Archie definitely brightened up. Ass.

Probably one of the reasons I liked him. He always came up swinging.

"So, what you're saying is we all try to date her?" Jake didn't sound so certain.

"What *I* am saying is that I plan to make it very clear to her how interested I am. That no one, not Frenchy, not any of you, is going to push me away. I want a chance, I'll fucking grovel if I have to in order to get the chance. If you don't want one—" Now I shrugged. "Then it's *your* loss."

"Fuck you, Coop." Jake scowled.

"No thanks, you're definitely not my type."

The ballooning tension in the room popped. Archie and Bubba both laughed, but I met Jake's glare easily even as he struggled to maintain his temper.

He lost and finally cracked a smile of his own.

"We're idiots," Archie admitted, still chuckling.

"Big ones," Bubba said, not unkindly.

Jake looked up. "So what now?"

Just like that, we were all on the same side again. Would it last? I didn't have an answer. I looked at the guys and thought about Frankie holding herself together with stubborn pride and sheer exhaustion.

Frankie, who backed us on every damn thing we wanted to do even when that involved dating other girls. Her comment about Laura still rang in my head.

Fuck. I needed to break up with Laura.

Again.

"We back off," I said, then raised a hand when all of them gaped at me. "Not leave her alone. Not abandon her.

But we stop trying to tell her what to do. We let her breathe. Let her *choose*, without all of us breathing down her neck.”

“And if she chooses none of us?” Jake asked, his voice rough.

“Then we let her.” Sure, it sounded simple. Except… “Even if she doesn’t pick me, I’m still her friend. I’m *always* going to be her friend. But I won’t assume anything unless she tells me to my face.”

Period.

They didn’t argue. Not anymore.

“Well,” Archie said. “Jeremy ordered pizzas. We should map out the rules for this so we avoid pissing each other off.”

“Much,” Jake said dryly. Yeah, he might not be mad anymore but he was still irked.

“Much,” Archie said almost agreeably. “Sometimes it’s fun to poke the bear.”

I rolled my eyes but left them to snipe. One of these days, that bear might just punch Archie.

TWENTY-ONE

FRANKIE

The air outside still held onto the day's heat like a grudge. Somewhere, someone was mowing a lawn too late, and the scent of cut grass mixed with the smell of whatever was burning on someone else's grill.

Mathieu's host family's garage always smelled like gasoline, old pine from the shelves, and the faint lemony cleaner someone used to clean up the mess. Somehow, despite the scent cocktail, it had become one of the few places that felt neutral.

Safe. The overhead fan clicked with every rotation, blades wobbling just enough to make me glance up every so often to see if it was about to fall.

Mathieu was cross-legged on the concrete, wearing one of my old band tees and a pair of jeans with paint flecks on the knee. I didn't ask if the shirt was deliberate. He had spent the night at the apartment a couple of times when Mom was gone. Once he really needed a shirt to borrow and he'd left me one of his. That should mean something, right?

"You're thinking too loud," he said, breaking the quiet with his soft, accented voice that had a way of making everything sound like a lyric.

"Not possible," I muttered, tugging at a loose thread on my cuff. "I barely think at all."

He smiled, dark lashes dipping low as he leaned back on his hands. "Then I'm listening too hard."

I snorted. "That I believe."

The silence between us wasn't bad. Not yet. But it was weighted. Tense. Like the kind of quiet that comes before a question you don't want to answer. Or one you're not sure how to.

Despite ditching with Archie, the day before, I'd managed to scoot out of the apartment after I fed the cats and head over here to meet Mathieu without the guys snagging me. It was hardly my first trip here, but it was the first time I felt like I was actually *sneaking* off to see him.

"So." I licked my lips. "Archie's party is tomorrow." If he hadn't mentioned it that morning, the text messages he'd sent over the last hour made it clear. Saturday afternoon, his place, pool party, pizza, music, and fun.

Mathieu's head tilted slightly, just enough to make a piece of dark hair fall into his eyes. "Yes. You want to go?"

I hesitated. "Do *you* want to go?" What did I want his answer to be? The fact that I had *zero* idea worried me more than the question.

He shrugged, which on anyone else might have seemed indifferent. But with him, it was thoughtful. "It is the senior party. It would be a good thing to do, no? Meet more people. See what this big American school experience is all about."

I sighed, staring at the oil stain near the door that looked suspiciously like a bear paw. "It's not just a party."

"I gathered."

He didn't press. That was the thing about Mathieu. He never demanded. Never pushed. He waited. And that, somehow, was worse. Because the pressure wasn't *on* me, it was *in* me.

"I'm not sure if going means I'm walking straight into a fire... or if *not* going is its own kind of disaster."

His brow furrowed, and he leaned forward. "Why would it be a fire?"

I opened my mouth. Closed it. Bit the inside of my cheek.

"Because... everyone will be there. Coop, Jake, Bubba. Archie." I glanced at him. Half the damn school. "And you."

Mathieu's smile was slow, but there was something guarded behind it. "That is a problem?"

I dropped my head back against the garage wall, exhaling hard. "You ever feel like no matter what choice you make, you're still going to screw it up?"

"Yes," he said instantly. "But that's just being human."

I gave him a look. "Well, right now, being human really sucks."

"Why?" he asked gently.

"Because..." I pulled my knees to my chest. "I care about them. All of them. In different ways. And they care about me, too. But this—this thing with you—it's real. It's new. It's mine. And still... I feel like I'm constantly waiting for someone to call me a traitor."

Jake had. At least, he'd reacted like I was one. That was bad enough. Archie didn't want Mathieu around and Bubba wanted me to not limit my dating options. Coop? Right now, I had no idea what Coop wanted.

If I were honest, I was half-terrified of even asking Coop. I hated that feeling more than anything.

Mathieu's jaw tightened subtly, but his voice stayed calm. "They had their chance."

It wasn't angry. Not quite. But it wasn't neutral either.

"They didn't know they needed to take it," I said quietly. If I'd learned nothing else over the past few days, I'd learned that. "Apparently—they had taken it and I didn't notice." Which was embarrassing enough. "Now everything feels... like walking across a glass floor. I keep waiting for the crack."

Mathieu stood slowly, brushing off his hands, and came to sit next to me on the old couch pushed against the wall. Our knees bumped. He didn't pull away. He never did.

"You are not glass, Frankie. You're not going to break."

"No?" I whispered, testing the answer. He believed in me a lot more than I did. "They might." Jake had been so angry Thursday morning. Not seeing him that afternoon had given me breathing room, but he hadn't been that friendly earlier today. If anything, he was distant as hell.

Mathieu studied me a long beat, then reached over and took my hand. His fingers were warm and strong and steady in a way that made my chest ache.

"You don't have to pick a side just to survive."

"But I might have to pick one to stop everyone else from bleeding."

He was silent for a beat, then said, "If I asked you to come to the party with me... as my date... would you say yes?"

My heart stuttered.

"I—" My mouth went dry. "It's not that simple."

"I didn't say it was," he replied. "But it is a question."

The empathy in his gaze that made me pause. Not the performative kind, not the kind people use when they're trying to look like they care. His eyes held something deeper. Understanding without judgment. Like he saw the pieces of me fraying at the edges and wasn't afraid to look directly at them.

"You okay?" he asked gently.

My instinct was to lie. Or dodge. Or laugh it off with something stupid.

But his eyes...

The way he looked at me like he *meant* it. Like my answer mattered more than the time or place or how I tried to pretend I was fine.

I didn't have the energy to pretend tonight.

"I don't know," I admitted. "I feel like no matter what I do, I'm going to mess it up." I looked down at our hands. "I want to go. But I also want to hide under my bed and pretend none of this is happening."

"Ah," he said, his voice dipping with something like amusement. "So you are like every other teenage girl in the movies, then."

"Rude."

"But true."

I elbowed him lightly. He didn't let go of my hand.

"Frankie," he said softly, "they are not your responsibility. How they feel, what they want—that is not yours to carry."

"But I still feel it." I swallowed hard. "Every look. Every question. Every time I get a rose on my windshield or someone calls and says 'you home yet?' I feel like I'm about to fail someone."

"Then fail them."

I blinked at him. "What?"

"If they put you in a position where your happiness depends on them not hurting—then let them hurt. Because that is not love. That is guilt dressed up in affection."

I looked away, jaw tight. "You don't know them." It felt disloyal as hell to talk about them now. Earlier in the summer, when I'd been so angry with them, I managed to avoid it. But now?

"No," he said. "But I know *you*."

Fuck, that was worse.

I let my head drop onto his shoulder, the only safe place I'd found in days. "If I—we go, it's going to be a mess."

"If you don't go, it will still be a mess," he said, light. "But you'll miss the pizza and I've heard American pizza is a reason to live."

I let out a weak laugh.

"I'll go," I said eventually, heart twisting. "But I'm not promising I'll survive it."

Mathieu kissed the top of my head—soft, careful, like a promise he hadn't said out loud yet.

"You will," he murmured, his voice all quiet certainty. "Even if you don't want to."

I huffed a laugh, because of course he thought he knew better than me. "I like your confidence."

He slid an arm around my shoulders, pulling me in until I was tucked into his side like I'd always belonged there. When I tilted my head back, I found his gaze waiting for me—steady, unshaken. Like he was already imagining the version of me that didn't flinch from the spotlight.

"It's a pool party though," I said, trying for casual, even though my heart had started kicking like it was trying to outrun the moment. "So that means... bathing suits."

A slow, wicked smile crept across his face. There it was —that spark. That Mathieu mischief that always made my stomach flip in dangerous directions.

"Could I persuade you," he said, drawing the words out

like a dare, "to wear the bikini you had on when we first met?"

Oh, hell.

My face went warm instantly. "Maybe?" It came out like a question I didn't know how to answer. That bikini had been a whole situation—and I'd only worn it because Schlitterbahn was two hundred miles away and no one there knew my name.

"I don't usually dress like that here," I added, like that might protect me from whatever reaction he'd give.

Mathieu didn't miss a beat. "Then all the more reason to wear it."

His voice dropped, and so did my defenses.

He brushed his lips over mine—light, teasing, like he was testing the limits of what I'd allow. Then he pulled back just enough to meet my eyes again.

"Tell me what I have to do to convince you," he whispered, like it was a secret only meant for us.

The way he said it wasn't about clothes or skin or poolside gossip. It was about shedding the weight I kept carrying around—expectations, fear, the version of myself I thought I had to be to survive high school.

Because *he* wasn't the safe option. Not really.

Safe didn't look at you like they knew exactly where you were most afraid and still wanted to stand there with you. Safe didn't ask you to be seen.

Mathieu wasn't safe.

He was *real*.

And maybe that was what scared me most.

The garage, with its familiar smells and the hum of the old fan, suddenly felt too small. I wanted more of him, more of this feeling. I reached up, tangling my fingers in his hair, and pulled him closer. His lips met mine again, this time with more urgency, more need. The kiss deepened, and I felt myself melting into him, the tension of the day fading away.

Mathieu's hands found their way to my waist, pulling me onto his lap. I straddled him, feeling the heat of his body through his jeans. His hands roamed over my back, tracing the curve of my spine, sending shivers down my neck. I could feel his heartbeat, steady and strong, matching the rhythm of my own.

When he broke the kiss just long enough to whisper, "Let's go inside," I nodded.

We stood up, our hands still entwined, and made our way to his bedroom. The house was quiet, the host family out for the evening. His bedroom was over the garage. It gave him privacy, and a door that locked. Right now, it was dimly lit, the soft glow of a bedside lamp casting long shadows across the walls.

Once locked behind that door, he slid his hand up to my ponytail and loosened the tie. When my hair fell free, he finger combed it. "You know you are so beautiful to me."

It wasn't a question, but I shuddered as his words seemed to caress that part of me that needed the acknowledgment. Needed to feel wanted. I never felt like I was competing with anything when it came to Mathieu. His eyes were dark with desire. Desire for *me* and that thrill ran through me.

"I wish I had your gift with words," I murmured. Because I did. Mathieu just always seemed to know the right thing to say. When I slid my hands beneath his shirt, he pulled it up and off.

Then he was lifting my shirt. Between us, we toed off our shoes, stripped each other naked and I shuddered when he dragged me closer for another kiss. The air conditioner, the older unit that kept this room comfortable kicked on and that rush of cold air over my overheated skin made my nipples pebble.

Wrapping an arm around my waist, he lifted me up and carried me over to his bed. Once he set me down, he straightened to look down at me. His eyes roamed over my body and I felt touched everywhere he gazed.

My heart accelerated at the open want on his face. Then he shoved down his boxers. The jut of his cock always surprised me. Even as he dropped down to cover me, I was rising up to meet him. Our mouths fused and Mathieu's hands were everywhere.

He stroked my skin, cupped my breasts, then teased the nipples with his fingers. When he kissed a path from my mouth to my chest, I sucked in a deeper breath. His breathing was ragged and a thin line of moisture dribbled over my leg as his cock dragged over it.

"Frankie…" The harsh whisper had me clenching, then he cupped my pussy, before he pushed two fingers into me. For the first time, I was more than wet enough. We wouldn't need the lube. Still, he pumped his fingers as he licked and sucked at my nipples like they were his favorite treat.

Right when I was so close, he dragged his fingers away and I dug my hands into his shoulders. Frustration welled up, but he stole another kiss, then grabbed for a condom from the drawer of his nightstand. Between us, we rolled it on him. I loved how velvety soft the skin of his shaft was, but we always used condoms.

"Ready?" He asked, returning to the cradle of my legs and at my nod, he positioned himself at my entrance. The first push was still a bit of a sting. Not the sharp pain of the first time or the ache of the second. Just the pressure of the stretch, the soreness of not being used to it. Still, I craved this, wanted this... wanted him.

He was almost too slow as he eased himself inside, and when I moaned, he drew back and thrust in again. He caught his rhythm swiftly, increasing his pace and then he moved up to his knees, hands on my hips as he dragged me forward and up.

At this angle, I felt him everywhere as he pulled out and then it almost hurt every time he slammed back inside. The tension was right there, coiling tighter as he rocked his hips to mine. But his pace increased, he was so close.

When he pulled my hand to between my legs, I let his fingers guide me. Right, I needed to rub my clit. Between us, the coiled tension exploded into electric sensation. The first clench of my inner muscles had Mathieu shouting.

His was always so much more intense than my own, but there was still a hazy drift of pleasure that came from being with him. We lay there, wrapped around each other for a long time. I'd have to go home soon, but right now, I wanted to be right where I was.

TWENTY-TWO

BUBBA

The house always looked expensive. It didn't matter how many times I'd been here—every visit reminded me. The lawn out front was its own kind of smug. Stupid green despite the summer heat and trimmed to perfection. No dandelions. No dry patches. Not a single leaf where it didn't belong.

Even the damn fountain out front burbled with judgment.

Jake parked closer to the garage, and I slid the bike right up next to him. Coop climbed out before Jake even shut off the engine. He was already in swim trunks and an unbuttoned Hawaiian shirt. His grimace told me all I needed to know about Jake's mood before Jake slammed out of his Jeep.

Definitely *not* improved.

I had a change of clothes in my backpack. The air practically sweltered and sweat slicked my hair back as I pulled my helmet off. We looked like the before picture to Archie's after. But whatever. That wasn't new.

What was new? That sick twist in my gut.

This wasn't just a party. This was the night.

Frankie was coming—with *him*. And no matter how many times I told myself his name was *Mathieu*, my brain still spit out *Frenchy* with a snarl. Some habits died harder than others.

Archie's house was already buzzing when Jeremy opened the door to greet us in a wash of cooler air. The guy wore an immaculate suit despite the heat and a mild expression that said he'd seen it all and wasn't impressed by much. But he nodded at us in welcome, unfailingly polite. Then again, Jeremy could cut as neatly with a kind word. I had no doubt where Archie learned his skills.

"Mr. Bubba. Welcome. Mr. Jake. Mr. Coop. Mr. Archie is outside by the pool." A pause. "He asked me to remind you to pace yourselves with the bourbon and the sarcasm."

I huffed a laugh. "So, no fun at all."

Jeremy didn't smile, but I swore his eyebrows did.

We moved through the house like we owned the place —which, technically, only one of us did—but that was the thing with Archie. His world bent around him, and somehow it made room for the rest of us too.

Outside, the pool shimmered in the sun, lounge chairs scattered like thrones. The bar setup looked legit. Fairy lights were strung across the yard, already glowing. Music pulsed low from the outdoor speakers. Classy. Controlled.

This wasn't a kegger. This was curated. I diverted to the pool house to change. It didn't take long. When I came back out, Archie was lounging under one of the umbrellas, drink in hand, sunglasses on.

"About time," he called, raising his glass. "The rest of my court arrives."

"Who died and made you king?" Jake grumbled, still tense.

Archie didn't flinch. "Just go with it. The vibe works better when I'm monarch."

I dropped into a seat beside him. "Then who are we? Jesters?"

He gave me a sly look. "You're my favorite general."

That earned him a scoff. Jake muttered something I couldn't hear and stalked toward the drinks.

Coop stayed close, eyes flicking over Jake like he expected him to combust.

"Still think he's gonna throw a punch?" I asked Coop quietly.

"He wants to." Coop's voice was low. "But he won't. Not tonight."

"Because of Frankie?"

"Because of you." He gave me a look. If Jake threw down, I'd have to get in the way. We never had figured out which of us would win in a straight on fight. I still didn't want to know. "And because she's bringing him."

Right. *Him.*

I hadn't realized I was grinding my teeth until Archie nudged me with his foot.

"Relax, Bubba," he said. "You're going to break your molars."

"Easy for you to say," I muttered. "You already had your date."

That got me a grin.

It was different now—between all of us. We'd said what needed to be said, but that didn't mean it was resolved. It just meant it was out in the open. The silence was less dangerous, maybe. But the tension still simmered, low and steady like the beat of the bass-line behind us.

People started arriving in trickles at first—Sharon, with her perfect nails and fake laugh. She gave me a too-long look, but I just nodded and turned away. I wasn't going to get pulled back into that.

Patty showed up in a dress I was sure was chosen specifically to ruin Archie's night. Judging by the twitch in his smirk, it was working.

"Exes," Jake muttered under his breath as Maria came through the gate. "Like roaches. They come out for the snacks and the fire."

"Some of them *are* the fire," Archie quipped.

Laura came next, wrapped around some senior guy I didn't know, all legs and lip gloss and zero shame.

Coop's jaw clenched. "Why the hell did you invite her—"

"I didn't." Archie cut him off, voice syrupy. "She's *not* a senior, remember? Must be her new ride. Hopefully, he noticed that she's hitched herself on."

"Oh my god, let it go," Coop groaned.

"Did you actually break up with her?" Call it morbid curiosity, but Laura looked very attached to Baker? Braden? I couldn't remember the guy's name.

"Don't ask," Coop muttered.

"She doesn't look like she's upset, so maybe you're off the hook." Jake shrugged. It was about as philosophical as he was going to get.

Then Rachel Manning walked in.

She wore black, like she was attending a funeral. A one piece with a sarong. Classy, and as far from slut as you could get. Hair up. Lips sharp. Eyes sharper. She clocked Archie immediately.

"Oh good," she said, strolling in our direction. "The peacocks are in formation."

"Rachel." Archie tipped his glass like he was genuinely delighted. "Come to add poison to the punch?"

"No need," she said. "I brought my own."

I liked her less than I respected her, and I respected her a lot. Probably more than I wanted to admit.

"What are you doing here?" Jake asked, not even pretending to be polite.

She arched a brow. "Is that any way to speak to the girl who's been keeping your secrets?"

That shut him up. For a second. Which secrets was she referring to?

Coop gave her a warning look, but Rachel just continued past, plucked a drink off the table, and headed for the deep end of the pool like she, not Archie, ruled here.

"Why do I feel like she's going to murder someone before the night's over?" I asked.

"She won't," Archie said. "She likes an audience too much."

"She could always murder *him*." Jake sounded almost cheerful. "I'd help."

I snorted. "Dude, you have got to chill."

"Fuck you, Bubba." There went the cheer.

I took a swallow of the cold beer and just shook my head.

More people arrived. The volume picked up. Football players. Cheerleaders. That weird group from theater who somehow got the invite and were now reenacting Hamilton by the fire pit.

And still—no sign of Frankie.

The longer we waited, the tighter the knot in my chest pulled. I didn't even know what I expected to feel when she walked in with Frenchy. Anger? Jealousy? Regret?

All of the above, probably.

I spotted Sharon laughing with Mitch. Patty was holding court near the bar. Laura was already tangled up with her new distraction. Maria and Jake were pointedly not looking at each other.

Everyone was circling. Shifting. Waiting for the spark.

Archie grabbed me a fresh beer when he got a refill. He'd sauntered right up to the bar, ignored Patty and company and drifted back. I could wish I was that cool about Sharon's presence. But it was a challenge—we had more than one mistake milling around, dancing, or swimming.

"You ready?" he asked.

I took the bottle but didn't drink.

"Not even close," I said.

Because I wasn't.

Because the moment she walked in, everything would start.

Jake

It was too hot.

The kind of sticky that made shirts cling and tempers snap. The kind of heat where every breath felt like it weighed something. It clung to my neck, coiled around my spine, made the anger feel louder in my skin.

I shouldn't have left Frankie's place like that.

Hell, I shouldn't have spent the night in the first damn place. But she was Frankie. She was mine... I kept half hoping she'd *remember*—whatever the hell I thought she was supposed to remember. How much I cared? How long I'd waited?

Now, maybe I just wanted her to hurt like I did.

Which was bullshit. That wasn't me. That wasn't who I wanted to be, especially not with her. But lately? It was easier to be angry than admit I'd screwed up. Easier to hate Frenchy and his smug little smile and perfect pronunciation than admit *I* was the problem. That I let her drift and didn't fight hard enough to keep her close.

God, I was a cliché. A walking, talking teenage cliché with clenched fists and a bad mood.

I'd barely said two words since we got here. Bubba had taken point, as usual. Coop was trying to keep the peace. Archie was... being Archie. Smug and ridiculous and half a second from getting punched if he smirked at the wrong time.

People swam in and out of my line of sight. Party sounds blurred into each other—laughter, music, the soft splash of the pool, someone screaming about flip cup. But none of it settled.

I was too aware of the *gap*.

She wasn't here yet.

That space where she *would* be had its own gravity, pulling all my thoughts in like a black hole. She was going to walk in, her hand in his, and I was going to feel like I had when we moved to Germany. Cut off and alone.

"Earth to Jake."

Coop's voice dragged me back, annoyingly chipper.

"What?"

He was holding out a plate with two slices of pizza like it was a peace offering. "You've been glaring at the pool like it owes you money."

I took the plate and muttered a "thanks."

He settled beside me at the table under the awning, biting into his slice like we were just two dudes enjoying the party.

"This is good pizza," he said, chewing. "Jeremy probably ordered from that bougie place with the wood-fired oven."

"Pizza's pizza."

"That's not true. Some pizzas are cardboard lies."

I glanced at him. "Are you trying to distract me?"

Coop gave me a look. "Yes. Am I failing?"

A pause.

"Yeah," I admitted.

He sighed, leaned back in the chair. "She's coming. You know that, right?"

"I know."

"And you know she's going to be with him."

I didn't answer. I didn't have to.

"I know you're pissed," he continued. "But the enemy isn't Frenchy. Or Archie. It's definitely *not* Frankie."

I raised an eyebrow. "Then who the hell is it?"

His gaze met mine, calm and steady. "At the moment? You."

That hit harder than I expected. Not because he was wrong—but because it was *too* right.

"Thanks, Dr. Phil."

"Hey, I didn't say it to be a dick. You're just better than this. You're not the guy who blows up and ghosts her and then acts surprised when she doesn't crawl back."

"Jesus," I muttered, but it wasn't angry. Not really.

"Look, you are the guy who blows up and decks people. But never her. That part—that has to stop."

Asshole wasn't wrong.

"Just..." He stood, crumpling up his paper towel. "Don't make her pay for the stuff you never said."

Then he walked off.

Which was good, because I needed to breathe.

I headed for the drinks table near the corner of the pool

area, bypassing the bar. Too many damn people there. The drinks table was mostly abandoned—just a few stragglers hovering near the coolers and mixers. I dug through the ice for a can of Coke, more for something to do with my hands than anything else.

"Still like yours flat and warm?"

I stiffened.

Maria.

I didn't have to look to know that voice. Sweet on the surface. Razor underneath.

"That was once." I reminded her, and it was after we'd banged the fuck out of each other and I needed a drink.

She stepped up beside me, leaning one hip against the table. "Seems like I recall it being more than once. A lot more."

Of course she did. That was the problem with Maria. She remembered every kiss, every fight, everything I said or didn't.

"I didn't come over here for a trip down memory lane," I said, trying to keep it neutral.

"Yeah, well, memory lane has better lighting than whatever brooding cave you've been living in."

I turned to face her. Same glossy hair. Same sharp stare. Even her suit, a single piece sheath, fit her like blue-scaled armor. Different vibe. She didn't look like she wanted me back—just wanted to *poke the wound*.

"Don't," I said quietly.

"Don't what? Remind you that you used to smile? That you didn't always look like you were two seconds from decking someone?"

"I'm not in the mood."

"You haven't been in the mood since May." Her voice dropped, and suddenly there was no bite—just truth. "You were better when she was around. Frankie... you were softer. Kinder."

"That was before—" I stopped. Shook my head. "Doesn't matter."

"Before the French guy?" she asked, her smile turned sharp like a blade. "Before she picked someone else?"

I didn't answer.

She reached out, brushed a hand down my arm. Not flirty—almost *sad*.

"She's not trying to hurt you, Jake." Those were the very last words I'd ever expected to hear from her. "Frankie has never tried to hurt anyone."

No, that was all me. "I am not talking to you about her."

"You never did," she murmured, head tilted as she gave me this long assessing stare. "But I always knew. Always knew where I fell in the line of things. Second best." A half-snort of laughter. "Didn't care so much when it came to sex, at least then you were focused on me."

I fought to keep my expression neutral. "What do you want?"

"It would be easy for me to hate her." She raised her eyebrows as if daring me to deny it. "So easy to, especially if I let myself wonder how many times you pictured it was her you were drilling when it was me."

The barb landed. I didn't think I had, but at the moment... *Fuck*.

"That wasn't her fault then or now." No, Maria was right. It was mine. "Her dating someone else isn't a fault either. You're acting like she stabbed you in the chest."

"Feels like it." It rankled. It rankled because she'd let him touch her. Let him take what should have been...

Maria nodded. "Then maybe stop standing still and bleeding. Do something about it."

Then, just like Coop, she walked off before I could say anything else.

I stared at the can in my hand. I hadn't even cracked it open.

Footsteps behind me, a whisper of sound over the music.

Then a voice.

"She's here."

Bubba.

Just that. Two words. No fanfare. No prep.

My pulse spiked anyway.

I turned, slow, like maybe if I took long enough it wouldn't hit as hard.

But there she was.

Frankie.

Looking too good. Smiling like she wasn't about to shatter every piece of me. There *he* was beside her, perfect posture, stupid accent, hand on the small of her back like he'd earned it.

My grip tightened around the can.

Fuck.

Coop

I heard her before I saw her.

A laugh—light, easy, familiar—and the low hum of Frenchy's voice cutting through the music. It froze me. Like my brain registered her before my body could catch up.

I turned.

Everything else dropped out.

Frankie stepped into the backyard and it was like being

on a dolly zoom in a movie, everything in me lasered toward her.

Sunlight wrapped her in this soft glow that made her skin look even warmer, like she was built from summer. Her bikini was red—*deep*, bold, impossible to ignore. The top cut just high enough to drive me out of my damn mind, with this barely there strap that wrapped around her neck and made it obvious just how much skin she wasn't covering. The bottoms were mostly hidden by the sarong knotted low on her hips, but that didn't stop my brain from short-circuiting.

Her legs went on forever. That fabric slit high up one thigh, and when she shifted her weight, I caught the curve of her hip, bare skin that used to be mine to make her laugh when I poked it. Her belly, toned and smooth, caught the light when she moved.

And her hair—God, *her hair*—was braided down over one shoulder, thick and gleaming like gold thread, loose pieces escaping to kiss her cheeks and collarbone.

She was stunning.

Unfairly, unreasonably, *end-of-the-world* stunning.

I forgot how to speak. How to breathe. How to *exist*.

Frenchy had his hand on her back like it was natural. Like it belonged there.

Jake was stock-still near the drinks, his jaw set like stone. Bubba muttered something I didn't catch. Archie looked like someone had just served him the best and worst surprise of the night as he drifted toward us.

Me?

I just stared. Couldn't not. I was drowning in every inch of skin she dared to show.

I *liked* her covered. Loved her in jeans and her oversized hoodies. But this? This was *intentional*. This was Frankie stepping into the spotlight and letting the world see exactly what we'd all known for years.

She was beautiful, and she *knew* it.

"Coop," Rachel said from beside me, low.

I blinked. "What?"

"You're staring."

"No shit."

She smirked, but there was no humor in it. Or if there was, I didn't notice.

I watched Frankie thank someone for a drink, her fingers brushing Frenchy's arm as she took it. She glanced around—eyes searching, scanning—and I didn't even realize I was holding my breath until her gaze landed on us.

On *me*.

One second. Two.

Then she smiled.

Not the polite kind. Not the oh-you're-here smile she gave to classmates, old teachers, and strangers at Target. It was small. Quiet. Personal.

My heart stuttered like it forgot its damn job.

She started walking toward us, slow steps, Frenchy beside her, his hand *still* on her back.

"I'm going to die," I muttered under my breath.

"No," Bubba said, having somehow replaced Rachel while I gawked at Frankie. "But you might wish you had."

When she finally reached us, standing there in that barely-there bikini and smile that felt like a secret—*I still couldn't find a single, non-drooling coherent thought.*

TWENTY-THREE

FRANKIE

He told me I looked beautiful.

Twice, actually. The first time, it sounded like reverence. The second, it sounded like a warning.

But no matter how many times Mathieu said it, I still felt like I'd stepped out in lingerie and labeled myself *Target Practice*.

The bikini seemed like a good idea when I bought it. Bold. Red. Confident. Like maybe if I wore something that said "I'm fine" loud enough, I'd start believing it. But now, walking into Archie's pool area with a silk sarong barely hanging on and my stomach exposed to the entire senior class, I felt... hunted.

"Don't trip," I muttered under my breath.

"What was that, *mon cœur*?" Mathieu asked, voice light, fingers steady against the small of my back.

"Nothing." *Everything*. Kill me.

I could feel the eyes. Girls assessing. Guys staring. Friends frozen. Maybe worse.

But it wasn't just the crowd—it was them. Jake, Coop, Bubba, and Archie.

The boys I'd grown up with. The boys I used to share snacks and secrets and summer storms with. The boys who came along later with games, challenges, and fun. The boys who damn near broke my heart.

I wasn't sure they hadn't actually broken it. As much as it hurt with each beat, they'd definitely done damage. Or maybe I had. I really didn't know who to blame for it.

Jake looked like he might actually combust. Coop's mouth was slightly open, like he'd forgotten how to shut it. Bubba… looked resigned. Like someone had handed him a bomb and told him to hold it, again. And Archie? Archie looked amused. Which was its own kind of terrifying.

It was the slowest walk of my life. I could hear my heartbeat in my ears, thudding against the bass line of the party music like a countdown.

They'd shifted to one central location, sitting in a loose circle like kings on a damn patio throne. All I had to do was walk right into the court.

Fantastic.

No pressure.

Mathieu leaned closer. "You're doing great, by the way."

I shot him a look. "Easy for you to say. No one here wants to murder you with their eyeballs."

He grinned. "Disagree. Your Mr. Jake looks seconds from violence."

"Stop calling him *my* anything."

"I will when you stop flinching every time you look at him."

I didn't respond. Because he wasn't wrong. The fact he could offer the response in a tone that wasn't one of reprimand but filled with enough sympathy and teasing made it easier to swallow.

As we reached the edge of the group, I felt my mouth stretch into a smile. I had no idea if it looked genuine, but I was pretty sure my face was about to cramp from the effort.

"Hey," I said, trying for casual. "Hope we're not late."

Jake didn't answer. The ice stung.

Coop nodded, eyes flicking down and back up like he couldn't help himself.

Bubba gave me a grunt that might've been a greeting. Though, to his credit, he also struggled to give me a smile. Probably didn't look any better than mine, but it was there.

Archie stood, fluid and smooth, and kissed my cheek like we were old Hollywood friends reunited after scandal.

"Frankie, darling," he purred. Alarm bells went off in my head. It was easy to forget just how dangerous Archie could be. "You've outdone yourself. Mathieu, welcome to the chaos."

"I feel very... observed," Mathieu said lightly, releasing my back so I could sit. Only, now I had to figure out *where*.

Between Coop and Bubba? No.

Next to Jake? Hilarious.

The empty lounger near the bar? Safe, but cowardly.

I perched on the edge of a chair across from the boys instead, tugging the sarong tighter around my waist.

"I like your suit," Coop said, voice a little rough.

I met his gaze, surprised. "Thanks." Then, softer, "It was kind of a leap." Bikinis were never my thing. I wasn't altogether comfortable *now*.

"You stuck the landing."

Jake made a noise like he was choking on sarcasm.

Mathieu shot him a look, then smiled at me. "Do you want something to drink?"

"I—yeah, thanks."

He left with a parting brush of his hand on my shoulder, and suddenly I felt even more exposed. Like the only thing between me and an emotional firing squad had just abandoned me.

Jake stood too abruptly. "I'm getting another beer."

"You just got a Coke," Bubba said.

"Now I want a beer." Then he walked off like we were personally offensive.

Archie sank back into his seat. "Well. That went well."

"I told you not to bring him," Coop muttered.

"You didn't *tell* me." I didn't mean to snap, but it still came out that way. Sucking in a deep breath, I fisted my temper. I didn't come here to fight. "You *asked*. Nicely."

"You knew what it meant." While the look he gave me bordered on scathing, I shrugged.

"I did. I also ignored it." They brought their girlfriends places. How many parties had they thrown with them there? Just a few weeks earlier at Bubba's birthday, they'd all been there and it wasn't like Sharon and Maria weren't here *now*.

They all stared at me. Or near me. Or over me. It was a miracle I hadn't melted into the pool from sheer discomfort.

I rubbed my hands on my knees. "I wasn't trying to throw it in anyone's face."

"No," Bubba said. "But it hit, anyway."

If he wanted an apology—if any of them did, they weren't gonna get it. I exhaled slowly. "What did you expect me to do? Stay home and hide?"

"No one's asking you to hide," Coop said, too quickly.

"Really? Because the stares suggest otherwise."

Archie snorted. "They're just not used to seeing you dressed like a Bond girl."

"I'm not dressed like a Bond girl."

"Trust me, babe, *you're* dressed like the reason Bond loses focus."

I rolled my eyes, but the heat crept up my neck anyway. God, why did I come to this party?

I felt something brush against my bare ankle, and I glanced down. Bubba had nudged me with his foot, eyes steady, mouth in a grim line.

"We're not mad you came," he said. "Just... trying not to make it worse."

"I didn't think it could get worse."

"Don't challenge the universe," he said dryly. "It loves a dare."

Mathieu returned with a drink, handing it to me like nothing had exploded in his absence.

And maybe, somehow, it hadn't.

Maybe the fire hadn't fully caught.

Yet.

No way he didn't notice the awkward party silence hovering around us like secondhand smoke. The hum of the music, the others splashing in the pool or drinking or dancing all seemed to fade into the background. There, but dialed down because it wasn't part of what was happening right here. No, Mathieu had to notice how tense everyone was.

How tense *I* was. Anyone with a pulse would notice.

Still, he wore a relaxed smile as cool as the citrus twist in the glass he'd brought me. "They had cucumber, but that seemed sweeter and summery."

"Thank you." I took a sip and nearly sighed. It was ice cold, and sweet. Wine. He'd picked one I liked and, of course, Archie just gave me a knowing look. The wine was only available cause Archie knew I liked it.

Suddenly, the cold glass felt like a grenade.

Mathieu dropped to sit on the edge of the lounge beside me. He slouched like he belonged right there. He did. It still made the tension spike. You couldn't miss Jake's reaction. His reflection in the sliding glass door showed him freezing where he leaned against the bar on the far side of the pool with the bottle almost to his mouth.

"So, Mathieu…" Archie was the first to break the silence, all easy charm and subtle menace. "You're not from around here."

"No," Mathieu answered, easily enough as he folded his sunglasses and hung them off his shirt collar. "I've been enjoying my stay. It's a very nice area, except for one neighbor who mows at six a.m. He can eat a brick."

A laugh startled out of me before I could stop it.

Archie's smile didn't move. "Glad we're making a good impression. Frankie's always had a way of bringing people together." He spared me an enigmatic look. "Or starting fires. Sometimes both."

"She's been very kind to me." Mathieu tilted his head. "I get the sense that kindness is more radical here than it should be."

"So," Coop asked, leaning forward slightly. "How long do you plan to be here?" Translation: *How long are you planning to be around me like a security blanket?*

Unperturbed, Mathieu shifted his focus to Coop. "I came here for school. I'm staying for other reasons."

Jake scoffed from across the patio, but didn't say a word. That was somehow worse than yelling. We were getting a lot of attention. The rumble of so many voices had dropped off, but people were still looking and leaning into each other to whisper.

Others had their phones out.

I hated it here.

"Other reasons." Bubba drained the last of his beer. "Right."

So much for behaving…

I tugged my sarong a little tighter. "Can we not do this?"

"Do what?" Coop asked, all wide-eyed innocence. Like he wasn't vibrating with tension. That look didn't work on me in kindergarten and it definitely didn't work on me now. Like I couldn't see his knee bouncing like he did when he wrestled with his own temper.

"This," I gestured vaguely to the testosterone fog clouding the patio. "This weirdly polite gladiator match."

Archie smirked. "Gladiators wore less clothing."

I glared at him. "Don't encourage them."

Mathieu shifted next to me. "If it's a problem that I'm here—"

"It's *not*," I said quickly. Maybe too quickly.

"No, it's not," Bubba echoed my words, but not my tone. His clearly stated *it totally is*.

"Can we just *all*, try not to be jerks for one night?" My voice was barely a whisper, yet it felt like I had a microphone and shouted it to everyone present. "Please?"

The silence that followed was so pointy I could've stabbed with it.

"God." Rachel's voice sliced through the quiet like a glass dagger. "It's like watching a pack of golden retrievers realize their favorite chew toy started dating someone else."

I nearly choked on my wine. Rachel strolled up with a chilled drink of her own and zero patience in her eyes.

"Hello, boys," she said with a hint of a drawl. "Still sulking like prom got canceled?"

Bubba sighed and Coop looked down like he either bit his tongue or swallowed it. Across the pool, Jake glared. But at this point, he could shove it. Either join the damn conversation or shut up. Archie, though, smiled and those internal alarms of mine clanged loudly.

"Rachel," he said, smooth as silk. "You look like violence in a cover-up."

"I aim to please." She shifted her gaze to me. "Frankie, looking lethal. Need an exit?"

I didn't hesitate. "God, yes." I was on my feet so fast, I almost spilled my wine. Mathieu started to follow, but I brushed his arm. "Just give me a minute, please."

Guilt nibbled at me, but I really did need a minute.

His brow furrowed slightly. Not offended, just... watchful. "I'll be here."

Of course he would. Too decent for his own good. Too calm in a minefield. God, I was an asshole to leave him.

Rachel gave the guys a little two-finger salute, then turned on her heel before leading me toward the far end of the pool away from the guys, Jake, the other party-goers. Everyone.

As soon as we were out of range of prying ears and had our backs to prying eyes, I blew out a breath so hard my lungs protested.

"That was *excruciating*."

"You were doing great until you started begging for decency," she said dryly. "They don't have any left. Testosterone and repressed feelings burned them out a long time ago."

I huffed out a half-laugh. It was too sad to be really

funny, but I'd rather laugh than cry. "Why are you helping me?"

Head cocked, she spared a look back toward the others before studying me again. "Because I don't like you when you're pathetic."

"Wow." Ouch. "Thank you?"

Rachel shrugged. "I don't like them when they're smug. This new brooding, angsty gumbo they've cooked up? Unbearable. You're the common denominator."

"Fantastic."

She handed me her drink before plucking the wine out of my grip. "It's water. Hydrate. You're going to need it."

"For what?"

Rachel smiled without any teeth. "Because you've officially entered your villain era. Trust me—everyone just noticed."

CHAPTER

TWENTY-FOUR

FRANKIE

We slipped away from the open pool area and into the hedge garden beyond. The noise from the party faded to a dull throb behind us. Here, with the string lights casting soft shadows as the sun continued its descent. The hot breath of the air decried any cooling temperatures. Still, the low hum of cicadas filled the silence.

Rachel had downed the rest of my wine and left that glass behind. A sip of the water turned into a much longer drink for me. She was right, I needed it. While I had to fight the urge to gulp it down, I did press the ice-cold glass against my face. We wandered through the hedges to a stone bench where Rachel took a seat, leaned back on her hands and stared at me.

She wore a look you only get from someone who knew all of your secrets and wasn't impressed by any of them. Not that I had *secrets*. "So," she said, her voice as dry as ever. "You want to tell me what the hell you're doing?"

"What do you mean?" I blinked.

"Nope," she said, rolling her eyes. "You're not dumb,

Frankie. Blind? Sometimes. Oblivious? Way too damn often, but you can't walk into this party wearing a bikini that Aphrodite would envy and in Archie's *favorite* color, dragging French Vogue's wet dream with you, then play shocked when the guys are two seconds from solving their issues with a fist fight."

The judgment landed like a slap. "I didn't *drag* him." Defensiveness was my first instinct. "I didn't even want to come, but he asked me to, to be his date."

"And you said yes." Rachel tilted her head. "To *this*. You've been emotionally entangled with four human hurricanes who would happily kill for you and have beaten the shit out of others on your behalf."

Embarrassment went out the window. "I *never* asked for that. I would never." Hell, I hadn't even known how often they'd chased off others. "Something, I think you damn well know. Because you were the one who *told* me."

"I did tell you. I told you because you deserved to know. So, while you may not have known *then*, you *do* know now."

I stared down at my drink. Guilt soured the water. "It's just a party."

"Frankie," Rachel said my name on a gust of a sigh so deep that I almost wanted to apologize for frustrating her. "It's never just a party when feelings are involved. Especially not *that* many feelings."

I hated how that landed, because she wasn't wrong. Tears burned in the back of my eyes, but I blinked furiously to keep them in check. Then I downed more water.

"Look," Rachel said, shifting forward and patting the bench next to her. "I'm not judging you for moving on or for dating the hot French guy. Really, I'd buy the guy a drink myself and toast him for getting through those blinders of yours if I weren't worried Archie would slip cyanide into both of our drinks."

I frowned at the description, but Rachel's bland delivery made it hard to argue. Needing a break, I sat next to her. The stone was still warm from the sun, almost too warm but the sarong helped.

"Here's the thing," Rachel continued, and her voice softened, almost gentled like she was comforting me. "You didn't just move on. You detonated a landmine, then walked away like it wasn't going to blow everything up behind you."

I winced. "I didn't—" I sighed. "I was mad." Was? "Correction, I'm still mad."

"I know," she said, looping an arm over my shoulders. "You have every right to be pissed at them."

"Then why are you defending them?" I slanted a look at her.

"Oh, honey, I am not defending them. They are big boys with big balls, or so they act. They can take the kicks to the crotch they earned." She snorted a half-laugh. "Before you think I'm blaming you for picking someone else, I'm not doing that either."

"No?" I wasn't so sure about that.

"No," she said firmly. "Are they crazy about you? *Yes*. Did they date other people even while they were hung up on you? Also a yes."

That stung. That *really* stung.

"They aren't virgins, Frankie. They aren't innocent in any of this."

The fury in Jake's eyes coupled with the hurt flashed through my mind. "Jake's really mad at me because I had sex with Mathieu."

"No, he's not," Rachel said easily. At my askance look,

she gave my shoulders a squeeze. "He's mad that you didn't have sex with him. That you looked to someone else."

"I didn't—"

"You did," she corrected. "There's nothing wrong with that. He did."

Grimacing, I stared at the glass then downed the rest of the water. I kind of wished it was alcohol. "Why is it okay for them and not for me?"

"I never said it was okay for them." Rachel eyed me for a long moment, then she sighed. "Frankie, I think they're fucking idiots. They're crazy about you but couldn't figure out how to tell you. I almost feel sorry for them though because I get how that feels."

"Rach..."

"Ahh," she said, letting go of my shoulders to press a finger to my lips. "Don't go feeling sorry for me. I wasn't sure if you were into girls or not. You're not. That's fine. And you're really lucky, I'm an *excellent* friend."

"Even when you're a pain in the ass." I could admit that and Rachel's sudden smile almost made me laugh.

"Thank you." Like it was a compliment, but she was probably right about that too. Then she sobered. "You can be excused for missing all the signs before now, *but...* This is the big one, you can't pretend you don't know. Being surprised that they don't want to be extras in your new rom-com, that's kind of dense."

"That's not fair."

"Nope." She agreed way too easily. "Life isn't fair. I'm also not wrong."

The silence stretched out between us. Thick. Heavy. The weight of it threatened to crush me.

"You love them," Rachel said in a whisper. "All of them. You love them so much it hurts you."

I bit my lip.

"That's not the problem," she said, pressing onwards.

"Then what is?"

"You don't love yourself enough to believe you deserve any of them."

I looked up. Her gaze met mine, steady and unblinking.

"You keep making choices based on how little you think you matter," she said quietly.

"I didn't even think they cared *that* way." I'd always known they cared. They were my best friends which was what made all of this hurt so damn much.

"Of course you didn't. One, you're kind of oblivious. I adore you, but you really are. And two, at the risk of repeating myself, you don't think you deserve to feel that way. To feel like someone else believes you matter."

Those words lingered like a bad scrape, stinging where they ripped me open. I wanted to argue that it wasn't true, but the words all died unspoken.

"Mathieu makes you feel safe." Rachel said with another sigh, then wrapped her arm around my shoulders again. "That's not nothing. I'm *glad* he does. But with the guys? You'd have to admit you're worth breaking rules for. Worth staying for. Worth the fallout."

Tears pricked at the corners of my eyes before I could stop them. Of course she saw it. Of course *she* would say the thing I couldn't.

"I didn't mean to hurt them," I said, voice small. Even when I wanted to punch them, I didn't want them to feel like nothing.

To feel like I had.

"I know," she said. "But you still are. And until you figure out *why* you're so scared to be chosen—truly, unapologetically chosen—this is going to keep happening."

A long beat passed, and I sighed. She didn't ask me to do it, but I leaned my head against her shoulder and closed my eyes for a moment. Just leaned on the strength she offered. When she pressed a kiss to the top of my head, I felt small, but also... cared for.

"Okay, take another breath. Then we go back out there and pretend we're normal. Tomorrow? You start figuring out which life you actually want—then we make sure you get it."

"You make it sound so easy."

"I like having a plan." Another light kiss to the top of my head and a squeeze of my shoulders. I sat up straighter and met her gaze. "Also," she added, dry as the desert, "if you're going to be the center of a love pentagon, at least own it. Don't half-ass your scandal."

A laugh burst out of me even as fresh tears slipped down my cheeks. "God, you're terrifying."

"I'm honest. People confuse the two."

She wasn't wrong.

We stayed there for a moment longer. The truth wasn't going anywhere and Rachel let me wipe away my tears and put myself back together without any rush. I had a feeling, she'd sit there all night if I needed it.

I had no idea what I'd done to deserve a friend like...

What I deserved.

"I like that you're honest," I admitted, because Rachel was right. I didn't think I deserved to be chosen and she'd chosen me anyway. "I like that you're my friend, too."

"Me too," she said. "But don't go telling everyone. I'm a bitch and I like my reputation."

Another smile escaped me. "Pretty sure that's safe."

"Probably," she agreed. "Also—" She bumped my shoulder. "You're welcome."

I couldn't help it, I laughed.

TWENTY-FIVE

JAKE

I watched her walk away.

Correction—*they* walked away. Rachel and Frankie. Like they were going off to scheme world domination or a takedown playlist or maybe just to get away from all the testosterone that had choked the patio into a silent standoff.

Probably the third one.

Didn't matter.

What mattered was that *he* stayed.

Frenchy. Mathieu. Whatever the hell name he went by. Sitting there like he belonged. Like he hadn't touched her. Kissed her. Been *inside her*.

I clenched my fist so hard my beer bottle cracked under the pressure.

No one seemed to notice. Not really. Coop was avoiding my eyes, probably hoping I'd cool down. Bubba was half-turned, pretending to look at the pool, but his attention kept flicking back to me like he could feel the fuse burning down. Archie... Archie didn't say a word. Just watched.

That stung worse than I wanted to admit.

Because if he *knew*—if Archie knew the truth—he'd be on my side. No question. He'd throw that smug bastard out of his house so fast Frenchy would still be spinning by the time he landed on the sidewalk.

But Archie didn't know. Nobody knew.

Except Frankie.

Me.

And *him*.

Goddamn it.

I slammed the rest of my beer and tossed the broken bottle into the recycling bin. It hit the edge and shattered louder than necessary, but nobody flinched. They all saw this coming.

Especially him.

I stalked across the patio.

"Jake—" Coop started.

"Not now," I snapped.

Frenchy stood as I approached, like he was preparing for a conversation. A calm one. A normal one. That made it worse. That made me *livid*.

He had *no right* to act like this was anything close to civil.

"You think you're smooth, huh?" I said, low and dangerous.

He blinked. "Excuse me?"

Coop stepped in, his hand brushing my shoulder. "Let's maybe not—"

"Move," I said without looking at him.

He didn't. But he didn't say anything else either.

Frenchy's gaze sharpened, mouth tight but not surprised. "I think maybe you've had enough to drink."

Oh, *that* was the wrong thing to say.

I shoved him.

It wasn't a hard push. Not really. Just enough to break his balance, enough to tell him exactly where we stood. The pool crowd quieted around us, sharks sensing blood.

Coop grabbed my arm, tugging. "Jake, c'mon—"

"I said move!" I snarled.

Bubba stepped in this time, wedging himself between us. "You don't want to do this."

"Don't tell me what I want."

"Then let me remind you what happens if you *do* this." Bubba's voice dropped low, his eyes sharp. "You swing on a guest at Archie's house, and you're not just dealing with Frenchy. You're dealing with *Archie*."

My eyes darted over Bubba's shoulder. Archie hadn't moved. He hadn't said a word.

But he *was* watching. Still and silent, like a storm cloud just waiting for thunder.

God. That hurt more than it should.

Frenchy straightened his shirt, shoulders square, voice steady. "If you want to talk, we can talk. But I won't fight you."

That was the moment I realized: he wasn't scared of me. Not in the way I wanted him to be.

I didn't want calm. I didn't want understanding. I didn't want this guy offering to talk like he was the damn victim.

I wanted him to *regret it*.

"I know what you did," I said, voice like smoke.

He frowned. "What are you talking about?"

"You think you can just come in here, charm everyone, touch her—*fuck* her—like she's a vacation fling?" My voice dropped then cracked, rage boiling over. "You think I wouldn't figure it out?"

His face went tight, controlled. "That's between me and Frankie. Not you."

"She's not *yours*," I spat. "You don't get to *have* her."

Frenchy didn't move. "Then neither do you."

That was when I lunged.

Bubba caught me before I got more than half a step. Coop backed him up, grabbing my arms while I twisted, shouting, "Let me go! Let me go, dammit—!"

Archie still didn't move.

He just watched.

Watched while I fought everyone who wasn't her. Watched while my control shredded into nothing. Watched while I lost the one thing I still thought I had—*dignity*.

"She *loved* me!" I half-yelled at Frenchy over Bubba's shoulder. "She *loved* me first!"

Frenchy's voice came quiet. "Maybe she did. But that doesn't give you ownership."

Coop flinched like that line hit *him*, too.

I stopped fighting.

Suddenly, I was so damn tired.

Bubba let go first. Coop second. Frenchy stayed rooted like he didn't trust me not to go for it again, and honestly? Smart man.

I looked at him. This stranger who somehow knew her in ways I didn't anymore. Who had pieces of her I used to guard with my life. And now?

Now he had her trust.

And I had my rage.

Cool. Great trade.

"I'm not done with you," I said, voice dead even.

Frenchy nodded once. "I believe you."

The silence between us stretched. Thick. Oily. Choking.

And then someone laughed.

Not close — not right here — but close *enough*. A ripple of noise from the pool, a sudden swell in the music like the DJ sensed the temperature spike and hit shuffle on something poppy to compensate. But it didn't work. Not for me.

Because I could still *feel* the eyes.

Girls lined along the pool in their bikini armor and smirks. Sharon, Bubba's bitch of an ex, in her green wrap and sunglasses pushed into her hair like a damn movie star, looked *amused*. She whispered something to Patty, who full-on grinned like this was the best part of the evening. Popcorn-worthy drama.

But it was Maria who undid me.

Maria, who stood near the lounge chairs with a drink in her hand and *pity* in her eyes.

I'd take anger. I'd take disgust. I'd take her calling me every name in the book, throw her drink in my face, flip me off. But not *that* look.

Not like she already thought I lost.

I turned away from them, heat crawling up my neck. My hands were shaking. I flexed them and shoved them into my pockets like that would stop the tremble.

"Let's go," Coop said, voice low in my ear. "Before this gets worse."

"It's not worse yet?" I muttered, still not looking at anyone.

"You tell me, man," Bubba said from my other side. "'Cause right now it's looking a whole lot like a meltdown in surround sound."

He wasn't wrong.

The music didn't cover it up. The laughter didn't erase it. We'd pulled attention like a black hole in the middle of a sunny backyard. Even the people pretending not to watch were *watching*. You can always tell when someone's listening — the stillness gives them away.

We had *a lot* of stillness around us.

"C'mon." Coop gave me a light shove. "We'll go out front. Cool off. Reassess the war plan."

Bubba snorted. "It's not a war, Coop."

"The hell it isn't," I snapped, finally facing them. "You didn't hear what she said. About him. About them."

"I *heard* it," Coop said, tight. "Doesn't mean you get to go nuclear at a *pool party*."

Bubba tipped his head toward the gate. "Let's take a walk."

I looked back once, just once, and saw Frenchy sitting again. Calm. Composed. *Still there.*

And Archie?

Archie was leaning back in his chair, nursing a drink and watching the world burn like he'd lit the match himself.

I hated them both in that moment.

But I hated myself more.

I followed Coop and Bubba around the side of the house, past the hedge line and the speakers and the patio lights strung like fairy dust illusions over a night gone sour. The second we were out of sight, I dragged both hands down my face, trying to pull myself out of my skin.

Bubba popped open another bottle of beer he must have grabbed on our way past and handed it to me like it was a peace offering.

I didn't take it.

"I shouldn't have lost it," I muttered.

"Nope," Bubba agreed. "You really shouldn't've."

"But also," Coop added, "he *is* kind of a smug asshole. So, like... partial credit?"

I almost laughed. Almost.

Instead, I dropped to sit on the edge of the fountain. The line of cars around us provided some kind of cover, but it wasn't like the bricks or stone or even the chrome had any answers.

"She didn't even *look* at me," I said. "Not once."

They didn't answer.

They didn't have to.

Because I already knew.

I leaned forward, elbows on my knees. The sun-warmed stone made my legs sweat, but maybe if I roasted my ass enough, I'd just burn up.

Coop sat next to me and sighed. Bubba stood off to the side, popping open another bottle of beer. The one he'd left next to me began to sweat. I could hear the music drifting around the side of the house, something fast and upbeat, a total contrast to the black pit in my stomach.

The silence was heavier now. Not just uncomfortable, but *weighted*. All we needed was someone to acknowledge the blast radius.

I was the first to crack.

"I said it out loud."

Coop didn't look up, but I could see his jaw clench. Bubba let out a slow breath and finally walked over, picked up the bottle next to me and pressed it into my hand. I closed my fingers around it reflexively.

"I said it," I repeated, quieter. "I *actually* said it. In front of everyone."

Bubba rubbed a hand over the back of his neck. "At least you didn't *shout* it?"

That almost made me laugh. Another almost.

Instead, I winced. Hard. The moment replayed in my head like a glitchy projector, overexposed, off-kilter, all sharp edges. *She loved me first. You touched her. Fucked her.* I hadn't just lost it. I'd detonated.

The word hung in the back of my brain now, echoing: *fucked*. In public. At a party. In front of our entire class, half the swim team, and probably some freshman with a TikTok account.

My stomach turned. "Shit."

"Yeah," Coop said. "You, uh… kinda announced it."

I gritted my teeth. "God."

Bubba finally looked at me, steady and unflinching. "You didn't just say it, man. You *gave it to them*. Every guy in that backyard who's been wondering what went down between them just got their answer. From *you*. Not her. Not him."

I swallowed hard.

"Now she has to walk back into that patio," Bubba went on, "and every single person out there is gonna know something that was never supposed to be public."

"Worse," Coop added. "They're gonna *talk* about it. Twist it. Use it."

I covered my face with both hands and groaned into my palms. "Jesus Christ. I didn't even think—I just—"

"Yeah," Bubba said quietly. "That's the problem."

It hit like a punch to the throat. Frankie's face flashed in my memory, right before she walked off with Rachel. That high, brittle smile. The tight grip on her sarong. The way she never once looked my way. And now?

Now I'd made it worse.

No—not worse. *Unfixable.*

"She's gonna hate me."

Neither of them contradicted me.

Coop shifted, exhaling hard. "I don't think she hated you before."

Great. "And now?"

Now, maybe she should.

The ground should open and swallow me whole. Or maybe like I should just get in my damn car and leave. Drive until I could forget. Forget her laugh. Her skin. Her eyes the last time they were on me and not filled with pain.

Instead, I sat there, on the edge of the fountain as if the world hadn't just *shifted*.

"I've ruined everything," I said. Not to them. Just... to the air. To the night. To myself.

Bubba looked up at the sky like maybe he was hoping for divine intervention. "You can't un-say it."

Coop stood, brushing off his hands. "But maybe you can *own* it."

I looked at him like he'd lost his mind.

He shrugged. "Don't hide from it. Don't pretend you didn't screw up. *Don't make her carry it alone.* You want to fix it? Then start by not making it about you."

The last of the rage burned out of me like an ember dropped in a puddle.

Just steam and silence.

And the sound of laughter, echoing from the party I wasn't sure I still belonged to.

TWENTY-SIX

FRANKIE

Rachel was right. Hydrating helped.

For about five minutes.

Until we came back around the hedges and reentered the pool area.

The change in temperature was immediate. Not the air. That was still humid and thick with chlorine and spilled alcohol. The *vibe*, though? It felt like someone had hit the dimmer switch on fun and cranked the gossip dial to max.

The bass was louder. The pool had more people in it. Laughter still floated above the music like bubbles popping in the sun. But beneath it, there was something else.

Eyes.

Too many of them.

Lingering on me just a second too long. Shifting away when I looked back. Faces half-turned toward their friends as whispers caught the wind.

I slowed automatically, instincts prickling. "Something happened."

Rachel barely blinked. "Of course something happened.

You're not there to absorb the tension like a human light-ning rod anymore, so someone else had to short-circuit."

My stomach dropped. "Jake."

"Ding ding," she said dryly.

I tugged my sarong tighter around my waist. Like that would protect me from the aftershocks of whatever he did. "What did he do?"

"Dunno yet," she said. "But people are looking at you like you walked in while on fire, so I'm guessing it wasn't subtle."

Great.

Just what I needed.

I straightened my shoulders and kept walking. The only way out was through. We moved past the lounge chairs and toward the drinks table, and I could *feel* the energy shift around me.

Like air pressure.

Like everyone was holding their breath and waiting for me to explode.

"Mitch," Rachel muttered under her breath. "Three o'clock."

I turned slightly, and there he was. Mitch, linebacker, too tan for someone who claimed to hate the sun, wearing sunglasses *at night* and sipping from a red Solo cup like it made him cool instead of cliché.

He grinned when he saw me.

Nope.

"Frankie," he drawled, too loud, too pleased with himself. "Looking *real* good tonight."

Rachel slowed beside me. "Oh my god," she muttered. "Did your girlfriend fall down a well, Mitch?"

I flinched. "He's dating Cheryl."

"*Exactly,*" Rachel said. "Which makes this extra gross."

Mitch gave us both a cocky little shrug like this was all some inside joke we weren't smart enough to get. "Can't a guy give a compliment?"

Rachel turned to him, one hand on her hip. "Sure. If the guy's single, and the compliment doesn't come with a side of *regret sex fantasy*. Try again, wide receiver."

"I'm a linebacker," he muttered.

"Not in the *moral* sense."

I nearly choked on a laugh.

Mitch looked like he wanted to say something else but thought better of it, especially as Rachel stared him down like she'd be happy to turn his ego into a lawn dart. He slunk away, muttering something under his breath, probably about feminists or sharks or whatever scared him less.

I blew out a breath. "Okay. That wasn't normal."

"Nope," Rachel agreed. "Which means the fallout *definitely* happened."

I glanced across the yard, scanning for Jake. Coop. Bubba. Even Archie. But none of them were where we left them.

Instead, I saw Sharon, Patty, and Maria sitting near the shallow end, legs dangling in the water. Sharon caught my eye, smiled faintly, then leaned toward Patty and whispered something that made her smirk widen.

But it was Maria who looked up and didn't look away.

She didn't smile.

She didn't smirk.

She looked... *sad*.

My stomach turned. "I think they know."

"Oh yeah," Rachel said. "The jungle drums are beating, and guess whose name is in the lyrics?"

I pressed a hand to my temple. "I need a drink."

"You need to *breathe*."

"I *was* breathing. Then I came back here."

She steered me toward the cooler anyway. "Sip something cold, keep your head high, and whatever happens next, don't give them the story they want. You're not a scandal. You're a *main character*."

I wasn't sure I could do any of that.

But as the music thumped louder and the stares got heavier, I straightened my spine, took the water she offered, and reminded myself not to run.

Even if I really, *really* wanted to.

I took one more sip of the water before it hit me like a brick to the chest.

"Wait," I said suddenly. "Where's Mathieu?"

Rachel stopped mid-reach for a lemon slice. "What?"

I turned a full circle, scanning the crowd again — the patio chairs, the drink table, the poolside, even the shadows near the speakers. *Nothing.* The lounge where we'd left him was empty. The spot beside Coop and Bubba was vacated. And the fact that Archie wasn't smirking in my peripheral vision anymore?

Also missing.

My heart kicked up a notch. "Where the hell is he?"

Rachel blinked once. "You're right. He's *not* here. None of them are."

She meant it. *Jake.* Coop. Bubba. *Mathieu.* And Archie, apparently.

Gone.

The ground didn't tilt, but it felt like it *should've.*

The bad kind of silence was seeping back into the edges of the party. Had someone pressed pause on the vibe and forgot to hit play again?

"They're together," I said slowly. "Aren't they?"

Rachel gave a long, low sigh. "Well. That narrows it

down. Either we let the boys figure it out the old-fashioned way via passive-aggressive grunts and bruised egos—or…"

I didn't even let her finish.

"Rescue," I said immediately. "It's a rescue."

Rachel grinned like a lion. "Knew you'd say that."

I made a beeline for the girls by the pool, with Rachel on my heels and the knot in my chest twisting tighter. Sharon spotted us coming and arched one perfect eyebrow.

"Looking for your boyfriend?" she asked, all casual venom. "Or *boyfriends*? Hard to keep track lately."

I stopped dead in front of her, blood simmering just under my skin.

But I didn't get a word in before Rachel stepped past me, all teeth and velvet steel.

"Hey, Sharon?" she said sweetly. "Maybe worry less about her love life and more about the SPF rating on your entire personality. Now." She clapped her hands once, sharply. "Where'd they go?"

Sharon scowled. Patty let out a snort that she didn't bother to hide.

Maria, to her credit, sat up a little straighter and answered without waiting. "Archie and Mathieu went inside. Jake, Bubba, and Coop took off around the front of the house a few minutes ago."

That meant *they'd* all been gone long enough for people to notice.

Long enough for *this* mess to spread.

My throat was dry again.

"Thanks," I said, my voice a little raw. I started moving before I could overthink it. Rachel caught up with me halfway to the back steps.

"Game plan?" she asked.

"Find them before Jake does something he can't come back from," I said. "Before *any* of them do."

"If the damage is already done?"

"Then I make sure they know who really started the fire."

Rachel grinned again, but this one was different. More steel. More sisterhood.

"Let's go crash a testosterone summit."

The second we stepped through the sliding glass door into the house, the noise dropped by half. The party muffled behind glass, the air cooler and scented with cedar and citrus. Archie's place always smelled expensive, like it came with a cologne subscription and secrets sealed in wood paneling.

Rachel peeled off to scan the front hall while I paused just inside the kitchen, trying to get my bearings, and saw Jeremy.

Archie's butler-slash-caretaker-slash-wizard of all things elegant, stood near the wet bar with a folded cloth in hand and an unreadable expression.

But when he saw me, it softened.

"Miss Frankie," he said, with the gentle kind of smile that made me feel ten again and pretending the world wasn't hard. "You're looking radiant tonight."

"Thanks, Jeremy," I said, though the compliment landed sideways with everything else clawing at my nerves. "Have you seen Archie? Or Mathieu?"

He nodded, serene as ever. "Mr. Archie took your guest into the study a few minutes ago. For a private conversation."

My spine straightened like someone pulled a string.

"Private," I echoed.

Rachel muttered, "That's never good."

Jeremy tilted his head. "They didn't appear hostile. But I trust you'd prefer to check for yourself."

"Very much," I said. "Thanks, Jeremy."

He gave me a slight bow, and we were already moving, past the marble counter, past the gleaming art deco light fixture I'd once heard Archie call "bourbon glam," down the hall where the light dimmed and the sounds of the party receded entirely.

Rachel's sandals clicked against the hardwood beside me. "You don't think Archie would actually—"

"I don't know what he'd do," I said tightly. "That's the problem."

We were almost to the study door when another swung open at the far end of the hall.

The *front* door.

I turned just as Jake, Coop, and Bubba stepped into the foyer. Jake looked like a thundercloud wrapped in cotton, clearly still angry, but muted. Contained. Coop looked exhausted. Bubba, as always, wore the grim patience of someone cleaning up after a mess he didn't start.

Jake's eyes locked on mine instantly.

I didn't flinch, but I didn't look away either.

Let him see I wasn't afraid.

Let him feel whatever consequence he'd invited into this night.

I turned before he could say anything, lifted my hand, and knocked once on the heavy oak door of the study. No response.

So I pushed it open.

Without waiting.

Inside, the room was low-lit and cool, the soft scent of old paper and whiskey wrapping around me like a memory.

Archie was perched on the edge of his desk, long legs stretched out, glass of something dark in his hand.

Mathieu sat in the leather armchair across from him, one ankle propped on the opposite knee, head angled slightly like he was in the middle of saying something important. Comfortable, but serious.

Both turned when the door opened.

They *both* looked like I'd just caught them red-handed, not guilty, exactly, but intense.

Wary.

Too quiet.

"Sorry to interrupt," I said, voice flat but controlled. "But I figured whatever this was, I should be in the room."

Rachel stepped in beside me and shut the door behind us with a soft *click*.

Archie smiled, slow and deliberate. "Hey babe, just in time."

Mathieu stood immediately, hands open at his sides, brows drawn with concern. "You okay?"

I didn't answer him yet.

I looked at Archie instead.

And waited.

Archie didn't blink.

Didn't move, either.

He just sipped his drink like we were interrupting a dinner party instead of a strategy session. The amber liquid caught the light, and I wondered for a beat if it was the same bottle he cracked open the night he told me he didn't trust easy, but he trusted me.

Did that mean anything anymore?

I stepped farther into the room, keeping my eyes on him. "What's going on?"

Archie set the glass down on the desk with a quiet *clink*,

then folded his hands in his lap like a man preparing to deliver a lecture. "We were having a conversation."

"And?"

"I wanted to get to know your friend a little better," he said evenly, like this was just standard protocol. "Given the… circumstances."

I turned to Mathieu. "Are you okay?"

He nodded, stepping forward, his gaze softer when it landed on me. "I'm fine. Archie was being… thorough."

I looked back at Archie. "Thorough," I repeated. "That your new word for intimidation?"

His smile didn't quite reach his eyes. "He's the one who sat down, sweetheart. I just asked questions."

"What kind of questions?"

Mathieu exhaled through his nose, not annoyed, just tired. "About school. Family. Intentions. That sort of thing."

Rachel made a sound behind me like she was choking on invisible champagne.

"I see," I said slowly. "And what's the verdict?"

"That he's not as foolish as he looks," Archie said, standing now, reaching for his drink again. "I'm sure you knew that already, didn't you?"

The way he said *you* as though I was the wildcard in the deck made something sharp twist in my stomach.

"I didn't know anyone needed a vetting process," I said tightly. "I didn't realize I needed your approval."

"You don't," he said, almost kindly. "But you should've expected the scrutiny."

"I did," I snapped. "But you guys? Really, Archie?" I laughed once, bitter and low. "You've had *five* girlfriends in the last year and *two* were sisters."

Rachel winced beside me. "Oof."

Archie smirked. "That was a misunderstanding."

"You mistook one for the other?" I shot back. "Sure."

He didn't rise to it. Just sipped his drink again, slow and thoughtful. "I'm not judging your taste, Frankie. I'm trying to figure out if your new attachment's going to get himself torn apart out there."

Mathieu's jaw twitched, but he stayed quiet.

"I can fight my own battles," I said.

Archie gave me a look that was far too close to sympathy. "You shouldn't *have* to."

I blinked.

That... landed.

Soft. Quiet. Awful.

Before I could decide whether I wanted to be angry or grateful, Rachel spoke up, voice drier than the gin she liked to fake-drink when boys got on her nerves.

"Well, this has been *adorable*, but in case anyone forgot, the other three Stooges are still just outside this room, probably deciding whether to knock or punch something."

I turned to the door, pulse picking up again.

Right.

Jake.

Now that I was inside, now that I'd seen Mathieu standing here, calm and intact and *not* furious, another weight dropped into my stomach like a stone.

"What happened out there?" I asked them both. "Because the whole party's looking at me like I lit a match in a firework factory."

Mathieu shifted. "You didn't. He did."

Archie raised his eyebrows. "Loudly."

Rachel crossed her arms. "Define 'loudly.'"

Mathieu gave me a look I couldn't quite read. "He told them."

For a second, I didn't understand. Told them what?

Then the bottom fell out.

He told them.

The weight of it hit me so hard I had to sit.

Jake had told them. Everyone. That Mathieu and I had slept together. That *he knew*.

I pressed a hand to my stomach. It didn't help.

"Frankie—" Mathieu started.

I shook my head once. "I need a minute."

Archie handed me his glass without a word.

I didn't drink it.

But I held it tight, like it might steady me.

I didn't drink the whiskey. Not at first. It was too damn much, but I held it like it might anchor me. Like the condensation on the glass could trick my palm into thinking something was steady today. That my friendships were absolutely detonating around me and that there was something worth salvaging.

I wasn't so sure on any of these topics.

The truth was a knife in my ribs. Digging. Poking. Prodding. Leaving me to bleed out slowly.

Not because I was ashamed of sleeping with Mathieu—God, no. He had been amazing. That was mine. Ours. Private. It only came out with Jake because we'd been—Fuck I didn't even know what we'd been about to do. He'd been wrapped around me, then kissing me and it felt so good and then...

Then he stormed out. Angry didn't seem to even cover it. He'd barely said even two words to me *since* he left. Now, he took what I told him and turned it into some kind of punchline. A spectacle.

Rachel seemed to be watching me carefully, all sharp lines and silent support. Archie, on the other hand, wore an expression that looked like he waged an internal debate on whether to say something comforting or scathing. Honestly, he could probably do both in one laser-focused sentence. Archie's intelligence was matched only by the candid, sharp-witted nature of his often-biting commentary.

Frankly, it was a toss-up between Archie and Rachel who could land the most strategic verbal blows.

Mathieu moved closer, cautious as though I might shatter. I hated that. I hated how small I felt. I'd fought past this all summer and one of the reasons I'd succeeded had been *because* of Mathieu. Meeting him, getting to know him, and building this relationship... it had done more than rebuild my confidence.

"Frankie," he said in a low voice, his French accent softening each syllable. "I didn't know he was going to—"

"How could you?" I said quickly. Too quickly. When I told him about my confession to Jake, I hadn't hid the circumstances and Mathieu had taken that so damn well. He owed me no apologies.

Jake might have been hurt, and possessive. He might even have been jealous and pissy, in the worst way. But I never would have expected him to attack me so publicly, not even to get at someone else.

"Was it mean?" I had to ask. "Or strategic?"

"What?" Rachel blinked even as Mathieu looked puzzled.

"Jake outing us," I explained, locking my gaze on Archie's. "Was it because he wanted to hurt *me* or was it about humiliating *Mathieu?*"

"A little of column A," Archie said grimly. "And a little of column B. Except... I don't think he thought before he said it. I don't think it was that simple. Maybe."

"It's not about simplicity," I continued, not once looking away from Archie. We didn't lie to each other. Not when it mattered. There were little lies, little mistruths about day-to-day stuff. But the big things? Archie never lied, not when I asked him straight out and I'd done my damnedest to do the same thing. It might be weird to the others, but it worked for me and Archie. "It matters because if it was just about hurting me, then it was because Jake was angry." Then I could deal with that. Deal with Jake. "If it was about humiliating Mathieu and not giving a damn that I was collateral, then it's a lot worse."

"They're both bad, Frankie," Rachel murmured in a voice that was both sympathetic *and* empathetic.

She wasn't wrong except... "I know. But only one of those means he's not done yet."

Archie sighed and I read the answer right there in the anger in his eyes. It was definitely both. Jake had been—*was*—angry with me. But he also wanted to punish Mathieu. He was far from being done.

Disappointment was a living, breathing burn in my stomach. Mathieu brushed his hand against my shoulder, supportive. Present.

Before any of us could say anything further, the door to the study swung open again.

Jake stood there, jaw tight and expression unreadable. Coop hovered right behind him, his gray-green eyes were fixed on me and filled with apology. Bubba stood back, his arms folded and his expression grim. Neither of them wanted to be there with Jake. Not right now.

Probably didn't want to be painted with the same brush.

Jake swept the room with a glance, pausing only when he got to me. His eyes cooled as he focused on me. He blew out a breath then his gaze dipped to the glass in my hand. "Really?" He sliced at me with one word. "You're going for hard liquor now?"

"Watch it, Jake." Rachel surged forward, getting between me and Jake like a lioness. "You already set fire to one bridge tonight. Maybe avoid torching whatever you have left."

He barely even paused on her, his gaze staying fixed on me. "Why didn't you just tell me?"

"I did tell you," I snapped. God, he made me so mad. "Or correction, I tried to tell you. Then you decided to be a bitch about it and tell everyone else."

Jake flinched like I'd slapped him.

"But to be clear," I continued. "It was *my* business. Mine and Mathieu's. Not yours. Not yours to give permission or to pass judgment or to announce to everyone in the damn senior class. You want to flaunt your sexcapades, feel free. I know *none* of you are shy."

Bubba winced and Coop's mouth tightened. I couldn't see Archie from where I faced Jake, but I could imagine his expression.

"So—you just decide to act like none of this affects me?"

I pressed my tongue to the back of my teeth. "How do I say this?" A part of me wanted to make peace, to smooth this over, because that was better than fighting. I hated fighting. But when Jake snorted while glaring at me, I lost that particular battle. "I don't care."

Those three words slashed through the air between all of us.

"I don't *care* how it affects you. Just like you didn't give a damn about how you sleeping with Maria or Sharon or Laura or Patty or any of those girls affected me."

"Bullshit—" It was Jake who snapped this time, stalking forward, but I was too damn angry to back off. Not now.

"Why?" I demanded, glaring at him. "Because I'm a *girl*? Does that make the rules different for *me?*"

Jake clenched his hands into fists at his side. "You slept with him." He practically spat out the words.

Mathieu took a slow, measured step forward until he was right at my side. Jake might outweigh him and have more muscle mass, but Mathieu didn't back down at all. "You just wanted to make me look foolish." It wasn't a question. "It never occurred to you that it would hurt Frankie, did it?"

A muscle twitched in Jake's jaw, but he didn't answer.

"Guess we can take that a yes," Rachel said with a sigh.

The pounding of my heart was a dull beat in my throat. It had slowed from anxious racing to just sick little thuds. I wasn't sure whether I wanted to slap Jake, punch him, throw my drink in his face, or just run away and cry.

Honestly, at the moment, it might have been all of the above. He looked at me again, something raw in his eyes now. Not rage. Not jealousy. Just a hollow realization. God, we were so shattered.

All of us.

He opened his mouth, then closed it. One harsh exhale later, he said, "I didn't mean for it to go that far."

Silence stripped us all bare.

"But you did," I said, all the tears I didn't want to shed

clogging my throat. As much as I believed he didn't mean to do it, didn't mean it didn't hurt. "You did."

I held his gaze for another long moment. He didn't say anything else and I didn't want to talk anymore. Twisting, I handed Archie his drink back then stepped past Jake with Mathieu keeping pace with me. He never stopped touching me. Never stopped supporting me. Rachel followed us both as Coop then Bubba stepped aside.

Unspoken apologies lingered in the air already stinking with regret, testosterone, and too many bad damn decisions. Behind me, I heard Coop say, "Goddammit Jake, you need to fix this."

Then the study door closed behind us. I didn't stop walking until we were halfway down the hall again. The music from the party filtered through the windows, still thumping, still bright, like nothing had changed.

Except... *everything* had changed. I stopped and turned to Rachel and Mathieu.

"So what now?" Rachel asked.

"I'm going back out there." I hadn't even been sure of my answer before I actually said it. "Head high. Shoulders back. Let them look or talk or speculate or whatever the hell they want to do. I'm not ashamed of anything."

Brow furrowed, Mathieu tipped his head. "Are you sure? You have nothing to prove to anyone."

Except to myself. "I have nothing to hide."

Rachel grinned, but the smile didn't quite touch the grimness in her eyes. "You never did. Besides, maybe someone will say something stupid and I can smack a bitch."

All at once, the knot in my chest loosened. "Rach?"

"Hmm?"

I clasped Mathieu's hand, treading my fingers with his. "Thank you for being my friend."

"You're welcome." She was so magnanimous. "I'm a treasure, never forget it."

A real laugh broke out of me. "I wouldn't dare." When I held out my free hand to her, she clasped it and they moved with me back out to the party.

TWENTY-EIGHT

ARCHIE

The door clicked shut behind Frankie, Rachel, and Mathieu. The silence they left behind was heavier than anything else said in this room.

Jake stood there like he wasn't sure how he got there, his fists still clenched, chest rising and falling like he'd just sprinted ten blocks and still couldn't outrun himself. Coop leaned against the door, arms crossed and a stony look taking over his usually easy-going demeanor. Bubba hadn't moved from the place he'd taken near the cold fireplace upon coming into the room. He seemed shellshocked by the bomb that had just detonated in the middle of our lives.

I couldn't say he was wrong. The fact we were all still standing was surprising enough. Downing the last of the whiskey in the glass, I tried not to think about how I wished Frankie had taken a drink. It burned its way to my stomach. God, I needed the burn.

Crossing to the bar, I refilled my drink. "You shouldn't have done it."

Jake let out a bitter laugh. "So now it's my fault?"

I turned then, leaned back against the bar and looked at

him. Really looked. Jake hadn't always been the easiest of guys to get to know. From the first moment I met him, he'd been territorial where Frankie was concerned. It wasn't hard to see why. Except—she wasn't dating him. She wasn't dating any of us.

But Jake was a power player on the football team, could keep up with me in engineering and was right up there in most of the honors classes with Frankie. He was smart as hell. Or usually, he was. Right now?

The charming hardass was gone and there was something a lot darker and cracked in his eyes than had been there before. "You aren't mad she didn't tell us," I said, particularly because she had to have told *him*. How else would he know? "You're mad she didn't *pick* you."

That, I got. Was I mad that some guy we'd never even heard of had his hands on her? Had kissed her, much less had sex with her? Yeah. I was pissed. Because I wanted to be that guy.

So yeah, I got it.

His jaw tensed. "That's not—"

"It is," Coop cut in sharply. "It is *exactly* that."

Jake looked at him like he'd been slapped. "You're supposed to have my back."

"I *do*," Coop said. "Which is why I'm telling you the truth. You screwed this up. Badly. I think we all get it. I hate that this guy has that in with her, but what you did? Right now, I wouldn't be surprised if she cut us off again."

Me neither. Still wasn't going to let that happen.

Bubba finally spoke, voice quiet. "You didn't just humiliate her, Jake. You made her *unsafe*. You made Mathieu unsafe. You know how far that kind of rumor travels."

Jake looked down. "I didn't mean for it to be like that."

"Intent doesn't erase impact," I said. "You know better."

He did. We all did.

High school came with its own etiquette and unspoken rules. I'd grown up with kids who made a regular habit of destroying the reputations of others around them just to prove a point. Leaving behind private school and privilege hadn't meant that I was abandoning everything I knew. Kids in public schools did the same shit. They just did it with less finesse.

Image was everything. Control was currency. And Frankie... she was the one thing none of us could control. None of us *should* control her either. As much as I hated her sleeping with Frenchy, she had a right to do whatever she wanted.

I walked over to him slowly. Not threatening. Just close enough that he had to hear me, had to really *listen*.

"She still loves us, you know," I said. "Not the same way, clearly. Not like *that*. If she did, maybe she would have noticed us long before now. I'm not proud of it, Jake. I hate that she picked someone else. But she loved us enough to stay quiet about our secrets. Even when we messed up— hell, especially when we screwed it up. She stayed quiet. She shielded us. What did you do? Torched her reputation in front of half the damn school."

Jake's throat bobbed.

"But here's the part you're not really going to like," I continued. "She's still going to walk out there, head high, with people whispering, and she's going to win. Because she's Frankie. And you?"

I let the words settle.

"You're the guy who couldn't handle losing her without making sure all of us, including her, lost something too."

Jake closed his eyes. Tight. Like maybe if he kept them shut long enough, this would all go away.

It wouldn't.

I turned away from him and grabbed the door handle.

"You want to fix this?" I asked. "Start by apologizing. Not just for what you said. For the *why* behind it. For the part of you that thought you owned a piece of her."

I opened the door.

"And Jake?"

He looked up.

"If you ever pull a stunt like that again…" I smiled, but there was no warmth in it. "You won't be welcome in this house. And when I'm finished, I won't be the only one who sees you differently."

Then I left him there.

Because there were still people out by the pool waiting for a show. Still eyes that would follow Frankie, still mouths ready to spin stories that weren't theirs to tell.

But I wasn't going to let her face them alone.

Not anymore.

I found her on the patio, standing near the pool like a queen surveying her court, Rachel at one side, Mathieu at the other. People still whispered. But no one dared approach.

She looked over her shoulder when I stepped outside.

I didn't say anything.

She didn't need me to.

She just gave me a tiny nod. The kind that meant thanks, and don't push your luck, and maybe, just maybe, we were still on the same team.

Frankie didn't look at me again after that nod. She didn't have to. At the same time, I couldn't miss the way her spine was still locked straight, too straight. Like she'd coiled herself so tight she might shatter if anyone pushed the wrong way. The whispers had softened, sure, but they hadn't stopped. And everyone was still watching like she was a live grenade with a mascara wand.

No.

Not tonight.

Not *my* house.

I glanced at Rachel. She raised one perfect eyebrow, like she knew I was about to do something reckless and was already half-proud.

Good.

I cut a glance to Coop, who had trailed me out and was now standing awkwardly near the bar, clutching a cold Coke like he wanted it to be a teleportation device.

Right. He might not be much help at the moment. Fine. I'd do it myself.

I jogged up onto the pool deck, grabbed the mic from the DJ booth we hadn't used since the first hour of the party, and gave it a tap. The sharp feedback squeal made heads whip around, conversations pause, and several people visibly wince.

Perfect.

"Ladies and gentlemen," I said into the mic, voice smooth, rich, *loud*, "and all gorgeous troublemakers in between."

A smattering of laughs. Confusion. Curiosity. Frankie turned slowly, arms crossed, head tilted in that way she did when she was bracing for chaos. I gave her a wink.

"Since we seem to have forgotten the purpose of this evening—and have instead turned it into a half-baked high school tabloid—I figured I'd remind you all that this is, in fact, a *party*."

A few cheers, weak and scattered.

I tsked into the mic. "No, no, no. That was lukewarm at best. This is *my* house, *Frankie's* party, and you are all dangerously close to being the worst crowd this zip code has ever seen."

Rachel whooped. Bubba let out a bark of laughter. The DJ hit the volume on the music. Good job!

The bass thumped louder. The beat kicked up. Lights that had been set to moody golds and muted pinks shifted suddenly—neon blues and sharp white pulses painting the backyard like a beachside rave.

I pointed to the pool. "I want cannonballs, I want bad decisions, I want someone to start a synchronized swimming team in the next ten minutes."

Then, my voice dropped just enough to draw focus like a magnet. "And if any of you are still more interested in talking *about* Frankie than talking *to* her, let me remind you—she didn't light the match."

I let that hang. Sharp. Clear.

"She's just fireproof."

There was a beat of silence.

Then someone—maybe Maria, maybe that sophomore who always tried too hard—started clapping. Then more joined in. Laughter, cheers, a whistle from the shallow end. Someone launched a pool float like a missile.

The energy flipped like a switch.

And Frankie?

She smiled. Not big. Not for everyone. Just for me.

It was sharp-edged and weary and a little disbelieving, like she couldn't decide whether to kiss me or kill me. I raised my brows. Offered a shrug. *You're welcome.*

Setting the mic aside, I jogged back down and crossed over to her and held out a hand.

No mic now. Just my voice and her name.

"Dance with me."

She blinked. "You're kidding."

I stepped closer. "Have I ever looked like I'm kidding?"

Rachel groaned behind her. "Constantly. It's infuriating."

Frankie still hadn't moved. "You hate dancing."

"I hate standing still more."

Another beat.

Then, finally, she took my hand.

We didn't really *dance* so much as sway lazily near the fire pit while the chaos bloomed around us—someone did, in fact, start synchronized splashing, and someone else found the fog machine. But I kept her close, one hand on her waist, the other twined through her fingers.

"Epic move," she murmured, just loud enough for me to hear.

I leaned in, brushed a strand of hair behind her ear. "You deserve nothing less."

She didn't pull away.

I didn't let go.

And as the lights spun wild across the backyard and the gossip drowned under a tidal wave of bass and tequila, I thought—maybe this was what power looked like.

Not control.

Not fear.

Choice.

I'd choose her. Every time.

TWENTY-NINE

FRANKIE

I woke up to a text from Rachel, five missed calls from my mom beginning the night before, three absolutely starving cats who were wasting away to nothing thanks to me not getting up with the sun. There was even a bag with two apple fritters in it taped to my back door with a note that read: *Eat, you're a war hero - R.*

They smelled great. But I was still on autopilot. I'd left my phone in do not disturb while I fed the cats, made coffee, ate half of a fritter before throwing myself into a shower. It wasn't exactly *late* morning but it was just barely eight. My brain started winding up as soon as the hot water hit me.

Everything from the night before rushed back in. The stares. The whispering. *Jake.* The study. *Jake again.* Archie with the microphone playing it up like he was some drunk socialite Bruce Wayne capturing everyone's attention and more, their obedience. The whole tone of the party flipped on its axis because he took up my defense.

The chaos didn't rattle me so much. It was just so *Archie* and then he asked me to dance. We had, several times. I danced with Mathieu too, but Archie kept coming back and by the time Mathieu and I were leaving, I wasn't as mad anymore.

While I could handle the chaos, the quiet left me floundering. Today was the day *after* and that always meant choices. It meant social media posts. It meant the casual little digs and the gossip that would roll through the school like some majestic dominoes display tumbling brick by brick.

After my shower, I took turns drinking my coffee and drying off before I got dressed. Coffee made the brain cells work. I would need them working today for sure. Once I was dressed in shorts and a tank top, my damp hair combed and hanging free to dry, I finally started scrolling through the messages on my phone.

Mathieu sent me a text around midnight right as I was falling asleep. *Let me treat you to breakfast tomorrow. No secrets. Just us. Okay?*

I hadn't answered him then. Mostly cause my brain had been shutting down, but we'd talked some when I drove him back to his host family's house. Didn't make the knots in my stomach any less tense.

Back in the kitchen, I refilled my coffee and finished the first fritter. I wrapped the other one up in its paper bag. I would save it for later. The cats had begun to scatter after they'd eaten, though Tiddles hung out with me, sitting on the windowsill and grooming himself.

It was a little weird how disconnected I felt at the moment. I wasn't broken or sick. I didn't feel like I'd won anything or survived it either. I was just *me*. A little more scarred, a little more alone, and little more certain that no matter what I did, my best friends might not be that for much longer.

At least, not all of them.

Jake.

A long sigh tore out of me, but it did nothing to ease the weight.

After draining the coffee, I washed out my cup, then checked Mom's messages. She was *still* away on business and wouldn't be back until Wednesday or Thursday.

Shocker.

I would need to do the shopping. There were a couple of things she wanted me to take care of, including dropping a couple of her dresses off at the cleaners. Rolling my eyes, I just sent a thumbs up to her so she would know I'd read them. Somehow, I doubted she was going to care much about a response right now. Done, I sent a message to Mathieu to let him know I was on my way.

By the time I made it outside, the day was already warm enough to make me sweat. The inside of my car was a damn furnace but I rolled all the windows down so I could let it out while the air conditioner coughed up some cooler air. Summer in Texas, even late summer, was its own personal circle of hell. If not for swimming pools, water parks, and ice-cold malls, it would be unbearable.

Mathieu was outside when I pulled up. It was funny, he looked cool and crisp like the weather didn't faze him. Grinning, he slid right into the passenger seat and leaned over to cup my chin with his hand. A brush of a kiss, light as butterfly wings, and then another, firmer kiss that had me curling my toes in my shoes.

"Bonjour chérie," he murmured against my lips before nuzzling another swoon worthy kiss.

"Bonjour," I answered with a little smile.

"Good day?" he asked as he pulled on his seat belt.

"It's definitely better now."

With the door closed and the a/c chasing out the swirl of warmer air he brought in with him, I could enjoy the crispness of his cologne. He didn't crowd me or reach for my hand, just settled back while I started driving.

It had only been a few weeks but it was already familiar and easy. That felt a little dangerous. Shaking that uncertainty off, I glanced over at him when we reached the light at the entrance to his host family's subdivision. "Where are we going?"

"I found a place," he said, a smile curving his lips. "It's a bit odd, but according to the reviews, it serves Vietnamese coffee and waffles shaped like dinosaurs."

Odd? I blinked. "That sounds like a fever dream."

Mathieu chuckled. "The reviews were all positive, though they mentioned the owner wears the obscenely bright Crocs and likes to speak in puns."

A real snort escaped me. "And you're sure all the reviews were *positive?*"

"Want me to put in the address?"

"Please." I handed him my phone after I unlocked it. The silence that followed as my phone directed me out to the highway. The place wasn't close, and I was okay with that. We had time.

The silence that followed wasn't awkward, though. It was... calm. Like we'd both earned a breath after surviving the storm.

Still, I had to say it.

"Mathieu?"

"Yes?"

"About last night."

He didn't flinch. Just waited.

"I'm sorry it got messy."

He shook his head. "*You* don't owe me an apology. Jake does. The rest of them do."

"But I didn't want that for you," I said quietly. "To be dragged into my drama."

I took the onramp and Mathieu waited for me to merge with the traffic as I floored it before he answered.

"You're not *drama*, Frankie," he said. "You're someone worth showing up for." Then he smiled—small, quiet, but honest.

And I felt it all the way to my ribs. I didn't answer right away. It just didn't seem fair. For him. "I want to say I don't know why they are behaving that way." But that would be a lie. "A few months ago, I had no idea that they chased off any guy who might have asked me out."

Every single thing they'd done the night before had just underscored the truth Rachel had shared with me. Well, except for Archie. He was different. I couldn't put my finger on exactly what. It was almost like he counterbalanced Jake's increasingly frustrating temper with a kind of sardonic playfulness.

"They are jealous," Mathieu said without an ounce of teasing or jest. "All four of them."

"But if they *liked* me, why date other girls?" Being told that I was oblivious was not really an answer to me. Not when I knew damn good and well not a single one of them had been chaste. That they'd enjoyed discovering sex. They'd *talked* to me about it. Trusted me, at least with their choices. Apparently, I wasn't to be trusted with mine.

Mathieu sighed. "*Chérie*, I will not say *all* men, but many of us are not terribly bright where women are concerned. At least not at first. Most of us have to learn, to listen, and to love."

The last word sent a shiver up my spine. We'd never said that particular word.

"Whether you care for the thought or not, you do love them." He sounded so matter-of-fact about it. "They clearly love you, though—I disagree with how they show it. There is a saying about a boy pulling a girl's pigtails when they are younger, it means the boy likes her."

I made a face. "Yes, though, I find it weird that we encourage the concept of boys being 'mean' to prove they like someone." Jake and Coop never pulled my pigtails, or in my case, my ponytail. Probably because I would have punched them and they knew it.

"It is not so much about encouraging a boy to be 'mean' as you say but because we are possessive. We want to be the object of your attention. We like to be pursued."

That made me *laugh*. "Seriously?"

"Oh, *oui*," Mathieu said with an easy smile. He pressed a hand to his heart. "We like to be chased, to be adored, to be wanted. That does not mean we don't like chasing as well."

"So, it's okay for you to have other girls?"

"Only if we are both open to such." He shrugged. "Commitments come in different shapes and sizes. Hmm..." He tapped a finger to his lips. "I am saying this poorly. So let me say it directly, it might be easier for both of us."

My stomach dropped and my heart pounded. "Okay."

"Do not react to what you *think* I am saying, listen to exactly what I say, please?" He brushed a hand against my thigh and I nodded. We were still a good fifteen minutes away from the cafe he'd found.

"I'll do my best."

"*Merci*." He took a breath, then said, "We are friends, you and I. We have many things in common and we enjoy talking, learning about each other, and sharing new experiences. *Oui?*"

"*Oui.*" That was not hard to agree with at all. "You're a lot of fun."

He answered me with a grin. "As are you. I have truly enjoyed getting to know you these past few months. Enjoyed that you let me touch you."

That sent a scalding hot blush racing over my whole body. "No complaints here." It had been awkward, there was no getting around that.

Another smile. "We have never discussed exclusivity, merely that we continue to enjoy each other."

There went that sinking feeling again.

"I am not saying we need to discuss it now, however, I will flirt with other women—some men too—it is just how I am." The directness in the statement wasn't lost on me. "I will not, however, pursue another sexual relationship without discussing it with you first."

Oh.

"As I would expect if you wished something similar, you will also discuss it with me."

"I—"

"This is not judgment, Frankie." For a moment, it was like he chastised me, no matter how gently. "You told Jake about us because you were in a position where that might have been necessary."

Grimacing, I nodded. I couldn't really deny that. "It was —a little out of control."

"Accepted." Just like that, no temper at all. "I am only asking if you wish to pursue anything further with any of them, that you let me know first so we may talk. They are not as open as I am. I want you to only have positive experiences."

Direct. To the point. A shiver raced over my skin. "I really don't know what I want at the moment."

"That is fair." He quieted as I followed the directions to leave the highway and then we were pulling into the parking lot of what looked like a quaint little diner that occupied a corner of the strip mall.

After I parked, I twisted to look at him. "I like you."

He grinned. "I like you too."

A laugh escaped me. "Yes, you've shown me. We're being direct, right now?"

"Always." The emphasis on that word steadied me.

"Then right now, I don't know what I feel for them. Exactly." Rachel had called it. I loved them. "They are—they have always been my best friends. I miss them like I'd miss my arms. But the last few months have shown me that we have a lot we've never talked about. Jake's choices yesterday..."

They hurt. A lot.

"What I am trying to say," I pressed forward, then cleared my throat. "I don't want a sexual relationship with anyone else yet." It was weird enough to say that, like I might want another at all. Then all I had to think about was the way Jake had kissed me and... Yeah. I pushed that out of my head. "I don't know if that's going to change. I don't know if any of us will forgive each other after yesterday."

There were so many issues littering the ground between us. So much fallout.

"You don't have to decide anything," Mathieu said, leaning over to cup my face. "But don't ever be afraid to talk to me."

"Do you want to be open so you can date others?" It might gut me, but Mathieu didn't owe me anything.

"Not at the moment," Mathieu said easily. "No. It will

be a decision we make together, Francesca. Or we won't make it at all. *Oui?*"

I hated my full name so much but he made it sound like an endearment. Covering his hand on my cheek, I smiled. "*Oui.*"

He pressed a kiss to my forehead, lingering there a moment before dipping to brush another over my lips. "Good. Now, no more worrying or hurting yourself."

"Deal." My smile this time was real. "Dinosaur waffles?"

He laughed.

Unbuckling my seatbelt, I shut off the car before I opened the door and we were both climbing out. I let myself believe—for just one morning—that it might really be that simple.

THIRTY

COOP

By Sunday afternoon, the place still smelled like chlorine, cheap rum, and a mistake we all watched happen in slow motion. Or maybe that was just me. None of us had left. The only difference from every other back to school party was the lack of Frankie being present. She'd left with the new boyfriend, followed swiftly by Rachel. As far as I knew, we hadn't seen or heard from her since.

While Jake hadn't left, he hadn't really hung out with the rest of us. Not really. Not in the way he should've. He'd disappeared into one of the guest rooms after the party like a ghost who knew better than to haunt the rooms we were in, but not brave enough to leave the house.

I gave him space. Then I ran out of excuses.

"Talk," I said around noon, arms crossed, leaning against the doorframe like that would hold the tension back. It didn't.

Jake was sitting on the edge of the bed, elbows on his knees, staring at the floor like it had personally wronged him. He didn't look up.

"She slept with him," he said flatly. Did he think if he said it enough it would *change*?

"That's not the bombshell you think it is." Or it shouldn't be. Still, I'd told myself I would listen. With that in mind, I focused on him.

"It's not—" He finally looked at me. "It's not just that she did. It's that she didn't *tell* us. Tell *me*. Not even after."

I let out a slow breath, trying not to roll my eyes. "She didn't *owe* any of us that, man."

"We talked to her. We told her." His jaw clenched. "We were friends."

Maybe that was the problem, not that I said that aloud. "And now we're all stuck in the wreckage of what you did with that friendship," I snapped, then pinched the bridge of my nose.

He flinched. Just barely. But it was enough.

"I get it," I said, softer now. "You were hurt. You were jealous. You didn't know what to do with the feelings we've all had to deny because she didn't seem to notice." Holy shit did I get that. "So you exploded."

"I didn't mean to humiliate her."

"But you did." No matter how much I got it, I still wanted to slug him.

He didn't say anything. Just pressed the heels of his hands into his eyes like he could scrub the memory away. Like he could pretend the look on Frankie's face hadn't leveled all of us.

I wanted to be madder.

God, I *should* have been madder.

But being pissed changed *nothing*. What we needed to do right now was *repairing* that damage and rebuilding that connection. But as Sunday turned into evening, Jake dropped me back off at home. Archie and Bubba stopped answering group texts. Frankie wasn't home—her car wasn't there. Her car and her mom's cars were both missing.

Frankie was just *gone*.

No replies. No location tag. Just radio silence and the echo of that party still hanging in the corners of my head. She had every right to disappear for a day. I knew that. Hell, I respected it. But it still made my chest ache in a way that felt like punishment.

Because I hadn't said anything, not when it counted. Not when Jake opened his mouth and let the lie-that-was-also-true fall out. I hadn't stepped between them. I hadn't made it stop.

That was almost worse than the fight itself.

By Monday morning, I was raw.

Not tired. Not angry.

Just *done*.

Backpack slung over one shoulder, pretending like this was just another school day, I leaned against the side of her car as I waited for her to come out. The profound gratitude that ripped through me when I saw the car there had damn near taken me out at the knees.

I hadn't heard a word from Frankie since the party. Not a text. Not a meme. Not even the usual angry reaction when I sent her that picture of a raccoon wearing Crocs. Radio silence. Which would've been fine—normal even, for someone trying to reclaim her peace—but I knew her better than that. Silence wasn't Frankie's style. Not with me.

That's how I knew she was still hurting and maybe—just maybe—from *me* too.

When I heard the familiar jingle of her keys, I forced myself to not straighten up abruptly. Taking a deep breath,

I waited for her to spot me. Her expression transformed, briefly, to one of surprise. Then her face evened out.

Calm. Collected. Guarded.

"Morning," I said, trying to keep my voice steady.

"Hey," she said. She didn't smile. But she didn't flip me off either. Small win.

"You mind giving me a ride?"

Frankie arched one brow. "We doing this?"

"I mean, it's Monday," I said with a half-shrug. "I still don't have a car. So... if you wouldn't mind." *Please don't mind.*

She stared at me for a second, like she was weighing her options. Maybe deciding how much she wanted to punch me versus how much she didn't. Frankie had a pretty wicked right hook, but she had her backpack in that hand, so maybe I'd only get the left.

Finally, she exhaled and all the tension bled out of me. "Fine, but you owe me pizza or something."

"Done." *Whatever you want.* "Whenever. You name it. We'll make it happen."

I opened the driver's side door on reflex after she unlocked the car. When I held out my hand for her backpack, she gave me a brief look before she handed it over. "Thanks."

"Frankie?"

She stiffened and I nearly swore. But she braced a hand on the open door and met my gaze. The green of her eyes really was downright stunning. Frankie herself was a stunner, beautiful, long-legged even if she was shorter than the rest of us, lean, but fit and trim with a sweetheart face and a brain that didn't quit—unless it came to us flirting.

"I'm sorry." The words came out on a soft, slow exhale. "I'm really sorry."

She dipped her chin and blinked twice before she tugged her sunglasses out. Thankfully, she didn't slide them on and hide those eyes from me. "For what?"

"For not stopping it," I said. "For not stepping in when Jake opened his mouth. For letting you walk back into that party alone."

Her jaw tightened, just slightly. "You didn't make him say it."

"No," I said. "But I didn't stop him either."

The silence stretched again.

"I kept thinking about the look on your face," I said, voice lower now. "After. In the study. I've known you since we were five, and I've never seen you look like that."

She still didn't say anything.

"But I don't want that to be the last thing you remember when you look at me," I finished.

That got her.

She lifted her head then, enough to meet my gaze. The hurt was still there. So was the exhaustion. But the anger was gone.

I'd take it.

"We gonna stand here until graduation or are we going to school?" she asked, voice dry.

"Depends." I huffed a laugh, shoulders easing for the first time since Saturday night. I circled the car to the passenger seat and put both backpacks in the back seat before I climbed in.

"On what?" she asked as she clipped her own seatbelt on and started the car.

"How much coffee have you had?"

The curve of her lips robbed me of breath, but there was the smile I adored. "Nowhere near enough."

"Warning accepted. I'm texting Archie right now to

make sure he gets yours—" Then before I could think on it too much, I added. "What does Frenc—what does Mat drink? I'll make Archie get him one too."

Her smile deepened and the air between us shifted as she backed out of her parking spot. "Mathieu is not a fan of American coffee."

I gaped at her. "For real?"

"I know," she said, sniffing once. "You should be grateful he isn't perfect."

We were far from a full repair for the damage that had been done, but the door was open and I was welcome again. Right now, that was more than enough.

"I'll bow down and do a damn prayer." Then because I could resist, I added, "I *love* American coffee."

She laughed.

That was more than enough.

THIRTY-ONE

Monday hit like a poorly timed pop quiz—unexpected, irritating, and laced with passive-aggressive energy.

People weren't staring the same way they were at the party, but they were *still* watching. Just quieter now. Slanted glances over locker doors. A beat too long at the water fountain. And the whispers had evolved into speculation—*what happened, who was involved, was it really her and Mathieu, did Jake punch someone, did Archie host a secret trial in his dad's whiskey lounge?*

That last one might've been true. But none of it mattered as much as it did Saturday. I'd already lived through the explosion. The aftershocks? I could handle them.

Especially with Rachel at my side.

"People keep staring," I muttered as we made our way to third period.

Rachel didn't even blink. "Let them. They're just upset you had better drama than Netflix this weekend."

"Pretty sure I *was* Netflix this weekend."

She smirked. "Then start charging subscription fees."

I rolled my eyes but didn't argue. Mostly because a small part of me liked that she kept walking a step ahead—shoulders back, hair perfect, her aura set to do not cross unless you want your feelings rearranged.

Backup. That's what she was. Not just snark and fashion. Real backup.

And today? I needed it.

Because somewhere between first bell and lunch, the roses showed up again.

Instead of being on my car, though, they were tucked into the grate of my locker. Same corner. Same folded white card with no name, just the same slanted writing and another simple sentence:

"Still rooting for you."

I stared at it longer than I meant to. For once, I was glad Coop got stuck talking to Mrs. Fajardo. Normally I would have waited, but I needed the break. Even for a couple of minutes, a breather.

Rachel popped up to lean over my shoulder. "Alright, at this point, it's either a secret admirer or a very emotionally intelligent ghost."

"Could be both," I said, taking the card and sliding the rose into my bag. "Friendly poltergeist who follows teen melodrama."

She narrowed her eyes. "Could also be Archie."

"Too obvious," I said automatically.

She raised a brow. "So, not obvious enough to *not* consider it?"

I ignored her.

I didn't want to think about Archie right now. Not after the way he'd gone full Gatsby at his own party just to reset the narrative. Not after the way he handed me that drink in the study like it was an offering.

Not after the look on his face when I didn't drink it.

Instead, I focused on the familiar warmth settling at my side—Mathieu, appearing like he always did, hands in his pockets, that soft, slightly crooked smile on his face like I was still a good thing in a very messy world.

"Hey," he said, easily. He'd gotten a different ride into school this morning, because he had to be in earlier. I hadn't told Coop that at the time, but he had asked about getting Mathieu coffee and that was big.

"Hey," I said, trying not to smile too wide.

Rachel took that as her cue to wander toward the caf. Subtle like a wrecking ball.

Mathieu leaned in just slightly. "Can I walk you to lunch?"

"Sure," I said, bumping my shoulder lightly against his. "Unless it means wading through more people asking who you are and why we made eye contact."

"I don't mind the attention," he said. "As long as I'm standing next to you."

Okay. That wasn't fair. That should not have made my pulse skip like that. We walked down the hall, not quite holding hands, not quite *not*, and the looks didn't matter so much anymore.

Until Archie appeared around the corner near the trophy case, flanked by Bubba.

Of course.

They both looked like they were trying *very hard* to be casual. Bubba had a protein bar. Archie had a coke.

"Frankie," Archie said, slowing. "Got a minute?"

Mathieu glanced at me like *you good?*

I gave him a tiny nod, then turned to face the boys.

"What's up?"

Archie shoved his hands in his pockets, eyes unusually soft. "Wanted to say I'm sorry. For the way things went down. For not stopping Jake sooner. For getting involved with the interrogation."

Bubba added, "And for not telling him to shut up about it before he said anything. I was there. I could've... I should've said something."

I looked between the two of them. Bubba, sincere and solid. Archie, unreadable but trying—really *trying*—to let the wall down for once.

"Thanks," I said finally. "For saying that."

Neither of them pushed it. No guilt-trip. No expectation of forgiveness. They just nodded and stepped aside as I kept walking.

But even then... I saw Jake, further down the hall.

Alone. Sitting on the bench near the counselor's office, pretending to scroll his phone, looking like someone had kicked him in the chest and he still hadn't recovered.

He didn't look up.

Didn't say a word.

And maybe that was the most honest thing he'd done all week.

If Monday had been about testing the waters, Tuesday felt like wading directly into the current. Stronger. Colder. But not impossible.

Especially not with Coop waiting at my car just like the day before. It was *normal*. But it still didn't feel normal. The look he gave me said "I'm here," and I could accept that for now.

We walked into school together. Not quite shoulder to shoulder, but close. A few people noticed. More than a few whispered. But I kept my head up.

Coop stayed with me all the way to the cafeteria. I wasn't sure if I was really ready to be back at the table. But I also knew if I didn't show up now, the narrative would keep writing itself without me.

So I walked in.

And stopped short.

Mathieu was already there.

Sitting at our usual table like it was *his* usual table, an iced tea in hand, posture relaxed but not cocky. Bubba sat beside him, tapping something out on his phone. Rachel was mid-rant about Mrs. Kline's "butchered syllabus and toxic energy," and Archie had apparently decided to be normal today—well, normal for *him*, which meant classic rock band t-shirt, faded out jeans, and a tray of coffees.

He caught my eye as I approached and held out one like a peace offering.

"Morning, Frankie."

I raised a brow. "Am I allowed to sit, or do I need a vetting process again?"

Archie smirked, already pulling out the seat beside him. "You passed."

I took the drink without comment, but my lips twitched.

I slid into the chair between Rachel and Mathieu, and for a second, it was... good. Easy.

Mathieu leaned in. "I saved your spot."

That did things to my heart I wasn't proud of.

Coop dropped into the seat across from me and gave me a look—part protective big brother, part dude-still-holding-emotional-glue. "You good?"

"For now," I said. "Maybe until last period."

Bubba added without looking up, "Try to avoid punching anyone before noon. That's all I ask."

I would've laughed, except that's when it happened.

From the table just behind us, I heard it—half-sneeze, half-sneer.

"Achoo... slut."

I went still.

No one laughed. Not really. Just the kind of breathy, gross chuckles that always follow guys who peak at seventeen and don't know it yet.

Then came the second hit—louder, this time. Clearer.

"Careful, Frankie. Start charging for it and you could afford better shoes."

That voice.

Derek. Again.

Same Derek who tried it at the party. Same Derek who apparently hadn't learned what happened when you mouth off.

I didn't move yet.

Didn't have to.

Because out of nowhere—*literally nowhere*—Jake appeared.

I don't know where he'd been. Didn't even know he could move that fast.

All I saw was the moment he launched forward like something inside him had finally snapped.

A chair flew. Someone screamed. Derek barely had time to open his mouth before Jake *plowed* into him, shoulder-first, knocking both of them into the next table. Trays crashed to the floor. Juice cartons exploded.

Gasps rippled through the room.

And then chaos.

"Jake!" Bubba was already up, trying to drag him back by the collar. "Jesus, man—*stop!*"

Jake didn't answer. He wasn't even swinging anymore

—just had Derek pinned, teeth gritted, face twisted into something raw and cracked open.

"I told you to shut your *mouth* about her."

Archie was on his feet. Coop, too. Rachel was already in front of me, shielding like a reflex.

But all I could do was stare.

Jake.

It wasn't the punch that hit me the hardest. It was the *look* in his eyes when he said it. Fury, yeah. But also… shame.

Like he couldn't take back what he'd done before, but this—this was him trying.

Trying *too late*, maybe.

But trying.

Teachers burst into the cafeteria seconds later with a school resource officer coming in from the other side. Someone blew a whistle like we were in gym class, which was impressively useless.

Bubba finally wrestled Jake off Derek. Derek was swearing, bleeding from the mouth, and already blaming everyone but himself. But no one was listening.

Especially not me. Jake looked around the room, breathing hard, eyes landing on me as they dragged him away.

"I'm sorry," he said hoarsely. Then they were gone.

And the cafeteria buzzed like a kicked hornet's nest.

I sat there, heart thudding in my chest like it was trying to escape, and slowly reached for my coffee.

"I hate Tuesdays," I muttered.

Rachel handed me half her muffin without asking.

By noon, the story had already mutated into three different versions.

In one, Jake broke Derek's nose with a single punch. In

another, he slammed him into the vending machine and shattered the glass. In the last and most dramatic retelling, he whispered *"You deserve this"* before delivering a flying kick like some vigilante from a CW reboot.

None of those were true.

The truth was quieter. He'd snapped. Lost it. Let it all out in one sharp, irreversible moment.

And now he was gone.

Suspended.

Coop grabbed my arm on our way out of fourth period. His expression was unreadable, but his eyes were tired in that way only people caught in the middle ever really know.

"Hey," he said, voice low, already scanning the hallway like he didn't want to make a scene. "You hear?"

"Yeah," I said. "Suspension?"

"Three days," he confirmed. "Maybe more. Depends on how Derek's parents push it."

I pressed my fingers into my temple. "Of course."

Coop shifted awkwardly. "Bubba's dad showed up. He's advocating for Jake. Said he'd talk to the school board, make sure they keep it internal."

That surprised me. "Bubba's *dad?*" Maybe it shouldn't have, I knew Jake's dad and Bubba's were friends and Jake's dad was still on a base in Germany.

"Yeah," Coop said, a little amazed himself. "Said no one should be punished for protecting someone who's been through enough already. I think he meant you."

I didn't know what to say to that.

The idea of grown-ups stepping into this mess was already foreign enough. The idea that they might be *on my side?*

It just made the knot in my chest pull tighter.

"Thanks for telling me," I said, already backing away. "I have to get to lunch."

"Frankie—" Coop hesitated. "If you want to talk. Or yell. Or, like, rage-eat pudding cups again…"

I managed half a smile. "I'll find you."

Lunch was a blur. Rachel had claimed us a table near the courtyard windows. Bubba sat beside her, unusually quiet. Mathieu had an arm draped casually across the back of my chair, trying to make me feel grounded, present. It almost worked.

Until Archie appeared, perfectly pressed and slightly rumpled, as if he'd just stepped out of a courtroom or a Calvin Klein ad. Probably both.

He set a plastic coffee cup down in front of me. "Iced mocha. Your Tuesday order."

I blinked at him. "You're bribing me with caffeine now?"

"Not bribing," he said. "Strategically fortifying. You're about to hate the rest of your day."

I stared at him. "Thanks for the pep talk."

Archie sat across from me, elbows resting lightly on the table, all mock-casual confidence. But his eyes were sharp. Watching.

"Don't worry about Jake," he said, voice quiet but sure. "If Derek's family tries to press charges, I'll get a lawyer."

I blinked again. "What?"

"Just in case," he said, sipping his espresso like we were discussing weekend plans and not *actual legal consequences.*

I didn't have the energy to thank him or tell him he was insane. All I could feel was the slowly mounting pressure behind my ribs—like I was being squeezed from the inside out by things that hadn't even happened yet.

By the time the bell rang, I could barely taste the mocha anymore.

AP European History was tucked away in one of the quiet upstairs classrooms—windowed, vaulted ceilings, the kind of space that always smelled like old paper and stressed-out dreams.

It was also empty.

Just me.

Jake wasn't there.

His chair sat pushed back, one leg uneven on the floor. His notebook wasn't in its usual spot. The desk was too clean, too still.

He was *gone*.

Suddenly the silence felt brutal.

This class had always been our weird neutral zone. The place where we didn't have to perform for anyone else. We just read, scribbled in margins, argued about revolutions and dead kings, passed notes like no one was watching. Because Mr. G trusted us.

Now it felt hollow.

Like every unspoken thing between us had followed him out the door, and I was left behind in the echo.

I sat down anyway.

Opened my book and stared at the same paragraph about the Habsburg dynasty for twenty minutes without reading a single word.

When the bell rang, I jumped.

I hadn't written anything. I hadn't moved.

I just sat there in the ghost of what we used to be, feeling the weight of it settle deeper into my stomach.

We were gone.

And I wasn't sure how we were ever going to get us back.

THIRTY-TWO

FRANKIE

By Wednesday, the hallways had become a war zone.

Not of gossip or tension—though that still simmered like bad leftovers—but of glitter bombs, choreographed marching bands, helium balloons, and too many roses to count.

Homecoming proposal season had officially begun.

And as usual, our school didn't just lean in. We went full Broadway.

Archie and I walked into first period behind a girl holding a *live goat* wearing a t-shirt that said "Will you *bleat* my date?" and I wasn't even surprised.

With a snort, Archie dropped into his desk. At his lack of biting commentary, I raised my brows. "Too easy," he mouthed and I grinned. For a few seconds, we were just us again.

The only thing that shocked me at the moment was how quickly people forgot about the mess at lunch just days ago. Trauma had a short shelf life at Robertson High.

Rachel met me at my locker with a dry smile and a barely concealed eye roll.

"Three promposals by 8:20. A new record. I'm calling FEMA."

I popped open my locker and tried not to laugh. "You think they'd show up?"

"Only if someone sets off a pyrotechnic display. Which, honestly, give it until third period."

She leaned against the row of lockers beside me and tapped a notification on her phone. "Someone just posted that the mascot's doing a halftime proposal at Friday's pep rally. I give it ten minutes before we have a mascot brawl."

"Let me guess," I said. "Chad versus other Chad?"

Rachel gave a solemn nod. "The two species."

As we made our way to class, we passed a girl covered in rose petals from a "Love Actually"–style cue card proposal that ended in a fog machine fail and a minor asthma attack. A theater kid's a cappella group serenaded someone in the stairwell. And someone else, I swear, was building an actual *archway* in the quad. With scaffolding.

It was... a lot.

During lunch, things got even more chaotic.

A guy in a Cupid costume skateboarded into the cafeteria and nearly crashed into a lunch cart. A girl screamed as confetti rained from the ceiling. At our table, Bubba wore the expression of someone two seconds away from giving up on humanity altogether. He'd already stared down one guy carrying a bucket of *something* and they took a wide circuit rather than cut past us.

"You'd think they were proposing marriage, not a dance," he muttered, watching a junior literally unfurl a banner with a drone. "What happened to texting and keeping it casual?"

Mathieu, seated beside me with his ever-calm expression and a sandwich he'd been politely ignoring, gave a small shake of his head. "I didn't think this kind of thing was real," he said. "I thought it only happened in movies. The glitter. The signs. The livestock."

I smirked. "Everything's bigger in Texas."

He raised an eyebrow. "Even the romantic gestures?"

"Especially those," I said, a little rueful. "There's an unspoken rule here—if you don't rent a mariachi band or stage a flash mob, do you even like the person?"

Mathieu looked faintly alarmed. "I didn't realize there were… expectations."

Rachel snorted into her iced tea. "Don't worry. Frankie hates flash mobs. And mariachi bands. And public emotional displays. Basically, she doesn't like anything involving feelings in font size 500."

I gave her a flat look. "Thanks, Rach."

"You're welcome. Just keeping the emotional bar where it belongs: manageable, indoors, and slightly sarcastic."

"Add caffeinated," I said, raising my cup in a toast.

"Obviously."

Archie showed up halfway through lunch, plunking himself down with iced coffees for me and Rachel, much to her surprise, and a frap for Bubba. He even had a black tea with lemonade for Mathieu. The extra iced coffee had to be for Coop who strolled in. He'd disappeared after fourth, so I guessed he went with Archie or something.

"What did we miss?" he asked.

"Cupid wiped out," Bubba deadpanned.

"A drone banner nearly decapitated one of the lunch ladies," Rachel added.

"Someone's goat ate a geometry assignment," I finished.

Archie nodded, completely unfazed. "Ah. You should have let me make the bingo card."

I almost snorted my iced coffee.

Mathieu leaned toward me and whispered, "Are we supposed to start preparing countermeasures?"

I laughed—soft, involuntary.

The truth was, for a few minutes, it actually felt like a normal high school lunch. The kind with inside jokes and snack trades and the kind of absurdity that makes you forget you're holding your breath.

But it didn't last.

Because every time someone looked at me—*really looked*—I could still see it.

That question behind their eyes.

Who was I going with?

Was Jake still in the picture?

Was it Archie? Coop? The *French one*?

Had someone asked her already?

And worse—*had someone been rejected?*

Everyone had a theory.

I had none.

And as much as I hated to admit it… I didn't have an answer either. And I wasn't sure how we were ever going to get us back.

By Thursday, it felt like the school was actively auditioning for *America's Next Top Proposal*.

Someone installed a glitter cannon in the gym that misfired and dusted half the volleyball team like radioactive cupcakes. Another guy faked a pop quiz in English class just to slide a "Will you go with me?" note into the test packet. It wasn't romantic. It was mostly confusing. The girl said yes anyway.

And the banner drone? It came back. This time trailing a

six-foot heart and a QR code to a TikTok video of someone singing "Perfect" by Ed Sheeran in three-part harmony.

It was like watching a very sparkly apocalypse.

The weirdest part?

The roses didn't stop.

Every day—one or two at a time, tucked into my locker or resting carefully on my desk in AP Euro—wrapped in simple parchment paper, no glitter, no note. Just soft petals and the faintest trace of scent, like the sender knew I couldn't handle anything more right now.

Rachel thought it was adorable.

"I don't care who it is," she said Wednesday afternoon, plucking one from my backpack like she was inspecting a rare artifact. "This is emotional warfare. They're winning."

"I don't think it's supposed to be a war," I said, though my cheeks burned.

Rachel shrugged. "Everything's a war. This one just smells better."

Mathieu hadn't asked me to homecoming.

He hadn't mentioned it, either.

Which—I told myself—was *fine*. We weren't labeling things. We were going slow. Casual. It didn't have to be some dramatic thing.

Still, every time another flash mob broke into "Can't Help Falling In Love," I felt something sharp twist in my chest. Not jealousy, exactly. Just... something else. An ache.

I didn't want a parade.

But I wouldn't have hated a *question*.

By Friday morning, Coop had the look of a man on the brink of a carefully timed mission. He kept scribbling in a notebook during free period, tucking it away when anyone got too close. He'd stop mid-stride in the hallway and study the ceiling tiles like they were part of a secret map. It was kind of cute. Kind of terrifying.

Then, one by one, the unexpected started to happen.

Bubba tugged my arm after second period, drawing me away from the rush of kids heading to their next classes. He looked nervous. *Bubba.* The guy who once punched a hole in drywall because some jackass knocked me off my bike and I scraped up my arm. The move was way more Jake than Bubba, but he'd been *pissed.* I didn't think he even *had* a nervous expression.

But there he was, scratching the back of his neck, not quite meeting my eyes.

"Hey, uh—Frankie?"

"Yeah?"

He exhaled through his nose. "I know it's kinda last minute. And weird. And I totally get it if someone already— well. I just wanted to ask if maybe, *if* you're not already going with someone else... you'd wanna go to the dance with me?"

I blinked.

Then blinked again.

"Bubba..."

"You don't have to answer now!" he said quickly, voice low and awkward. "No pressure. I just figured, y'know, in case no one else—"

"Hey." I touched his arm lightly.

He gave me a sheepish smile. "I'm trying to be lowkey charming."

"You're doing great."

"Remember, I did ask that you not limit yourself?"

"I do."

"Then—think about it? If you want me to go bigger with the ask, just tell me. I'll do it." He blew out a breath and held up a hand. "I meant what I said, you don't have to answer yet."

That made my heart flip flop. "Okay."

He nodded once, then bolted like I'd just handed him a live grenade instead of a compliment.

I didn't even have time to breathe before it happened again.

That afternoon, in the art wing stairwell—quiet, echoey, usually where people went to cry or hide from pep rally sign-ups—Archie found me.

He didn't say anything at first. Just leaned a shoulder against the rail and looked at me like he was still figuring out how to begin.

Then, after a long pause: "I won't do glitter. Or drones. Or a six-piece jazz band."

I blinked. "Okay..."

"But if you'd rather skip the whole circus and go with someone who won't make you slow dance to *Jason Mraz*, I'm your guy."

My heart stuttered.

I opened my mouth, then closed it.

He gave me a smile. That easy, infuriating, *Archie* smile. The kind that said he wasn't asking for an answer right then. Just planting the idea like a seed in soil.

"You know where to find me," he said. "If the roses aren't a declaration you're already spoken for."

A beat of silence.

"Frankie?"

My heart beat so hard I worried it was about to punch its way out of my ribs.

"To be one hundred percent clear, this is me, once again, asking you out on a date. If you want to skip that dance and go play mini-golf, we can do that too. I just want the time with you." He stared at me so long, it was like he was trying to make sure I got the message in my soul.

I did.

"You have time and I'm patient." A whisper of a promise and a wink that was just all my Archie.

Then he was gone.

Just like that.

I had to sit on the steps for a few minutes after. Because apparently my heart had learned how to sprint without asking permission.

When we got to lunch, the courtyard had become a full-on stage.

Not metaphorically. Someone literally set up a platform.

Rachel and I hadn't even gotten our trays when a guy in a rented tuxedo climbed onto the stage with a mic and a giant sign that said, *RACHEL, BE MY QUEEN OF HEARTS?*

A cheer went up. The band struck a few clumsy notes. A tiara descended from the ceiling on fishing wire.

Rachel just stood there, unmoving.

She stared at him for so long the cheering faded into awkward silence. The guy shifted from foot to foot, his grin faltering.

I could feel secondhand embarrassment building like a wave.

Then Coop, who'd been watching from a nearby table, stood and walked over casually.

"Hey, man," he said, clapping the tuxedo guy on the shoulder. "Loved the performance. If you wanna live, I'd clear the stage."

Rachel still hadn't said a word.

The guy took one more look at her, wilted slightly, then

turned and fled, tiara bouncing behind him like a sad punctuation mark.

Rachel sat down without speaking.

I raised an eyebrow. "So. That was…"

"He brought up *Lewis Capaldi* last week," she said flatly. "It was already over."

Coop slid into the seat beside her, grinning. "I consider that a public service."

She sipped her tea. "You want a medal?"

He leaned in. "No, but I'll take the leftover tiara if no one's using it."

By the end of the week, I'd turned down two hallway serenades, avoided one locker flash mob—thank you Rachel!—and received six more roses.

No one signed them.

No one claimed them.

No one asked.

But my heart? It was getting harder to keep still.

Because the longer I waited, the louder it whispered:

Who are you hoping asks you?

And why aren't you sure?

The pep rally ended in a rain of glitter, sweat, and three sprained ankles.

Which, all things considered, was pretty mild.

I watched from the back row of the bleachers as the marching band blared something vaguely recognizable and the cheer squad tried not to kill each other with their own tumbling passes. My eyes kept darting toward the sidelines, toward the place where Jake usually stood—shoulders squared, face unreadable, adrenaline humming just beneath his skin.

Then, for the first time in days, he was there.

Back.

No fanfare. No entrance music. Just... Jake. In his jersey. Like nothing had happened.

He didn't look around. Didn't search the stands. But he was here. And that was enough to set my pulse fluttering like it didn't know what to do.

I almost texted him. Almost.

But my phone was already blowing up—from *Mom.*

MOM: Dinner's at 6:30. Don't be late, Francesca.

MOM: There's someone I want you to meet. This is important to me.

MOM: FRANKIE.

I stared at the screen, thumb hovering over the reply button. I could still make it if I left now. Put on the polite smile. Pretend everything wasn't chaos. Let her steer the conversation toward colleges and posture and posture and posture...

Or.

I could go to the game.

Mathieu had plans with his host family that night— some dinner at a steakhouse with his host dad's extended family—and he'd kissed my cheek before leaving the pep rally and said softly, "Text me if the glitter gets violent."

I promised I would.

But I didn't want to text *him* just yet. Not with all the nerves in my stomach bouncing off the walls.

I wanted to *move*. To *do* something.

And when Coop caught up with me in the parking lot and raised an eyebrow, I just blurted it out.

"You going to the game?"

He shrugged. "Was thinking about it. You?"

I hesitated. Then nodded. "Yeah."

He opened my driver's side door for me like it was the most natural thing in the world. "Then let's go."

It wasn't until we got to the stadium that I saw Archie waiting at the gate, leaning against the fence like he'd been born to look both expensive and slightly dangerous in school colors. Not that he looked bad in the purple. Archie didn't look bad in anything.

"Look who showed up," Coop said.

Archie gave a slow smile. "Couldn't let you two go unsupervised."

"Is that what this is?" I said. "Chaperone duty?"

Archie stepped aside to let us through. "Think of it more as quality time with my favorite girl in glitter territory."

I rolled my eyes, but my cheeks warmed anyway.

The stadium lights buzzed overhead, slicing through dusk with blinding force. The stands were already packed —students, parents, teachers, the marching band, and at least three local news cameras. Homecoming weekend was going to be here soon, and we were getting closer to the playoffs. Maybe. Pretty sure we were. It usually meant heightened drama. Honestly, I only paid any kind of attention cause Bubba and Jake played. I really didn't get football at all. Friday night lights meant someone was going to cry before the fourth quarter.

Probably me, if my heart didn't calm the hell down.

We found seats near the top of the student section, just high enough to see everything but far enough to avoid the accidental pom-pom injuries and class reps throwing out free school merch.

Coop handed me a cold soda. Archie settled his baseball cap on my head. Neither said a word about Jake.

I was grateful.

I leaned forward on the bleacher, chin on my knees, watching the game start. Jake was on the field, helmet on, shouting something to the offensive line. He moved like he never missed a day. Like the world hadn't tilted sideways earlier that week.

Maybe that's what made my stomach twist. Because *mine* hadn't leveled out yet.

"Is it weird being here?" Coop asked, voice low enough that I almost missed it under the roar of the kickoff.

I didn't answer right away.

Then: "Yeah. A little."

"Still glad you came?"

I glanced sideways at him, even as Archie bumped my knee with his, letting me know he was there.

"Yeah," I said. "I think I am."

The crowd cheered as Jake's pass landed with surgical precision into the receiver's hands. First down.

I watched him for a moment longer, breath caught somewhere between guilt and relief.

Then I leaned back into the night and let the game unfold in front of me, flanked by two of my best friends who weren't asking anything of me and felt like my best friends again.

Maybe, for just a few hours, that was exactly what I needed.

THIRTY-THREE

FRANKIE

By Monday, the school looked like the inside of a Pinterest board that got into a street fight with a Valentine's Day parade.

The glitter hadn't faded. The drones had multiplied. And someone had installed a rose wall by the cafeteria that was definitely not school-approved. But no one was taking it down. Because apparently, homecoming week had officially become a full-blown aesthetic war.

"I swear," Rachel muttered as we walked past it. "If someone suggests a coordinated color palette for the pep rally, I'm walking into traffic."

I offered her my coffee. "Mood stabilizer?"

She took it without protest. "You're a saint."

I was not. But I didn't say that out loud.

Because today... Today was already weird.

Not bad. Not good. Just weird in the way your skin feels right before a storm hits—electric and tight and too aware of itself.

It could have started with Mom's sudden disappearance over the weekend. After her repeated messages on Friday, she hadn't even been home when I finally got there. A note waited on the fridge, she had to go out of town for business. She'd be back. There was money on the counter for groceries if I needed them.

Despite the quiet weekend where I worked almost exclusively on my applications for colleges and holed up in my room, I still felt—off. The guys had all messaged or called. The vibe was "normal," almost too normal.

That added an element of strange. Because our normal hadn't been normal in months. Every conversation seemed to vibrate with all the things we weren't saying. Was the pressure there real? Or was I just imagining it? When did it become so hard to talk to them?

Maybe it was because Jake was back. Not just physically —he'd returned on Friday like nothing had happened—but emotionally, too. His participation in the group chats had seemed quiet, centered. Like he'd done some kind of soul inventory over the weekend and decided to try again. At the same time, he kept our interactions to the group chats only.

Was he waiting for me to reach out? Should I reach out? Over a decade of friendship said I should. Friends fought. We all did dumb things. But I couldn't say that his actions hadn't left a sting of pain that still burned.

Then there was Coop. I did see him over the weekend, as well as maintained an ongoing conversation we picked up in person then back to messages. Coop had been acting suspiciously chill for three days straight.

Too chill.

Like the kind of chill that always came right before he dropped emotional TNT in the middle of the living room. I hated thinking that. I didn't have many memories that didn't involve Coop in some way. He'd been my best friend from kindergarten on. We'd lived in this apartment complex for years, he was my closest neighbor, my summer buddy, and the guy I would say I knew better than anyone.

And I was right.

Because he found me during free period—in the back of the library, where no one went unless they were skipping or having a breakdown over college apps. (Both were valid.)

He didn't say anything at first. Just stood next to me, staring at the long aisle of reference books. I tended to study back here because it was quieter and no one bothered me.

Finally: "Hey."

I glanced up. "Hey."

"You okay?"

It was Coop, so I answered honestly. "I don't know."

He nodded like that tracked. "Me either."

We stood there for another minute. Then he turned toward me, hands shoved deep in the pockets of his shorts, gaze steady.

"So... I wasn't going to ask. Figured it didn't matter. Or that you already knew how I felt." He looked down, exhaled. "But I realized that wasn't fair. To you. Or to me."

I swallowed. The kick of the air conditioning coming on sounding loud in the quiet.

He pulled out something small—a folded note. He handed it to me without ceremony, though there was a hint of a familiar smile quirking his lips.

He hadn't passed me a note at school since—sixth grade? Maybe? I couldn't remember.

I opened it.

It wasn't a speech. Not a poem. Just a line in his handwriting.

If you're still figuring it out, I'll wait. If you already know... I'll still go with you anyway.

I looked up.

His eyes met mine. Calm. Steady. Not pushing.

"We've been friends forever, and I know I screwed up," he said softly. "But this? This isn't about that. It's about you. Wanting you to have someone who shows up without making it complicated. Just... me. No glitter. No conditions."

My throat got tight.

"Think about it," he said, backing away. "I'll still sit next to you either way."

Then he left, as easily as he arrived.

I didn't cry.

I almost did.

But the day wasn't done with me yet.

Jake found me. Right outside the AP Euro room. Mr. G wasn't there, but that wasn't unusual. That stupid desk he usually sat at was still empty like a ghost.

"Frankie."

His voice was quiet. Rough around the edges. Like he'd worn it down rehearsing.

I swallowed, then squared my shoulders to meet his gaze. If he could take the time to talk to me straight out, I could make the time to listen.

He didn't look like a guy with a plan. No speech. No props. Just Jake. T-shirt untucked from his jeans, hair a mess like he'd been raking his hand through it. A bruise still decorated his knuckles.

"I'm not gonna give you some grand proposal," he said, voice low. "I don't think I have the right to ask anything of you right now."

That should've hurt. It didn't. He looked so damn uncomfortable it made me ache.

He ran a hand through his hair. "But I wanted you to

know... I see it now. Everything I missed. Everything I said that was wrong. Everything I didn't say that mattered more. Where I fucked up—I don't think I can apologize enough for that."

I didn't breathe.

Jake reached into his backpack and pulled out something—folded parchment paper. A rose.

The same kind that had been in my locker for the last week.

He held it out.

Was he behind the roses?

"I was too much. Then not enough." He coughed. "Then too late. But I never stopped rooting for you, Frankie. I never will. I screwed up. I get that. I'll spend however long it takes to make it up to you."

My chest cracked.

"This isn't pressure," he added quickly. "You don't owe me anything. I just... I wanted to show you I'm still here. And if you want a date for homecoming, I'd be lucky as hell if it was me."

The rose trembled slightly in his hand.

I took it. Carefully.

"Jake..." I found my voice. "The roses?"

"I wish." His smile was bittersweet. "But they made you smile and whoever is doing it seemed to have more of a clue than I do. I wanted you to smile so—" He motioned to the rose. The slight trembling in his hand was still visible.

"Thank you." I managed to push the words out past the lump in my throat. "I do love it." I smiled. "See—it worked."

Jake gave a single nod. Not confident. Not cocky. Just... honest.

Then he turned and walked away.

No demands. No dramatics. Just a boy trying to unburn

a bridge. He should be in AP Euro with me, but he was just —leaving.

I leaned against the wall and stared down at the rose. Then slid a hand into my pocket for the note Coop had given me earlier.

Four asks. Four very different boys.

Somehow, for the first time in weeks, the question wasn't *who* I'd say yes to.

It was *who I wanted to be* when I said it.

I WASN'T until after school that I finally got to talk to Mathieu. He'd been too busy during third period with work for Madame to say more than a couple of words.

He found me in the hallway, right outside his last class of the day. With Mr. G out of the class and Jake absent, I dipped early to go find Mathieu. His smile buoyed me, the lack of tension in his relaxed expression helped to chase away some of my tension. The easy calm in his posture was... disarming. Like he wasn't worried about what came next.

"Hey," he said, stopping beside me. "Been trying to catch you all day."

I gave a small smile. "It's been a day."

"*Oui*," he said, the generous lilt of his accent kissed each word. "It looks like it."

He didn't say anything more right away, just walked with me a little until we hit the empty wing where the vending machines always ate people's dollars and hope. That's where we stopped.

"You talked to them?" he asked, not unkindly. "The guys?"

I nodded.

He tilted his head, like he could already see the gears turning in mine. "So who are you going to pick?"

That surprised me. Not the question. Just how gently he asked it. Like it didn't cost him anything to say it out loud.

I turned to face him. "Were you going to ask me?"

He didn't blink. "No."

My stomach bottomed out. "Should I have asked you?"

His smile was soft. A little sad. "No, Frankie. You don't need to."

A pause stretched between us. The kind you don't rush to fill.

"I adore you," he said finally. "You know that. I think you're—electric. But those guys? They're waging this kind of... intimate war over your attention. And honestly? I'm not interested in stepping into the ring."

Something tightened in my chest.

"It's not that I'm frightened or intimidated," he continued, "I just don't feel the need to fight for something that isn't meant to be a fight. The dance? It matters to them. It matters to you. That's okay. I'm not judging that. But it doesn't mean the same thing to me."

I looked at him for a long moment. "So... what does this mean? Are we breaking up?" I couldn't even wrap my mind around that. We'd had so little time since school started. And whose fault was that? The snide little voice in the back of my head needed to stuff a sock in it.

Mathieu didn't flinch. "We don't have to. I like being with you. I like what we are. But you need space to figure this out. To see where those relationships might go. I don't want you to regret anything."

That word hit like a slow echo. *Regret.*

"Regret is what drove you to me in the first place," he

said, voice like velvet on stone. "I don't want regret to be the reason you make any choice now. Not when you have this huge heart, Frankie. Not when it's trying so hard to be fair to everyone but you."

I swallowed hard.

Because he wasn't hurt.

He wasn't even trying to protect himself.

He was trying to protect *me*.

"I don't want to hurt you," I said, barely above a whisper.

"I know," he said. "That's exactly why I'm not going to let you turn yourself into knots to spare me."

He leaned in, brushed his knuckles against my cheek. His breath was a whisper against my lips.

"You'll make the right choice," he said. "Even if it's not perfect. Even if it's messy. You'll make it with your whole heart. That's enough."

Then he kissed me. Light. Sure. Like punctuation on a sentence that had already ended.

"I trust you," he murmured. "You need to know what could be, before you let anything go and if what could be is one of them, then I want you to have it."

I forgot how to breathe.

"I won't hold you back or make you choose." Another kiss. "I will, however, be here for you." The last kiss was almost butterfly light. "If they hurt you, I will find a way to extract violent reprisal."

For some reason, the ferocity in that last sentence just made me laugh even as tears sparked in my eyes. His smile grew and when he wrapped an arm around me, I burrowed into him. The hug was everything I needed. Wrapped up in his scent and support, I rubbed my cheek against his chest.

"Mathieu...I really don't know what I want right now."

"I know," he said, another smile kissing his words as he leaned back. "You are entitled. Maybe I will woo you to show them how it's done."

Woo. Who used the word woo?

Then he winked. "I'll call you later?"

"I'd like that."

Another brush of his knuckles against my cheek, then he walked away.

He didn't look back.

For some reason, that made me want to cry more than anything else.

THIRTY-FOUR

FRANKIE

We weren't even a full month into senior year and everything seemed to be upside down. I had a boyfriend who was taking a step back to let me explore things with my best friends. The same best friends who'd made me untouchable in the first place. They'd chased off anyone interested because they *thought* I wasn't interested in dating.

No matter how I twisted the thought, I couldn't wrap my mind around it. How had I missed them asking me out? Archie said all the times we went to mini-golf, but we'd literally gone *dozens* of times with and without the guys.

Bubba said he wanted me to keep my options open and he'd made a point to ask me to homecoming, quiet, and low-key so I wasn't embarrassed. Even Archie—the one I would have guessed at definitely going over the top but he'd kept it pretty normal.

I had to wonder how that had killed him to not go the extra mile. Then Archie had been the one to tackle all the staring at the party and asking me to dance. He'd had my back. It was almost like old times, if you didn't count the fact that Jake was the one who'd put me in the fire in the first place.

Instead of driving home, I drove out toward the lake just listening to music and trying to figure out where my head even was. For once, I was relieved that there was no Coop at the car and no one in the passenger seat. There had been no rose either, no the sender had taken to putting them in my locker now.

Someone knew my combination which made me suspect the guys even more, but you'd think if it was them, they'd have totally owned up to it. Yet, they hadn't. When Spotify hit the latest Torched release, I turned it up.

I had four invitations to Homecoming, none of which were from my boyfriend. At a traffic light, I beat my palm against the steering wheel. None of this was fair. Who did I say yes to? Which one? Or none? Because if I said yes to any one of them, the others would get hurt. Now that the dating genie was out of the bottle, it brought more than my wishes to come true.

The urge to scream was right there. An hour later with no easy answers, I swung back by the apartment to feed the cats, then finally opened our group chat. It had been wildly quiet all summer, because I'd muted it so I wouldn't be notified if they were talking.

Scrolling back, I could see a few messages. But right around the time they stopped talking in the group, they'd still be sending me individual messages and I'd just ghosted on all of them. All the outrage and justification I'd ridden on through the summer seemed to evaporate.

Tiddles wound around my right leg, his tail dragging as he purred. I crouched to pet him as I debated what to send. There really wasn't an easy way to do this. They'd all asked, even Jake, though his had also included an apology. Coop asked me to trust him, but even if I already had plans, he just wanted to be there.

God, I missed them all so damn much.

Me: *I know you guys are probably busy, but can we talk?*

I rose to grab a can of Coke from the fridge. I hadn't even cracked it open when my phone vibrated madly.

Archie: *On the phone? Via text? Zoom? Or you want to come over? We can meet somewhere too. Hell, I can come there.*

Coop: *I can be at your place in five, I just got home. But what Archie said.*

Bubba: *I'm game for wherever. I was just working on homework.*

Jake: *I'm down. Time? Place?*

A knock on my front door came hot on the heels of that last comment. I set the can aside as three little dots appeared to show someone was typing something. One glance through the peephole showed it was Coop.

I unlocked the door before opening it, letting him in along with a wash of sultry, sticky air. Ugh. He studied me with his gray-green gaze, his focus intent. "You okay?" He nudged me back before closing the door and relocking it. Then I had all of his attention.

"I'm—" I had no real answer for this. Was I okay? My phone vibrated in my hand.

Archie: *You know, why don't you guys just come here. I can get pizza ordered or Chinese or just about anything you want. We can lock ourselves in the game room for privacy. Edward and Muriel aren't here so we have the place to ourselves.*

I never thought I'd say this, but I was sick of pizza.

Bubba: *I can be there in thirty. Mom just asked me to do a couple of things.*

Jake: *I can head out now, if you want. But I can skip if you'd rather I didn't.*

The last line from Jake wrenched my heart painfully. Almost too painfully. How had we managed to get to *this* spot?

Coop: *Shut it for five guys, let me talk to her.*

I blinked, then let out a wet laugh before shooting a look up at Coop. "That wasn't subtle."

"I didn't need it to be subtle. Now, are you okay?" When he cupped my cheek, I wanted to lean into the contact. It was both oddly intimate and yet wildly familiar. This was Coop...

"Mathieu isn't going to ask me to Homecoming." The words sort of just fell out of me. "I told him that you guys asked me, but I wanted to know if he was going to and he said no."

Coop's eyes narrowed as he wiped away a tear that escaped from my watery eyes with a gentle thumb. "Do I need to kick his ass?"

A hollow, if wet laugh escaped me. "No, I mean—no." I shook my head. "He wasn't being mean. He isn't even breaking up with me, but he wants me to figure out what I want."

"So, you ask him if he's going to ask you, which is kind of like you asking him and he says *no*," Coop said slowly as if feeling his way through the situation verbally. "And you don't need me to kick his ass—question mark."

The fact he didn't sound certain about whether he was stating it or asking again made me smile. "No, you don't need to. He isn't being mean. I promise." I drew back and swallowed around the lump in my throat before I shoved the phone into my back pocket. Rubbing my hands over my face, I tried to chase the tears away,

I hated crying.

"No. We're not breaking up. Or at least, he isn't. He likes

what we have—which is pretty undefined at the moment so—" I spread my arms. "Whatever. I like him too. He's—he's a good guy."

"I'll take your word for it," Coop said easily and when I frowned at him, he spread his own arms. "I said I'd take your word for it. I don't know him, Frankie. I'm never going to think anyone is good enough for you. Hell, *we* aren't good enough for you."

I must have gawked at him, because my mouth dropped open, then I snapped it shut. Shaking my head, I tried to ignore the vibrating phone in my pocket. "You're such an idiot."

"Sometimes," he said, almost agreeably before he typed something into the phone.

"Be nice to them, I started this conversation."

"I'm always nice," he quipped, then paused a beat to meet my gaze. "Fine, I'm nice most of the time. What do you want to eat? Because Archie is about to order takeout from five different places if we don't tell him."

Exasperation underscored every single word as did the roll of his eyes that he punctuated the whole sentence with.

"He does that..."

"Yes, I know. It's how he tries to fix things. First, are we going over there? Second, are you hungry? Third, what are you hungry for? And lastly, are you sure I can't go kick Fren—Mathieu's ass for you? Maybe he needs it more than you know?"

"Yes. Yes. Chinese. Moo Goo Gai Pan. And no, you might need to kick his ass, but Mathieu doesn't."

His long-suffering sigh made me smile again. My emotions were just all over the damn place.

"I'm going to wash my face real quick." The last thing I needed to do was show up at Archie's with red eyes or looking like I'd been crying. Not everyone would listen to me. Hell, I wasn't even sure Coop would totally listen at the moment.

One step from the bathroom, the date hit me and I groaned. "Coop?"

"Yeah?"

"Can you ask Archie to order ice cream too?"

"Chocolate?"

"Or mint chocolate chip—no—both. Wait. Those and strawberry." That all sounded so good.

"I'm telling him to make sure he gets the works for sundaes."

"Yes!" I almost fist pumped then I hurried through washing my face. PMS sucked. Periods sucked too. But whenever I stressed, PMS just made it a thousand percent worse.

I was tempted to pull out my phone and check the messages, but I needed to get it all together before we left. 'Cause I had to talk to Coop on the way there. I hesitated— maybe I should wait until we were there.

Better to talk to them all at once? Yes, I could practice with Coop. But that wasn't really fair to the rest of them. Closing my eyes, I tilted my head back. Maybe dating was just a bad idea. Why did all of this have to be so hard?

"Done. I said we'd be there in thirty, and it only takes fifteen to get there, so we have some time." Coop was right outside the open bathroom door.

Turning put me face to face with him. "Thank you."

"You're welcome." In his short-sleeved dark gray t-shirt and dark cut-off sweatpants that he'd turned into shorts the summer before last because he shot up like six inches and they were too short. He was also bare foot.

"You forgot your shoes."

"I'll grab them before we go," he said with a shrug. "You want to come out here and talk to me now?"

"Not really." I twisted my lips, before I cleared my throat.

"Because...?" He prompted in that easy, coaxing tone that could usually convince me to tell him what I'd gotten him for Christmas or his birthday or just about anything even when I was trying to keep it a secret.

"Because, it involves all of us. Or at least me with each of you and talking to you first might give you an unfair advantage."

"I'm good with unfair advantages." His smirk was almost adorable. "However, I will make the great sacrifice of saying, I'm asking as your best friend and not as the guy who wants to date you. Or the guy who asked you to go to Homecoming. If you'll recall, I also said even if you picked someone else, I just wanted to be there for you."

He had said that.

"At the risk of shooting myself in the foot, you've had to listen to me bitch about relationship drama and stuff before. I'm offering to do that for you now, and I give you my word that what you tell me stays between us and I won't use even an iota of it in my campaign to win."

"You do, huh?" There was something utterly captivating in how direct he was being.

"Hey, for you? I can do anything." He checked his watch. "We have ten minutes, Frankie. What do you want to do?"

THIRTY-FIVE

FRANKIE

What do you want to do?

"That's kind of the ten-thousand-dollar question, isn't it?" I followed him back to the living room and sat on the arm of the chair. Tiddles immediately jumped up to get attention. He even gave Coop a *look* and a very irritated *meow*.

"Sorry, Your Highness," Coop responded. "I haven't paid the tithe yet." He added a long, slow stroke to the cat which had Tiddles purring on my lap and then turning in circles to keep rubbing against Coop's hand and mine.

"Demanding little thing," I murmured, but I also appreciated the company.

"I'd think you'd like to have at least one guy in your life who can ask for exactly what he wants." The dry comment had me meeting Coop's gaze as he looked down at me.

"From what you've all said, it's not that you haven't been asking, I've just not been hearing." *That* was a sore point. I didn't want to be the problem.

"I think it was a little from column A, a little from column B, and probably a whole lot from column C."

"C?" I tilted my head. "What was in column C?"

"We'll wait and see," he said, continuing to pay homage to the little purr engine that could, that was Tiddles. "I always thought it would be you and me. That you just needed the time. So maybe not freshman year, then not sophomore, then you know—junior was out. So maybe not high school at all. But there was always college, and after college."

I frowned.

"Frankie, you and me? We're cradle to grave, you have to know that. Hell, even if we end up going to different colleges, I am so going to show up regularly, call you, and see you on breaks." He made a face. "Not that I'm planning different schools. Who is going to be your best friend if I'm not there?"

The thought alone was enough to make my heart sink. "Who would be yours if I wasn't?"

"See." He grinned then scooped Tiddles off my lap to give him another loving pat before he set him on the sofa. Then Coop caught my hand and tugged me up from the chair. "You and me. We're forever."

"It sounds really good." Really, really good.

"But?"

At his prompt, I shrugged. "Do you know how small the percentage of high school friendships that last into adulthood really are?"

"Nope," he said with a wink, even as he threaded his fingers through mine. "Don't care about statistics either. We're not just not a number, Frankie."

"I want you to be right." I could admit that, then pressed my forehead against Coop's shoulder.

"It's going to be alright," Coop said, shifting so he could

slide his arms around me. When he wrapped me up in that hug, I gripped him back. "I mean it," he promised me against my hair. "When have I ever led you astray?"

"Third grade," I said against his shirt. "You said if we caught the ice cream truck just as he left the apartment complex, we'd get a buy one get one free." I'd gone up to wait near the sign that sat next to the turn-in while Coop "tracked" the truck inside.

"You got free ice cream," he reminded me.

"Cause you paid him," I muttered.

"Lies," Coop said lightly. "That all you got?"

A half-snort of laughter escaped me. "Sixth grade. Lia Baker."

"Who?" Genuine confusion filled his voice and he pulled back to squint at me.

"Lia Baker," I repeated. "Reddish-brown hair, always in braids, had a huge crush on you."

"Nope," he said, his mystified expression firmly in place as he shook his head. "Doesn't ring a bell."

"Really?" I met him stare for stare, not backing down. "You don't remember telling her that she couldn't crush on you because I had rules and the only person I allowed to crush on you was me?"

"Frankie, does that sound like me?" A light gleamed in his eyes. "If you had a crush on me in sixth grade, and I—"

I pinched him and he laughed.

"Hey, party foul!"

"You're an ass."

"But you're smiling. So, I did something right."

I opened my mouth to respond but then he kissed me.

It wasn't hesitant. It wasn't careful. It was like he'd been waiting to do it for years and now that the door had cracked open, he wasn't wasting a second. His hands slid up my back and into my hair, anchoring me as his lips found mine—warm, sure, and just a little breathless.

For a heartbeat, I froze. Then I kissed him back.

Everything else—the apartment, the years of friendship, the ridiculous stories we kept locked away like treasure—fell quiet. His mouth moved with a kind of familiarity that startled me, like he already knew how I kissed, like part of him had always known. It was soft, then firmer, a question and an answer all at once. I gripped the front of his shirt and let myself lean into him, into this, into everything that had always been just under the surface.

When we finally broke apart, I didn't move far—just enough to stare up at him.

"That was..." I whispered.

"About damn time," he murmured back, voice low and rough with something new. Something real.

And this time, I didn't argue.

When he swooped back down to kiss me again, I knew I should stop us but...

I didn't want to.

There were a hundred reasons why this was a bad idea —reasons I tried to grasp onto but every single one popped like a soap bubble as soon as I landed on it. We were best friends. He knew all my worst moments. We'd seen each other at our absolute lowest. This was the kind of line that once crossed didn't have a return path.

But none of that mattered when his lips found mine again.

This kiss was different. Slower. Like he was savoring it, like we had time to unfold everything we'd never said. His hand slipped to the side of my face, his thumb brushing just under my cheekbone, grounding me as my heart went chaotic in my chest. I felt like I was falling, but not in a panicked way—more like gravity had finally given up the fight and let me drift into the space I'd been orbiting for years.

My fingers curled into the back of his neck, and I leaned into him, into the weight of him, the warmth, the history. He knew how I took my coffee. He'd sat with me through fights with my mom, bad haircuts, and the death of my first cat. And now he was kissing me like he'd been waiting for me to catch up.

When we finally pulled apart again, it was slower this time, like neither of us really wanted to let go.

He looked at me—really looked—and his voice was quiet but steady. "You okay?"

I nodded, breath still shaky. "Yeah. Just... recalibrating."

A smile tugged at the corner of his mouth. "Good. 'Cause I'm not planning on pretending that didn't happen."

"I don't think I could if I tried."

He brushed a strand of hair behind my ear, his hand lingering. "Then don't."

And for the first time in a long time, the knot in my chest loosened.

"We still have to go to Archie's," I reminded him.

"Yeah, we still need to 'talk'?" He canted his head. "I mean, unless you've changed your mind on that."

Had I?

Running my tongue over my lower lip, I shook my head. "No, I haven't." As clarifying as that kiss had been, it also added a whole new layer of confusion. "Coop—"

"I'm right here, beautiful," he said, tugging me forward for another hug. Eyes closing, I firmed my grip.

"We're going to be late."

"Trust me," he said, amusement trickling into his voice. "They'll wait."

Both of our phones buzzed at the same time. The simultaneous vibrations had me biting my lip even as a snort of laughter escaped me. "Not patiently," I pointed out and Coop let out an aggrieved sigh.

"Have I ever mentioned how much simpler my life was when it was just you and me?"

Leaning back, I met the teasing light in his eyes. "No, but then—you'd miss the guys if they weren't around."

He held his thumb and forefinger together until there was barely any space between them. "Maybe this much."

"Coop?"

Our phones buzzed again and he rolled his eyes. With a groan, he kept one arm around me as he leaned away and dragged out his phone.

"Bets?" he said, pressing the phone against his chest.

"Archie." Not a doubt existed in my mind. "You?"

He tilted his head from side to side as if debating it even as I hooked my fingers around the phone in my pocket. "I'm going with Jake."

I frowned. "Because of the fight?"

"Because he was an ass and he's struggling with how to make it up to you." The directness there was not a surprise. "I told him he needed to grovel more."

"What are we betting on?" The Jake thing still stung and I wasn't even one hundred percent sure how I felt about it.

"I'm easy," he murmured. "If I win, I want more kisses."

"So, if I win, you don't get more kisses?"

"Not really a win," he said slowly. "I think you win, *you* get more kisses."

"Oh—so we're not kissing each oth—"

He pinched me this time but it just made me laugh. "You win, I kiss you." Firm, almost *authoritative*. "I win, *you* kiss me."

"Deal," I said, and we shook on it. Then because I couldn't help it, I added, "You didn't say when the kissing would occur, so I hope you take markers."

He let out a little growl that he only made when I really got him and delight unfurled in me.

"It's a good thing I like you," he muttered. It was. It really was. "At the same time?"

"One, two," I said, counting it down. "Three." We turned our phones at the same time and the name that popped up on mine and the name that popped up on his was "Bubba."

"Huh." Coop made a face. "Neither of us wins."

Then our phones buzzed again and it *was* Archie this time.

"Ha! Spoke to soon."

He dipped his head as if to kiss me and as tempting as that was, I pressed two fingers to his lips.

"We need to go." My heart did a fast little fist bump with my ribs when he pressed a kiss to my fingers. "Raincheck?"

"Definitely."

Retreating a step, I tried to get my breathing under control then opened the messages so I could let them know we were leaving now. Coop darted out to grab his shoes and said he'd meet me at the car. Though he did steal another fast kiss before he left.

Archie messaged again before I even made it to the back door.

Archie: *You okay?*

That was a loaded question, but I went with the only answer I had at the moment.

Me: *Working on it.*

Archie: *Get over here so I can help.*

That made me smile.

Me: On the way.

THIRTY-SIX

FRANKIE

I don't know what I expected when we pulled up to Archie's, but it wasn't for all three of them to be standing out front with the door open like they were air-conditioning the driveway.

Archie stood with his hands on his hips, and I swore I could practically feel his foot tapping impatience radiating off him in waves. Wearing a guarded expression, Jake stood near but not right next to him with his arms crossed. Bubba gave me a firm once over then a genuine, if relieved smile as I put the car in park.

"You'd think they've never had company before," I muttered as I turned off the engine.

"You're *not* company," Coop said, pushing his door open. "And you know it. If you don't—then you should."

That little comment shouldn't have made my stomach flutter. And okay—maybe it wasn't just the comment. Maybe it was everything. The kiss. The promises. The fact that Coop kept glancing at me like he wanted to pin me against the car and make me late on purpose.

Instead, we headed out to meet them together like

normal people. Normal people who were about to walk into a not-normal night.

Archie strode forward to meet us and gave me a very firm look. "You okay?"

That was going to be the question of the night, wasn't it?

"Peachy," I lied. "Cramping like hell but emotionally stable-ish."

The corners of his lips twitched as he gave me a measured glance. He didn't fully believe me, but he was going to let me get away with it. "We've got hot food and cold drinks. That should help."

When he held out a hand, I clasped it and let him draw me into the house. The others fell in with us. He took us straight to the dining room where the table was loaded with takeout boxes, french fries, pizza, salads none of us were going to eat and a giant-sized cookie loaded with chocolate chips.

The smell of it hit like a wave. Carbs and sugar.

"Okay," I said, blowing out a breath as I let go of Archie's hand. "I want to get part of this over with right now."

That earned me four matching expressions of confusion.

"I have a question," I said, pointing a finger around the room like I was conducting a very weird orchestra. "And I want an honest answer from each of you."

Jake frowned. Bubba leaned forward like I was about to reveal national secrets. Archie just lifted a brow. Coop flipped open a box of pizza and started filling a plate.

I zeroed in on all of them. "Are any of you Mr. Thorns?"

Jake blinked. "Who?"

"Mr. *Thorns*," I repeated. "The guy who's been leaving

roses. At school. At my door. Randomly in my locker like a very floral stalker."

"Oh." Bubba leaned back and squinted. "That's not creepy at all."

"It's not creepy, it's—" I stopped, because okay, *sometimes* it was creepy, but also it was a little thrilling in the romantic mystery kind of way. "It's a thing. Someone's been leaving roses and notes and I started calling them Mr.Thorns cause there's never a name."

"Not it," Coop said before he took a bite of pizza.

"Nope," Archie said, popping the *p*. "Not me."

I turned to Bubba.

He shook his head. "I have a black thumb. Plants fear me."

My eyes landed on Jake last. His gaze finally met mine for the first time since I walked in. "I told you already, wasn't me."

I didn't know what I was expecting. Relief? Disappointment? Proof one of them was secretly a romantic weirdo in disguise?

Instead, I just felt this hollow kind of thud in my chest. Like a door had closed before I even knew it was open.

"Well," I said, forcing a shrug. "That's disappointing."

Bubba actually looked down about it too. "I kind of hoped it *was* one of us."

"Same," Archie muttered, then cleared his throat. "I mean—not that it's not weird. Just that you've got this whole Jane Austen meets 'You' vibe happening and it'd be nice if the guy was someone we could yell at."

Coop set a hand on the small of my back. "Still cool if I punch him when we find out who it is?"

"Why do you get to punch him?" I asked. "Also, did you

have to bring up the Joe Goldberg of it all?" Now I really was a little freaked out.

"Cause I called dibs," Coop said with an oh so helpful grin.

I stared at the table as my lower abdomen reminded me that today was, in fact, a *situation*. The kind of cramp that felt like my uterus was trying to eat itself. I winced and grabbed a bottle of Coke, mostly for something cold to press to my stomach.

"You need something?" Archie was already heading for the kitchen. "We've got Midol. Or whiskey. Possibly both."

I stared at Archie for a long moment. "Do I want to know why you have Midol?"

One corner of his mouth curved upward into a teasing smirk. "For you, babe, obviously. You're the only reason I even know where that aisle in the grocery store is."

"That's—,"

"Creepy," Coop muttered as he pulled a chair out for me and I smacked his arm.

"It's not creepy."

"Fine, it's *not* creepy."

I didn't roll my eyes but I did sit down and then shot Archie a smile. "Thank you, I'm good. I'm just trying to keep it together." Frankly discussing my period was not something I wanted to be doing but the guys were not cringing away from it either.

Jake and Bubba hovered at the doorway but moved in as I took a seat. Archie came back to claim his own slice of pizza, but he didn't sit down so much as face me across the table like we were about to have a team meeting.

Which, to be fair... we kind of were.

"Okay," I said, setting down the drink. "We're all here.

We all know things need to be said. So—should we just rip the Band-Aid off?"

No one answered.

Great.

I sat back and let out a breath. "I'll go first, then."

Coop touched my arm, but didn't stop me.

"Things got messy. Really messy. Apparently, you were asking me out and I wasn't noticing."

I hated that I *missed* out on them asking me out. That I'd been utterly blind to their alleged devotion. How stupid was I?

"You were then dating other people and *that* I definitely noticed."

It stung too each time I thought about it. They were so crazy about me, that they ended up dating other people? Hooked up? Heat flashed through me and I clamped my jaw down before I could chase that thought any further.

"Then I find out that you guys have cut off others who might have been interested in me."

That *really* hurt when added to the rest.

"It hurt you." Archie echoed my unspoken thoughts. "All of it." He didn't deny it nor did he try to soften it. His bluntness helped. So did his lack of excuses, denial, *or* blame.

"Yes." Since he mentioned it. "I'm going to say that, my obliviousness and failure to notice your interest hurt *you*."

Folding his arms, Bubba frowned. "Frankie…" He blew out a breath. "I don't know that *hurt* would be the right word."

"Frustrated is a word," Archie volunteered, then he shot me a half-smile. "But babe, just—having you around was enough."

I raised my eyebrows and I wasn't the only one who just *stared* at him because Jake snorted and shook his head.

"Yes, having her around—"Jake began before he cut a look at me. "Having you around is more than enough. But I always wanted more. I just didn't want to put you on the spot when you didn't seem to want the same things."

"Maybe you should have been clearer then," I said, spreading my arms. "Why couldn't you have just said—*I am asking* you *out on a date? A real date?*"

"Because you laughed at us," Jake countered. "You joked and teased, then just turned it aside."

"Or—turned it into a group outing," Coop said with a faint grimace as he scratched his jaw. "I'm not making excuses, but if we're going to put cards on the table here then... we put them on the table."

"If you didn't want us dating other people," Bubba asked. "Why didn't *you* say anything to us when we did?"

"I didn't have the right to stop you from going after what you wanted." It would never have occurred to me that I did. "I've always wanted you guys to succeed at everything you wanted to do, even when I didn't get it. Not just where it concerns football."

Archie pushed one of the cartons of food over to me. "So... to be clear, we asked you out but you didn't think we were serious because we'd *always* been friends. That's what we're hearing you say?"

I flipped open the carton and stared at the moo goo gai pan and considered it. "Not really sure anyone saw me as attractive."

Literally, because I could feel the buzz in the room rising, I held up a hand.

"I'm not fishing for compliments. In fact, right now, I have cramps, I can't make up my mind about whether I want to cry or scream, and I really want to fall face first into ice cream, so let's just accept that I don't *think* of myself as gorgeous or attractive. Or any of the things that I would think guys want in a girl."

I locked gazes with Coop and to his credit, he just rolled his eyes and shook his head. "Fine, you don't see yourself that way."

"Not fine," Archie countered, but waved his hand. "But accepted. Eat that and we'll build sundaes in a minute. Also, I was serious about the Midol."

Instead of responding immediately, Bubba seemed to be staring at me intently like he was looking for *something* in the words. Jake, though, he scowled.

"You're fucking beautiful, Frankie. You've always been gorgeous. You were pretty as hell even when you were getting into fistfights in elementary school." Arms folded, he glared right back at me. "You don't have to fish for compliments and if we have to accept that you don't see yourself that way, then maybe you should have to accept that *we* see you differently. *I* see you differently."

I opened my mouth to argue, then popped it closed again. Head bowed for a moment, I turned the comment over in my head. "You know, point to you on that one." Because I couldn't tell them how to see me anymore than they could tell me how to see myself. "I'll accept that you see me one way and I see myself another."

"Thank you." It was quiet, but firm while lacking any kind of real triumph.

"The thing is—I think we all could have handled this better." Yes, I would lump myself into this category with them. "Maybe I should have just picked a fight with all of you when I found out what you'd been doing."

"I wish like fuck you *had*," Archie said, his gaze locking

on me. "In fact, from this point forward, if you're mad or hurt or confused or just generally uncertain about something, you throw things at our heads if you have to. No more ghosting."

I flinched, but he wasn't wrong.

"Hey," Coop said, shoving out the chair next to me and sliding his hand onto my back. "You do what you have to do, but the not talking thing has to be a no go. If we don't know what's wrong, we can't fix it."

'You can't fix everything," I reminded him.

"No," he said. "Maybe not. But that doesn't mean we can't *be* there for you."

I swirled my fork in the container of mushrooms and chicken. "You can't make more decisions for me."

"In our defense," Bubba said before the guys could jump in. "We thought we were just supporting *your* decision. Knowing what we know now, we'll work on that."

"Still not going to be on board with you dating other people." Archie leaned back in his chair, arms folded. "That's not negotiable."

"Really?" Was he serious right now?

"Yes, really. If you have to date one of these guys, fine. I don't have to like it as much but I *know* them and I trust them—" He cut a look at Jake. "Most of them."

"Archie—"

"It's okay," Jake said. "I deserve it."

"You do," I said, agreeing with him and met Jake's pale blue gaze as he widened his eyes. "Doesn't mean Archie gets to make those decisions *for* me."

"You have any idea how long you're going to be pissed at me?" Jake asked and I shrugged.

"Jury is still out. Be happy that I want to talk to you at all."

Lips pursed, he nodded slowly. "Point."

Rubbing a hand over my face, I sighed. "This is not what I imagined when I asked for this conversation."

"We are listening," Bubba said, and the intensity in his blue eyes promised he meant it. "I know we're all a little hard-headed." He bumped Archie with a light jab of his shoulder. "Some of us are a *lot* hard-headed. But we're here. And we're listening."

They were. Every one of them. For better or worse.

So I blew out a breath. "I asked Mathieu if he was going to ask me to Homecoming."

Everything at the table stilled. Forks paused midair. The rustle of pizza boxes went silent. Even Archie's chewing slowed like he was trying not to interrupt the vibe. The only one who didn't flinch was Coop—we'd already had this conversation, though saying it again in front of the rest of them made it feel brand new.

"He said he wasn't going to," I continued. "And before you offer to kick his ass, don't. He's doing it to give me space—to let me figure out what I want without him adding more pressure."

It was sweet. Frustrating. Fair. And deeply inconvenient for my heart, which still hadn't made up its mind.

I rubbed at my chest like I could smooth out the ache there. "Part of me wishes he *would* fight for me. But I get it. No one wants to throw themselves into a war if they're not sure they'll be welcome when the dust clears."

And that was it, wasn't it? The heart of all of this. Wanting to be chosen, but also needing to choose. Wanting clarity, when all I had was chaos.

"If I'm being honest," I added quietly, "I really like him. I do. He's easy to be with. It's fun and uncomplicated." Then I exhaled and looked down at my hands. "But I don't know if that's enough. Because the truth is—" I hesitated. "My lips are still tingling from Coop's kiss. And the rest of you? You're tying me up in knots."

The silence that followed was thick.

That feeling?

Yeah. Still *deeply* conflicted.

"You've all invited me," I said, finally glancing around the table. "I haven't forgotten that. I swear."

They were watching me like I was a live wire. Like one wrong move might burn the whole night down.

"I just…" I licked my lips. "I don't want to say yes to one of you and make the others feel like they don't matter. I don't want to be that girl who turns something real into a contest."

"So what girl *do* you want to be?" Bubba asked, voice gentler than I expected.

"I don't know yet," I admitted. "But I *do* know I want to go to Homecoming."

The truth slid into the air like a weight, solid and real.

"And… I kind of want to go with *all* of you."

I didn't look at them right away—didn't *dare*. But when I finally raised my eyes, the table was frozen like someone had hit pause on the universe. No one moved. No one breathed.

And that's when I realized—I hadn't just dropped a bomb.

I'd lit the fuse.

THIRTY-SEVEN

ARCHIE

The room was silent, but it was a silence so loud it was deafening. Frankie's words hung in the air like a challenge, a dare, and a plea all rolled into one. Tension radiated off each of my friends, and they had to be wrestling with the same thoughts I was. How do we make this work? How could we not screw this up?

I looked at Frankie, and for a moment, I saw the vulnerability in her eyes. She wasn't just asking us to take her to Homecoming. She was asking us to be okay with sharing her. It was a big ask.

While none of us expected this, here we were. I couldn't help but feel a strange mix of excitement and trepidation. Agreeing to share her now didn't mean a permanent state. It was a door that I'd leaned on for years finally opening.

"Frankie," I said, my voice steady despite the turmoil inside me. "You know we'd do anything for you, right?"

She nodded, a small, almost hesitant movement.

"Then let's figure this out," I continued. "Together. Because if you want to go to Homecoming with all of us, then that's what we'll do. But we need to be clear about what that means."

I glanced at Jake, Bubba, and Coop, each of them nodding in agreement. They were on board, but I could see the questions in their eyes. They were wondering, just like I was, how we did make this work without hurting each other or Frankie.

Jake, though, he looked away, a flicker of something—resentment? jealousy?—crossing his face. I couldn't blame him. He'd made his bed at the party and gotten himself tossed. It wasn't going to be easy on him.

Oh well.

"Okay," Frankie said, her voice a little stronger now. "So, what does that mean? How do we do this?"

I leaned back in my chair, trying to gather my thoughts. "It means we need to talk. Really talk. About what we want, what we're willing to do, and what we're not. It means we need to be honest with each other, even if it's hard."

Jake cleared his throat, his voice tight. "I agree. We need to lay everything on the table. No secrets, no hidden agendas. If we're going to do this, we do it right."

Bubba nodded, his expression serious. "And we need to respect each other. Frankie, you need to know that you're in control here. If at any point you want to stop, we stop. No questions asked."

Coop grinned, but there was a hint of nervousness in his eyes. "I'm in. Let's make this work. But Frankie, you need to be sure. This isn't something we can take lightly."

Frankie took a deep breath, her eyes scanning each of our faces. "I'm sure. I want this. I want to go to Homecoming with all of you. But I also want to make sure we're all on the same page. No one gets hurt, and no one feels like they're being left out."

I reached across the table and took her hand, gave it a gentle squeeze. "We're all in this together. We'll figure it out, Frankie. But we need to be patient and open with each other. This isn't going to be easy, but nothing worth having ever is."

Jake shifted in his seat, his jaw tight. "You sure about this, Frankie? Because once we start down this path, there's no turning back."

Frankie met his gaze, her expression steady. "I'm sure, Jake. But I need to know that you're sure too. This isn't just about me; it's about all of us."

I bit back the advice to tell Jake to shut up and take the offer. She was letting him back in, he'd be an idiot to turn it down. Still, I kept that to myself. If he cut himself out, one less person to worry about.

At the same time, I didn't want Frankie hurt by that rejection.

Jake held her gaze for a long moment before nodding, but the tension in his shoulders kept them rigid. He wasn't fully on board, and that was going to be a problem.

Bubba spoke up, his voice calm but firm. "We'll make it work, Jake. We just need to communicate and be honest with each other. No one said this would be easy, but we can do it."

Coop chimed in, his grin widening. "Hey, think of all the fun we'll have planning this thing. It's going to be epic!"

Frankie smiled, a small, tentative curve of her lips, and it was like the sun coming out after a storm. "Thank you. All of you. I know this is a lot to ask, but I couldn't imagine doing it with anyone else."

And there it was—the trust, the hope, and the promise of something new and exciting. We're standing on the edge of something unknown, and it was both thrilling and terrifying. But as I looked around the table at my friends and the girl who has captured all our hearts, I understood the reality that we *had* to be ready to take this leap.

"Let's do this," I said, my voice filled with determination. "Together."

Jake leaned forward, his elbows on the table, and fixed Frankie with a serious look. "Frankie, what about Frenchy? Does this mean you're done with him?"

Frankie's eyebrows shot up, and she looked taken aback. "Mathieu? Why are you bringing him up now?"

Jake's expression is tight, almost defensive. "I just want to know where I stand. If we're all in this together, does that mean we're all exclusive now? Or are we still seeing other people?"

The room went quiet again, the tension ratcheting up another notch. Valid question or not, I wanted to slug Jake. Uncertainty crept back into Frankie's eyes as she considered her response. That it took her time to answer was an answer.

"I... I don't know, Jake," she admitted, her voice soft. "I haven't really thought that far ahead. I just know that I want to go to Homecoming with all of you, and I want us to figure out how to make that work."

"Maybe we should take this one step at a time." Bubba took the reasonable route. "We can figure out the Homecoming thing first, and then see where we all stand after that."

Coop nodded in agreement. "Yeah, let's not get ahead of ourselves. We've got enough on our plates with Homecoming. We can cross that bridge when we come to it."

"Fine. But I want to know where I stand. If I'm in or out." Jake wasn't convinced but he didn't push the issue.

Frankie reached across the table and took Jake's hand,

giving it a squeeze. "You're in, Jake. We're all in this together. But we need to be patient and work through this as a group. Okay?"

He nodded but the hesitation was still there in his eyes. This wasn't going to be easy, and Jake's reluctance was just the first of many hurdles we'd have to overcome. But for now, we were all in, and that was what mattered.

If Jake kicked himself out the door later?

Well, his loss.

Archie: Alright, let's hash this out. Frankie wants to go to Homecoming with all of us. Thoughts?

Jake: I don't know, man. It's a lot to take in. And what about Frenchy? Is Frankie done with him?

Coop: She answered that. We need to trust her.

Bubba: I think we need to respect Frankie's decision. If she wants to go with all of us, then that's what we do. No questions asked.

Coop: I'm down for whatever Frankie wants. But Jake's right, we need to know where we stand with other people.

Archie: I agree. We need to have an honest conversation about exclusivity. But for now, let's focus on making Homecoming work. We can figure out the rest later.

Jake: I just don't want to get my hopes up and then have her pull away again. You know?

Bubba: I get that, Jake. But we can't let our fears hold us back. Frankie's being brave by putting herself out there like this. We owe it to her to meet her at least halfway.

Coop: Exactly. And think about it—going to Homecoming with Frankie and the rest of us? That's gonna be epic.

Archie: Coop's right. She wants Homecoming. We need to make this count, because if we fuck this up, I don't know how many more chances she'll give us.

Jake: She's already giving me another chance.

Bubba: Yes, she is. We have to be on the same page. We need to communicate and be honest with each other. No one said this would be easy, but we can do it.

Coop: And hey, think of all the fun we'll have planning this thing. It's gonna be legendary!

Archie: Remember, no pressure on Frankie. She's in control, and we respect that.

Jake: Got it. Let's make this work.

Archie: I'll take care of the limo...

THE HOUSE WAS QUIET, the kind of quiet that settled in after a storm. I was still in the living room, the soft glow of the lamp casting long shadows across the floor. I didn't usually bother to linger down here. I had my own rooms and a whole wing of the house. But Jeremy was out for the evening and I was flipping through photos from the locked file on my phone. So many pictures and moments spent with Frankie.

The weight of the evening's conversation with her and the guys still hung heavy in the air. The tension that echoed after the involved the awareness of having to rely on the guys to not fuck anything up, while at the same time—a part of me kind of hoped they would. I was in this for the long haul. I was playing to win. So if they screwed their chances, I would do everything to make sure she kept me as the ally, the one she wanted—the one who would always be there for her.

The front door opened, and in walked Edward, my father. He was a tall man, my mirror image in so many ways, with a presence that commands attention. There was a coldness in his eyes, a distance that had become all too familiar. When his gaze landed on me, a flicker of something—guilt, maybe?—appeared in his eyes. Yet it was gone before I could fully register what it meant.

"Edward," I say, my voice steady despite the turmoil inside me. I refused to call him "Dad." Not anymore. Not after everything.

He nodded, his expression unreadable. "Archie. How was your evening?"

I shrugged, not wanting to get into it. "Fine. Just hanging out with the guys."

Edward set his briefcase down on the entry table then crossed into the room, his footsteps echoing slightly on the hardwood floor. He didn't pause until he reached the wet bar where he poured himself a drink. "And Frankie? How is she?"

I tensed at the mention of her name, a protective instinct surging through me. Frankie was off-limits in this house, a safe haven from the toxic dynamics that rule here. "She's good," I said, my voice tighter than I intended. "Why do you ask?"

Edward paused, then turned. His eyes met mine for a long moment. "No reason. Just making conversation."

Lie.

It never changed. He always lied.

This new one just hung in the air between us, thick and heavy. He was banging Frankie's mother without a thought for how that might affect her. I clenched my jaw, pushing down the anger that threatened to boil over.

"Well, if that's all, I'm going to head upstairs," I said, standing. "I've got some stuff to take care of."

Edward nodded, a small, almost imperceptible movement. "Sure thing, son. Goodnight."

Not flinching at his use of "son" had taken me time to perfect. I barely even noticed it now. I turned and walked away, each step taking me further from the tension in the room. At the top of the stairs, I glance back down. Edward stood by the window, his back to me, his shoulders slumped slightly. For a moment, he seemed *almost* defeated, a far cry from the powerful, commanding figure he usually presents.

I shook my head, pushing the thought away. I can't afford to feel sorry for him, not when he was the one causing all this pain. Not when Frankie could get caught in the crossfire.

Before I could turn to head deeper down the hall to my wing, the front door opened again. This time, it was my mother, Muriel. Her heels clicked sharply on the floor, a staccato rhythm that matched the tension in her voice as she called out to Edward.

"Edward, we need to talk," she said, her tone sharp, demanding. I hadn't realized she was due back. Not like either of them ever read me into their schedules. At this point? I would rather stay out of it. No way this wasn't planned. They avoided each other with almost surgical precision.

Edward's response was muffled, inaudible. I could only imagine the storm that was about to break, the emotional shrapnel that would fly in every direction. In the middle of it all, Frankie, blissfully unaware of the storm brewing around her.

I needed to protect Frankie, to keep her safe from all of

this. Whatever it took, I'd make sure she didn't get hurt. Even if it meant continuing to keep secrets, even if it meant lying. She deserved better than this, better than them.

She probably deserved a hell of a lot better than me, but I was selfish. I refused to let go.

With a final glance down the stairs, I headed to my room, the weight of the evening settling heavily on my shoulders. As I closed the door behind me, I glanced down at the picture of her on my phone and made a promise.

No matter what happened, no matter how bad it got, I'd be there for Frankie. I'd be her rock, her safe harbor in the storm. And together, we'd weather whatever came our way.

With or without the others.

They were my friends, but she'd always been my forever.

THIRTY-EIGHT

BUBBA

I t was still early enough that the garage wasn't suffocatingly hot, but I had the outer door open to let in the semblance of "air." I also had the big fan on to keep what air was in here moving. The engine on my motorcycle purred to life under my touch, a satisfying rumble that always brought a sense of accomplishment.

In addition to taking classes on motorcycle safety and how to ride over the summer, I'd spent time with a couple of my dad's friends who worked on their own bikes. I'd learned enough to make sure I kept mine in good shape. It was a used bike, but in excellent condition. I wanted to know everything about the machine, from how it should sound to what maintenance it needed regularly.

It was less about the engineering than understanding the safety and making sure it was all done *right*. Turning the engine off, I shifted to tighten the final bolt. Changing the air filter had proven straightforward enough. A scuff of a shoe on the concrete and the skipping of a pebble rattling over the drive to the grass had me glancing up

Sharon stood in the open garage entrance, her blond

hair pulled back into a sleek ponytail that gave her face a severe look. If not for the light glow of her tanned skin, she'd look ill. Steeling myself with the familiar scents of oil and metal, I flicked a look over her then past her.

"Sharon," I said, wiping my hands on a rag and keeping my expression neutral. "What brings you here?"

Her presence was like a dark cloud, sudden and unwelcome. She crossed her arms, her expression a mix of boredom and something else—annoyance, maybe? Or was it jealousy? It could be both or neither, the past few months she'd grown more and more mercurial and impossible to read.

"Just thought I'd stop by and see you." She gave a casual shrug like it didn't really matter to her. "You know, catch up."

"Really?" It took physical effort to not *snort* and no, I wasn't buying this act for a second. "The last time we talked—correction, the last time *you* talked to me, you made it pretty clear you weren't interested in being friends."

Which, at the time, had been a relief.

"Maybe I've changed my mind." The corners of her pink-glossed lips curved upward into a sharp smile. All jagged edges and cutting as glass, it did little to diminish the sense of calculation. How I'd missed it when we were first dating? I had no idea. "Or maybe I just miss the good times."

"No, I'm not doing this." I shook my head. "I'm busy and there's a lot on my plate, right now, Sharon. So maybe..." I gestured for her to go.

Her eyes narrowed, and for a moment, a flash of the bitchiness that lurked beneath the surface peeked out. "Oh, I see. You're too good for me now, is that it?"

"Can we not?" I raked a hand through my hair, and if I got a little grease in it, whatever. "I mean, seriously, can we not?"

"Aww, poor Bubba, are you feeling on the spot?" She drifted into the garage, the drag of her shoes making me flick a look down at her bare legs then back up. The shorts and tank top were a damn good look on her, they emphasized the muscles in her legs, and the toned shape of her arms.

Blowing out a breath, I took firm hold of my temper. One of the things I used to enjoy about Sharon was the biting wit she often wielded like a scalpel to slice through conversations with surgical precision. It always seemed to fall just on *this* side of mean.

Most of the time.

"It's not that." I dismissed her observation of me being on the spot even if she *was* cornering me in my garage. "I just... I've got other things to focus on. Important things."

She stepped even closer, her voice dropping to a low, sultry purr. "More important than me? Really?" The soft perfume she favored wreathed the air around me, penetrating the dust, grease, and fainter hints of exhaust from where I'd had the engine on. But that delicate balance of floral scents had an underlying cloying sweetness to it that irritated my throat.

Taking a step back, I put the motorcycle between us. "Yes, actually." I gestured to the bike. "This is just the start of my day."

"Uh huh." Sharon studied me through narrowed eyes. With a huff, the tension burst and she relaxed into a real smile. "I suppose. I just—miss you."

That revelation slapped down my judgment. "We don't have that many classes together." Thank God.

"We don't have *any* classes," Sharon complained. Funnily enough, that wasn't my fault. She'd had to swap a class and that took her out of the two we'd shared.

She shifted her stance, refolding her arms as some of the confidence bled out of her and left a more uncertain girl behind. "That's part of the problem. We were so tight all summer."

"No," I said, correcting her gently. "We were both really busy this summer." I'd had classes, a couple of college visits, and Sharon had gone to Europe with her parents for three weeks.

"But we *made* time for each other." She closed the distance between us and planted her hands on the motorcycle. "You remember when you were looking at the different bikes with your dad?"

"Yeah." I wasn't sure where she was going with this. I'd never taken her on the bike. From the first day I got it. Sharon was not going to be my first passenger.

Period.

"So do I! You sent me photos, told me about the different ones and you let me help you pick."

I blinked slowly. That was not how I recalled that conversation going. At all. "What does that have to do with anything?"

Where was she going with this?

"It has to do with you and me. I miss you, Bubba. I miss hanging out with you. I even miss the guys sometimes." One corner of her mouth curved upward. "I miss the parties. Though—Archie's last one was a little... you know. Out there."

Every word she said, every smile she cast, every little gesture down to the way she lifted one hand and curled her fingers invited me to join in on the joke.

"Can you believe it with Frankie? Miss Goody Two Shoes took a dive and it only took a French guy to get her to go down on him."

The ice that slammed into my veins did very little to cool either the temperature in the garage or the spike in my temper. "Excuse *me*?"

"Oh come on, Bubba." She gave me a little pout. "I thought you and the boys got over that little crush finally. You definitely weren't thinking about her while you were fucking me."

No, I wasn't. "One has nothing to do with the other. Leave Frankie out of this."

Her expression darkened. "Why? Because you think you have a chance now that she popped her holy cherry with someone else?"

"Sharon." It came out in a snap. "Don't talk about Frankie like that."

All traces of her smile vanished. "You're a fool if you think her picking someone else means she's going to go for you now. Archie is right there and he's loaded, then there's Coop, and they might as well be twins for how close they are, and we all know Jake is not patient."

She struck a match to my temper with each name she ticked off in her little rant.

"One, I don't care what you think." I couldn't be much clearer on that. "Two, who Frankie chooses or dates is not and has never been any of your business." When she would have opened her mouth, I raised a hand and she silenced. "Third, most importantly of all, no one asked you for your opinion."

"You know, I'm going to do you a favor..."

"Don't." Because I couldn't think of anything I wanted less.

"Stop being such a child," Sharon commented with a toss of her head. "You want her, you have to make her jealous."

"Believe me when I say, I do not want your assistance or advice."

She leaned forward, elbows on the seat of my bike. "C'mon Bubba, you know I can make it worth your while. Not to mention the fact I know exactly how to suck your—"

"Shut up." The anger boiling in me went cold. "Don't talk about her like that. You don't know anything about her."

Reeling back like I'd slapped her, Sharon glared at me. "Oh, please. Everyone knows about Frankie and her little harem. She's just stringing you all along, Bubba. She always has been. All four of you trotting after her like good little puppies. Even when you were dating me, all she had to do was bat her eyes and off you went. Can't you see that?"

Jaw clenched, I counted to ten and then back down again. I didn't punch people. Striking someone meant you lost control, and the argument, if you needed violence. I sure as shit didn't punch girls.

I was the closest I'd ever come to it. Fortunately for me, Sharon stopped talking even if she kept giving me a death stare. Why I ever touched her, I had no idea. She'd never been less attractive.

After exhaling a careful breath, I said in the most even tone I could manage. "You don't know what you're talking about, Sharon. Frankie is one of the kindest, most genuine people I know. She's not playing games. That's your thing, not hers."

Sharon rolled her eyes, her expression dismissive. "Whatever. She's never wanted you. Too bad you can't see it."

With that, she turned and walked out of the garage, but paused as she stepped into the sunlight and slid her sunglasses on. Then she twisted to look back at me.

"You know, one of my favorite parts of the summer was when we played musical chairs…" She ran her tongue over her lower lip. "You remember, our little version of spin the bottle."

My gut tightened, a sour taste in my mouth. "Can't really say it stood out for me."

Her mouth went to a flat little line. "Then it's a good thing I have pictures and some video… you know, mementos."

Pictures—

"See you soon, Bubba." Then she strode away.

I forced the hand that had been curled into a fist to flatten on the bike's seat. Pictures. Video.

The relief trickling through me at her absence was poisoned with dread by those last words. I dug my phone out of my pocket and sent a message to the group chat.

Me: At any point over the summer, were we stupid and let the girls film us?

I couldn't get blunter than that. One of them had to know. I didn't remember any but, some of those nights, I didn't remember much beyond alcohol, a warm body, and some release. Not a good look for me. Not really.

Setting the phone aside, I got back to working on the bike. The unsettled feeling in the pit of my stomach wouldn't go away. We were making progress with Frankie. I was—I'd told her I wanted to date. Even if she kept seeing the French guy. If she wanted to date the other guys, just let me have a shot.

Don't limit herself.

She didn't actually answer me on that, though, did she?

No, she asked for all of us to take her to Homecoming. Was this really a date if all four of us were taking Frankie? Had we turned the potential date into a friend outing? What did that even mean? How do we make sure we're all included, valued, and get time with her if there's four of us?

Archie was no slouch. He was taking care of the car and he'd pour on the money and the charm. The minute he saw an opening, he'd wedge himself in there. That was who he was.

Jake already shot himself in the damn foot, but maybe he could fix it. If nothing else, he'd be in "make peace" mode so that potentially dialed down any violence.

Coop?

No, Coop wasn't going anywhere and he'd kissed her. They'd let that slip. He'd kissed her, but he wasn't bragging about it or using it to score points. He was just...

All of this was uncharted territory. I wanted Frankie. I'd always wanted her. The girls, the others, they were barely pale imitations, but my taste in blondes definitely came from Frankie.

My phone buzzed and wiped my fingers off with the cloth before snagging it. The heat out here was already dialing up to sultry. Sweat had my tank sticking to me.

The notification wasn't from the guys. It was from Post-it-gram, the current go to social media platform.

Sharon.

I hit the reel that had tagged me.

Tagged all of us.

Son of a bitch...

They had filmed it.

THIRTY-NINE

FRANKIE

It started with a ping.

Just one. A notification on my phone from a group chat I usually kept on mute. Then another. And another. Within thirty seconds, my phone was buzzing like it was having a seizure.

I glanced at the screen.

"WTF IS THIS???"

"Did you see Coop??"

"Frankie… girl… you might wanna sit down."

I didn't sit down. I opened Post-it-gram. Mistake number one.

The first clip autoplayed without mercy—blurry at first, then sharp enough to make my stomach drop. A video. Bubba. Shirtless. Sweat-slicked. Grinding against some random girl in what looked like the pool house living room while Jake egged him on in the background. Someone had added slow-mo. And a neon caption that read:

"SUMMER SLUT BOYZ 2025 "

I blinked. Hit pause. Tried to breathe.

Mistake number two? Checking the comments.

"Who knew golden boy Coop had a freaky side?"
"Is that Bubba in the hot tub with two girls? Omg."
"Wait… IS THAT ARCHIE??"

My thumb hovered over another video. I didn't want to look. But I did. Of course I did.

This one had all four of them—Jake with a bottle in one hand, pants suspiciously low; Bubba holding a phone and narrating while Coop and Archie—**Archie**—made out with girls in a club like they were in some kind of contest. There were flashes of skin. Moaning. A suspiciously familiar game room. It kept going. Longer than I wanted. Definitely not accidental. These were saved, curated, deliberate.

I backed out of the app. But it was too late. My pulse was already pounding in my ears.

I felt… sick. Betrayed. But mostly? Just upset. Because their summer of "missing me" had also been a part of these "legendary sexcapades" apparently. Bile burned in the back of my throat. It wasn't *news* to me. I had been blocking some of these parts out, but I had gone to Bubba's birthday "party" and sex had been in the air that night.

So, not surprising that it had been there all summer. I wasn't a total idiot. I should've stopped watching—but curiosity and anger kept my fingers moving. The next video showed Bubba in a pool, hands everywhere, tongue somewhere it definitely shouldn't have been, while someone— maybe the girl who leaked all of this—zoomed in and whispered,

"Frankie's gonna love this one."

Like it was a joke. Like *I* was a joke.

I didn't realize I was shaking until my phone slipped out of my hands and hit the bed.

I sat there, breathing hard, trying not to cry. Not because they had been wild or reckless or even gross—but because not one of them had thought for a second what this would look like. What it would feel like. For me.

This wasn't just about bad decisions or hot hookups. This was about the lines they crossed, the little lies they told me, told themselves, and then wrapped in charm to hand out like candy.

I was the one they wanted, but they had definitely not gone without. My heart kicked so hard at my ribs, it felt like they would crack. I had no idea which of the girls posted this, the "original" post was already down, but screenshots and screenrecordings were forever.

My phone began to vibrate again, but this time, I didn't dare look. Not yet. I still had to get to—

A knock on the bedroom door had me staring at it, almost owl-eyed. It wasn't even nine yet. I had to be at work in a couple of hours, and I'd gone back to bed after feeding the cats that morning cause I wanted the extra sleep.

Another knock.

Shaking off the distraction, I clicked the side button to shut off the screen and pushed out from under the covers. "Come in."

Mom opened the door to glance in at me. She was far more disheveled than I was used to seeing her. Dressed in a long-sleeved button-down shirt and little else, she gave me a sleepy grin. "Good morning, baby."

For the second time that morning, my heart stopped and then began to sink wrapped in chains of dread. Who was this woman and what had she done with my mother?

"I'm glad you're up. We got in really late last night and I didn't want to wake you. But get dressed. We're going to take you out to breakfast."

"I have to work—" The response was almost automatic but it came out in a croaky voice.

"Call out sick."

"What?"

She huffed out a dramatic sigh. "Call out sick, you never call out. This is important."

"Mom," I began, trying to search for the words.

"No," she said, holding up one finger. "Francesca, I ask you for very little. You will do this for me, because it's important and we have a lot to talk about. So call out, and get dressed. We're leaving in twenty minutes."

With that, she blew me a kiss and left the room.

If I called out, I was stuck with Mom and—wait, she said *we*. Who the hell was *we?* Gravity seemed to double the force it exerted over my chest.

We.

Fuck.

I pushed off the bed and got dressed. I braided my hair rather than try to tame any of it. Then I called Marsha and as soon as she answered, I apologized. "I know it's short notice, and I'd rather go to work but—"

"You sound terrible," Marsha said, her concern soaking me through with guilt. "Take the rest of the weekend sweetheart."

The manager was probably one of the nicest people I knew.

"I'll try to be there tomorrow." Missing one day was bad enough.

"No, you'll take it easy. You have a heavy course load. I don't want to see you before Wednesday. If you're still feeling rocky, just let me know. You have too much to do to be sick."

She wouldn't take no for an answer. The whole time I

was on the phone, the notifications kept coming in. Every short, sharp, and insistent buzz seemed to rattle in my bones before I heard it.

Off the phone, I went to disable the notifications because there were just too many. There were also messages from the guys. I needed to answer them.

Rachel's name popped up on the screen. She was calling. I declined and let it go to voicemail. I just couldn't yet.

"Come on, Frankie!" Mom called. "You're going to make us late."

How could you be late to a date you didn't even plan? But I kept the comment to myself as I headed out to the living room phone in hand. "I just need to—"

Mom had chosen a playfully ruffled sundress in green and some strappy sandals. She'd traded in her earlier disheveled appearance for something more elegant and yet relaxed. It wasn't her, however, that stopped me dead. It was the man she stood next to, with her hand on his arm.

"Mr. Standish?" I said slowly. Archie's dad. I'd met him a few times. He and Archie looked so much alike at times, it was eerie, but where Archie always seemed warm, funny, and witty, his dad was far colder and remote.

"Frankie," he said, his expression softening from the icy distance he usually wore. "You don't have to be so formal with me."

"Eddie's right," Mom said, sliding her arm firmly through his.

Eddie?

My stomach did an agonizing flip-flop as my gaze slid back and forth between them. A lot of little pieces were starting to make more sense. Mom's constant late nights and long "working" weeks away. She was in the middle of an affair.

It was hardly her first.

But this was…

"You know, I was going to wait until breakfast, but I think we've all waited so long that I don't want to wait anymore."

My mouth was suddenly dry. "Wait for what?"

"To introduce you to your father," Mom said, her smile so brilliant it bordered on blinding.

The dizzying spiral of the world threatened to suck me down into a vortex. A hot, icy sensation raced over me. "What?"

Happiness radiating off of her in a way I'd never seen it, Mom beamed. "Eddie is your father, Frankie."

To dive back into the secrets, scars, and slow-burn seduction—where every letter cuts and every lie costs—get ready for *Book 2 of What If: Letters, Lace, and Lies*… because the past isn't done, the heart isn't healed, and someone's about to pay the price.

AFTERWORD

This is me—did you really think I *wouldn't* do a cliffhanger?

Some things never change.

But here's what *has* changed: the path we've taken together. What started as a single *what if*—a quiet whisper of possibility—turned into a full-blown alternate journey. One with new choices, new dynamics, and unexpected opportunities that even *I* didn't see coming until I wrote them.

That's the magic of letting your characters surprise you. Of trusting that the story will show you where it wants to go, even if it means diverging from what you thought was set in stone.

To my incredible patrons: *thank you*. Your support, feedback, and sheer enthusiasm made it clear that this wasn't just a one-off experiment. You believed in this story enough to want more, and because of you, *Rules, Roses, and Rivals* doesn't end here.

Book Two begins *over there*—on Patreon—where it's already taking shape, chapter by chapter.

If this is your first time stepping into this world, I'm so

glad you came along for this version of the ride. And if you've been here since the original *Untouchable* days, I hope this twist on familiar faces has been as fun (and painful... in the best way) for you as it has been for me.

See you in the next chapter.

With love and endless plot twists,

Heather

Website:

heatherlong.net

Reader group:

facebook.com/groups/heatherspack

ACKNOWLEDGMENTS

Thank you to my patreon members for all you do!
Mo
Kim C
Carla Dianne
kmommy1417
Jac
Jen
Emily Cotler
Phoebe Galbraith
Kaeliebear
Rebecca Henderson
Adriana Smith
Kristen
Aishlling
Jennah Brown
Jessica Loughnane
Caitlin Hart
Annette Lyons
Belinda S Tasaico
Alice R
Sonya Smith
Bryn
carisa kerr
Jessie O'Malley
Melissa Casey
Amanda Taylor

Marissa

Daphnne

B Marshall

Amy

Jenn Fantasia

Kristine Beeson

JenJen

Deborah West

Zoe Corkhill

Dalila Gurney

Katie Simek

Shay

Heather Johnson

Lindsay Marshall

Dianne Tumbers

Leigh Graham

Stephanie Gharst

Cheria Coram

Terri Smith

Steph Heinritz

Gina Yingwane

Brenda Gervais

Vicki Perry

Kara Genan

Perla Blessley

JessieW

Laura

TL Reeve

Kyan Wolfe

About Heather Long

I *love* books. Not just a little bit, but a lot. Books were my best friends when I was growing up. Books didn't care if I was new to a town or to a class. They were always there, my trustiest of companions. Until they turned on me and said I had to write them.

I can tell you that my own personal happily ever after included writing books. I've always said that an HEA is a work in progress. It's true in my marriage, my friendships, and in my career. I am constantly nurturing my muse as we dive into new tales, new tropes, new characters and more.

After seventeen years in Texas, we relocated to the Pacific Northwest in search of seasons, new experiences, and new geography. I can't wait to discover what life (and my muse) have in store for me.

Maybe writing was always my destiny and romance my fate. After all, my grandmother wasn't a fan of picture books and used to read me her Harlequin Romance novels.

Follow Heather & Sign up for her newsletter:
www.heatherlong.net
TikTok

ALSO BY HEATHER LONG

82nd Street Vandals

Savage Vandal

Vicious Rebel

Ruthless Traitor

Dirty Devil

Shamelessly Loyal (Novella)

Brutal Fighter

Dangerous Renegade

Merciless Spy

Reckless Thief

Fierce Dancer

Dirty Dancer

Bay Ridge Royals

Shamelessly Loyal (Novella)

Battle Lines

Deceptive Truce

Wicked Surrender

Violent Chaos

Desperate Victory

BLOOD Brothers

Burn

Lure

Own

Oath

Dare

Blue Ivy Prep

Problem Child

Mad Boys

Party Crashers

Money Shot

Bravo Team Wolf

When Danger Bites

Bitten Under Fire

Cardinal Sins

Kill Song

First Chorus

High Note

Last Word

Chance Monroe

Earth Witches Aren't Easy

Plan Witch from Out of Town

Bad Witch Rising

Fevered Hearts

Marshal of Hel Dorado

Brave are the Lonely

Micah & Mrs. Miller

A Fistful of Dreams

Raising Kane

Wanted: Fevered or Alive

Wild and Fevered

The Quick & The Fevered

A Man Called Wyatt

Going Royal

Some Like it Royal

Some Like it Scandalous

Some Like it Deadly

Some Like it Secret

Some Like it Easy

Heart of the Nebula

Queenmaker

Deal Breaker

Throne Taker

Lone Star Leathernecks

Semper Fi Cowboy

As You Were, Cowboy

Shackled Souls

Succubus Chained

Succubus Unchained

Succubus Blessed

Shackled Souls (Omnibus)

STANDALONES

Kiss of Fate (w/Blake Blessing)

Taste of Karma (w/Blake Blessing)

I'll Be Home... (w/Tate James)

Overexposed (w/Tate James)

Switchboard Duet

Talk to Me

Don't Let Go

Untouchable

Rules and Roses

Changes and Chocolates

Keys and Kisses

Whispers and Wishes

Hangovers and Holidays

Brazen and Breathless

Trials and Tiaras

Graduation and Gifts

Defiance and Dedication

Songs and Sweethearts

Legacy and Lovers

Farewells and Forever

Hellos and Happily Ever Afters

Wolves of Willow Bend

Wolf at Law

Wolf Bite

Caged Wolf

Wolf Claim

Wolf Next Door

Rogue Wolf

Bayou Wolf

Untamed Wolf

Wolf with Benefits

River Wolf

Single Wicked Wolf

Desert Wolf

Snow Wolf

Wolf on Board

Holly Jolly Wolf

Shadow Wolf

His Moonstruck Wolf

Thunder Wolf

Ghost Wolf

Outlaw Wolves

Wolf Unleashed

www.ingramcontent.com/pod-product-compliance
Lightning Source LLC
Chambersburg PA
CBHW021438310726
48971CB00005B/1416